I0583899

# A HOME FOR THE
## Windswept

### KARRI L. MOSER

Black Rose Writing | Texas

©2021 by Karri L. Moser
All rights reserved. No part of this book may be reproduced, stored in a retrieval system or transmitted in any form or by any means without the prior written permission of the publishers, except by a reviewer who may quote brief passages in a review to be printed in a newspaper, magazine or journal.

The author grants the final approval for this literary material.

First printing

This is a work of fiction. Names, characters, businesses, places, events, and incidents are either the products of the author's imagination or used in a fictitious manner. Any resemblance to actual persons, living or dead, or actual events is purely coincidental.

ISBN: 978-1-68433-678-4
PUBLISHED BY BLACK ROSE WRITING
www.blackrosewriting.com

Printed in the United States of America
Suggested Retail Price (SRP) $18.95

*A Home for the Windswept* is printed in Book Antiqua

*As a planet-friendly publisher, Black Rose Writing does its best to eliminate unnecessary waste to reduce paper usage and energy costs, while never compromising the reading experience. As a result, the final word count vs. page count may not meet common expectations.

Credit for author photo: K. Liz Photography by Kate Wilson

*Behind every young child who believes in herself  
is a parent who believed first*

I could not complete this book, or any other, without the support and encouragement of my family. I've always been lucky in that department right from the start. I think that's why I've never settled for being discouraged by anyone. I was taught young by my parents that my pursuits, my ideas, my dreams, my hopes mattered. I was lucky. I was heard. I was free to pursue who I wanted to be and what I wanted to do in life. My parents believed in me. Because of them, it never occurred to me that I *couldn't* do anything I wanted to do, including being a writer. That alone has made all the difference in my life and it's a gift I hope I've passed on to my own children. That is why this book is dedicated to my first and most important encouragers, John and Patricia Russ.

Thanks Mom and Dad!

# A Home for the Windswept

# PART I

# CHAPTER 1

Darcy leaned her forehead against the picture window that faced the paper mill. The cold glass soothed her headache. The steam billowing and the faint sound of valves releasing pressure settled her nerves. Darcy rubbed her protruding belly. "Don't worry, Elara. People will always need paper. That mill isn't going nowhere."

Darcy's breath left a circle of fog on the window of the single-wide trailer. She glanced behind her at the two little ones cuddled on the couch. She hoped they'd stay suspended in the bliss of their afternoon nap longer. Darcy wanted more quiet time before Basil and her brother finished their shifts, and her father started his. They would get news about the mill's future by the end of the day. The mill was all they had. It was all anyone in Winsockette, Maine had.

Basil's truck door slamming shut snapped her out of her reprieve from pregnancy headaches and the demands of two kids under five. She blinked to see him emerge from the snowflakes racing to the ground of their dirt driveway. The sun was trying to peek through as he walked toward the front porch steps. Darcy wanted to believe the streaks of sunlight were a sign that everything would be okay, but her heart sank when she saw his face emerge from the white blanket unfurling around him. Cassiopeia and Orion both stirred as their father entered.

"So? Any word?" she asked as she pulled the curtain closed. Darcy stepped over a pile of matchbox cars to take Basil's coat as he stomped snow off his boots.

"Yeah. Exactly what I expected. Looks like we've got three months of work if we're lucky, then nothing." He leaned down to peel his boots off and shook snow from his dirty blond hair. When he stood and stretched his long arms over his head, his hands touched the ceiling. His shirt lifted enough for Darcy to see the scar just below his belly button. Defeat filled his icy blue eyes. "That's all she wrote, Darcy. The mill will close. All of us will be out of work."

"No. They'll get another contract, merge with another Canadian plant just like in 2000 when they got bailed out at the last minute." Darcy leaned down to straighten his wet boots. He stepped past her towards the kitchen.

"This ain't like 2000. People don't need us anymore in 2008. They don't need paper. With phones, computers, cheaper paper across the border, and all, the mill is dead, or so it will be soon." He threw his arms up and tapped the threshold between the living room and kitchen with his hands.

Darcy scooted across the living room in her worn-out slippers from two Christmases ago. She lowered herself onto the couch and ran her pale, puffy fingers through Orion's black hair. The two-year-old reached up and moaned as he gradually woke. Basil opened the fridge and took out a beer. Orion rubbed his eyes and sat up looking for his dad when the cap popped and hit the linoleum.

"We're gonna be okay. Right, Basil? We'll figure out something." She said into the air not making eye contact as Basil huffed. She glanced down at her belly then at both kids. She knew he didn't have an answer, but the question floated out of her mouth anyway. Basil paced and swigged. Her eyes followed his lanky frame around their tiny trailer. She wanted to grab his arm, steady him, but she realized it was pointless. He needed to pace just as she needed to be still.

Darcy thought back to the high school dance when she first kissed Basil as they awkwardly swayed back and forth, trying to stay in step with each other. She told him about her plans to go to college to study astronomy to discover and name a new star. She wanted to peer at something no one else had ever seen. Darcy remembered Basil smiling at her before he leaned down for that first kiss. He whispered as he drew her chin up towards his mouth, "Winsockette ain't a place for stargazers and dreamers." He was right.

Seven years later they were up to one lost scholarship because of one unplanned pregnancy right before graduation, one single-wide trailer, two more pregnancies, one part-time job at the only grocery store in town, and now one lost job—the only real job in town. Those were all numbers she unwillingly to let sink in as her headache roared back.

Darcy pushed herself up from the old sunken couch and shuffled to Basil as he stood in front of the refrigerator. She reached up to his shoulder. He cringed.

"We'll be okay. We have to be." She whispered into his back. He exhaled a deep breath and his shoulders sunk as his head fell forward against the fridge door. "We'll leave here if we have to," Darcy said. She was startled by how easily that idea rolled off her tongue. Despite the last few years of living the exact life almost every girl in Winsockette was destined to live, Darcy was still a stargazer and dreamer who wondered what was beyond the mountain on the other side of the mill.

After she and Basil got Orion and Cassiopeia into bed for the night, they stood side by side looking out into the night sky and the steely clouds that hovered over town. She reached for his hand. He squeezed hers. Despite the condition of the trailer, the leaks in the roof, the cold Maine air that blew in from the old windows, and the carpet that would forever smell musty, they had a view unlike any other. Their trailer was perched on a small hill above the others in the park. It was positioned at the right angle so they could see over most of the town, past the mill, and onward to the mountain. Right before their wedding as the word was spreading that Darcy was pregnant and would be showing at graduation, Basil took her to the trailer to show her the view. At that time, she had already turned down her scholarship and resigned herself to the very life she swore she'd escape. But something about that view gave her hope that the world would still be out there if they ever found a way out together. If she couldn't leave Winsockette right after graduation as she had planned, at least she could stand at that window and see past her hometown. For five years now, she had been looking at Mount Katahdin, the highest mountain in Maine. Everything else was on the other side of that mountain even if she wasn't, and somehow that had become good enough.

A few stars poked through the lingering snow clouds. She let go of Basil's hand and rubbed her belly as Elara kicked. Darcy smiled. Elara was the name of a moon of Jupiter and also one of Zeus's lovers. Darcy loved the idea that someday she'd be able to show Elara her namesake. Basil bought her a decent telescope after she had Cassiopeia and promised to buy her a stronger one someday. On clear nights, Darcy made a point of showing the kids the constellations they were named after. Even though they were both too young to understand, Darcy needed them to know they were her tiny slice of the universe, her own stars and moon.

"Basil, what are we gonna do? And don't say 'I don't know' or 'we'll be fine'. I mean it. I really mean it." Darcy swallowed a lump in her throat, the kind she hadn't felt since she discovered she was pregnant for the third time in five years.

"Well, for one thing, there's gonna be a meeting about it all. We'll go. We'll hear what the company and selectmen have to say. Until then, I'll keep going to work and well, we just gotta save what we can. Maybe you can pick up more hours at Bakers?"

"More hours? Hell, Basil, he already gives me extra now cause he knows I'm gonna be out for God knows how long once Elara comes."

Basil leaned his head on the glass. Darcy looked to the floor.

"I knew I should've taken those online classes before I got pregnant again. Then at least I could get a better job and let you stay home more with these guys for once. You've given the mill everything for the last five years."

"We all have, Darcy. Me, our families. Jesus, this whole town has." Basil turned to her. "I'm going out for a smoke."

He slipped away from her side. The wind whipped through the living room and cold slithered up Darcy's back as Basil struggled to close the front door against the wind. Darcy squinted as she looked past the smokestacks. She couldn't wrap her mind around the thought that the world would no longer need the mill. At one point, the mill produced more paper than any other mill in the world. Thousands of people, at least five generations worked at that mill over the years. Because of the power it gathered from the river and the never-ending supply of Maine woods, the Great Northern Paper Mill of Winsockette was the heartbeat and lifeblood of the town. It gave rise to the opera house, a railroad station, and a grand hotel primarily used by industry executives and groups of tourists anxious to climb Mount Katahdin.

To think the roar, steam, and hum of the mill might cease, dry up, and be silent forever boggled her mind. The town would wither up and die without it. Darcy thought of all those catalogs, fliers, reams for newsprint, coupons, phonebooks, paper for books and letters. She knew business had slowed and layoffs rippled through the town. Some blamed foreign competition. Other companies produced more paper cheaper. It was simple math. Others blamed the technology boom. Newspapers and magazines tanked as people relied on cell phones and laptops for news and communication. Some blamed fuel costs. Others blamed mismanagement and failure to adapt to a changing world. Darcy understood it was a mix of all those, but she still hoped it was all temporary. The recession dominated the news. Winsockette proved just as susceptible to the economic collapse as any other small town. However, Darcy thought they were still far removed from the immediate impact. Plus, she thought, there was still an abundant supply of woods for as far as the eye could see. People would always need paper and the trees of northern Maine was the best resource to make it.

"Love letters" Darcy whispered to herself. "People will always want to write love letters." She smiled as she realized how immature and idealistic that sounded. But that simple thought gave her a spark of hope that the closing would be stalled. A deal would be made. Basil would continue to work at the mill for another few years. They'd save more for a house out of town. A real house, not a single-wide trailer made of creaking metal and musty carpet. They'd have a foundation, a yard, maybe a skylight, and a better telescope so they could sit on the deck and watch the stars as a family. She glanced down at her arm. Her tattoo of Cassiopeia was across her nearly translucent forearm. Orion was on her back. She needed to pick a spot for Elara once she was born. Suddenly spending money on another tattoo seemed as frivolous and as immature as thinking the need for love letters would save the paper industry.

Darcy saw Basil's lanky frame on the small front porch. She watched the cigarette dangle from his lips as he squinted into the night. It was hard to remember a time she wasn't sneaking glances at Basil Sullivan. They shared a few classes in junior high. They had mutual friends and their respective cliques grew closer as high school began. Her twin brother, Jackson, was soon in Basil's inner circle. While Darcy and Jackson didn't associate too much in school, it was hard to avoid each other's friends when they brought them home. Basil and Jackson would play video games for hours. They also got suspended together a few times, which made Darcy both leery of Basil and enticed by him at the same time. Basil stayed the night a few times when his dad would kick him out, seemingly for no reason other than drunken anger. When they'd cross paths in the kitchen, Basil would joke with her, tease her about always doing homework. She knew it was his way of flirting even if he didn't. Darcy liked him in that bad boy kind of way. Basil was known for fights in the school parking lot and smoking in the bathrooms, often with Jackson. If Basil wasn't the ringleader of whatever trouble was caused around Winsockette, Jackson was. But Basil was quick to turn on Jackson when it came to Darcy. If Jackson teased her in front of the others, Basil would immediately shut him down. He gave her a sense of protection even when she didn't need it. It didn't hurt that he had piercing ice-blue eyes and always ran his hands through his wavy blond hair.

She hated that he smoked, but also hated to admit she liked the way he'd wink at her with a cigarette dangling from his lips. She hated his fighting, but something about his fearlessness enticed her. Plus, she understood he needed to get his pent-up anger out somehow. Boys like Basil, or anyone in Winsockette for that matter, didn't go talk to a therapist or anyone. They didn't discuss what happened at home. They didn't explore their feelings of worthlessness with their friends. They drank, smoked, fought, suffered the consequences, then repeated the pattern.

Despite the obvious trouble that was Basil Sullivan, when he was around, she didn't feel so out of place in her own home, her own skin. She wasn't invisible. While Darcy knew she was the smartest girl in the house, she could never outshine her mother. She was no Gemma. From the time she was a baby, everyone would promptly say, "She doesn't look a thing like you." Hearing you don't look like someone else might be fine until you start to realize that someone else is regarded as the most beautiful person in the tiny world of northern Maine. Gemma wasn't just pretty; she was certified beautiful and had the sashes and crowns to prove it. She was a beauty queen. Darcy learned at an early age her mother was universally regarded as the epitome of physical beauty. And simultaneously, Darcy learned what it meant to *not* look anything like her.

Darcy never felt ugly and certainly wasn't treated as such. She just wasn't 'Gemma pretty' despite being Gemma's only daughter. She tried to be once she grasped Gemma's disappointment in this fact. Darcy unsuccessfully colored her hair blond. It turned orange with black streaks and fried ends. She tried to copy her makeup, which also failed as Darcy was stark white with coal-colored hair, not a natural blond with a perfect tan who rocked hot pink lipstick at any age or in any lighting. She tried to keep her weight down. But Darcy's curves had a mind of their own, as did her bones. She only grew to be 5'2 while her mother was a long, lean, and fit 5'9.

Occasionally, Darcy would try on Gemma's crowns and look in the mirror. They never quite fit. She never quite fit unless Basil was in the house. Somehow unlike every other friend of hers and Jackson's, Basil never seemed to notice the beauty queen fixing dinner or watching soap operas in the living room. He never asked Gemma questions about her childhood in South Carolina, the pageants, or her beauty regime like Darcy's friends did. He didn't raise his eyebrows as she sauntered by in a halter top or another piece of inappropriate clothing for her age. Basil noticed Darcy and seemingly nothing or no one else.

Now, as Darcy stood watching him having a smoke outside years later, she knew he still noticed only her and their soon-to-be three kids. Nothing else mattered to him. She recognized the thought that he was going to fail to take care of them was the worst thing that could happen to Basil Sullivan. Darcy looked down and whispered, "Don't worry, Elara. Your daddy will figure something out."

# CHAPTER 2

After a restless night of sleep, the sun peered in through their tiny bedroom window, Darcy heard Basil groan minutes before the alarm was set to go off. He was always up before the alarm. She nudged him. The days came early and dragged on in the winter. Every February in northern Maine seemed to last forever. The world was frozen, and the body felt that way too. They each stretched and tried to get their blood warm. Darcy slid her hands along Basil's back. The icy touch made him cringe.

"I'm up. I'm up. Don't do that." He said as he tossed the blankets over top of her. She giggled as she tossed them back on his side. Basil stretched his arms above his head. As he showered, Darcy started the coffee. Neither she nor Basil started the day without black coffee. It was one thing they never knew they had in common until he stayed the night at her parents after being kicked out by his dad for a week. As the maker dripped and churned, the phone on the wall rang. She exhaled as she saw her mother's number on the tiny screen.

"Hey, Mom." She said. "Yeah, of course, he told me." She cradled the phone on her shoulder as she poured herself a cup. "Yeah, I'm going to the meeting. Yeah. I know." As Basil made his way to the kitchen, she poured him a cup and mouthed 'mom'. He kissed the top of her head. Basil turned up the thermostat.

"I gotta go get the kids up. Basil is set to leave in a minute." She rolled her eyes after another sip. "Yes. My appointment is at one. I'll call you after." Darcy hung up and sipped more coffee.

"I didn't sleep much."

"Yeah, obviously," Darcy said. She could tell by the scattered look in his eyes.

"We'll just save what we can right now and hold tight to what we've got saved already for the house. After that meeting, we'll decide what we need to do. But I'll tell you this one thing, Babe. I'm going to take care of you and these kids. I promise. I don't want you worrying about none of this." Basil said. He tipped his cup back the rest of the way.

"I'm not worried. I know we'll be okay. We've got enough oil for the rest of the winter. We've got savings, which is a lot more than the rest of this town can say, you know?"

"Yeah, thanks to you being a tightwad." He said with a sly smile. "Once this whole thing goes down, we'll get unemployment for a while, too." The wind whipped and they both turned their heads to the front door as an icy breeze squeezed through the unsealed frame. Winter always had a way of reminding them who was in charge. "I should've resealed the storm door in the fall. Dammit. We lose so much heat through that door. I gotta go." Basil grabbed his coat and kissed her goodbye.

After the kids were fed and dressed, Darcy loaded them into her old Jeep, her gift for her 16th birthday and her first day working at Bakers. Darcy put it in four-wheel drive to get down the hill and into town. Without four-wheel drive, there was no way to be sure the vehicle would stop at the stop sign or if it would gently coast through onto Mountain Spring Road, the main road in town. Orion and Cassiopeia grumbled about being cold.

"We're almost there, guys." She said into the rear-view mirror. As Darcy parked and got out, Cassiopeia undid her seatbelt and then reached over to undo Orion from his booster, too. "Thanks, Cassie, you're such a big help to Momma," Darcy said as she plucked them from the seats and down onto the sidewalk. She squinted as the February wind smacked her in the face. It was stinging and relentless. Darcy lifted Orion to her hip and grabbed Cassie's hand to lead her down the street faster than her little feet could go. "Momma's late. We gotta hurry." She said with the wind at her back as she pulled up on Cassie's arm. The toe of Cassie's snow boots scraped the chunky salt grains on the sidewalk as she was hoisted up by her arm.

The dry heat of the office lobby fell over them like a blanket once Darcy got them inside. Orion slithered down her side and made a bee-line for the play table in the corner. He was building a tower of blocks before Darcy made it to the front desk. Her appointment was standard. She had gained the correct weight. Her measurements where spot on for 20 weeks and an ultrasound would be scheduled in two weeks to confirm the doctor's assessment of her third textbook pregnancy. Darcy took great pride in being referred to as 'textbook' at each appointment. It gave her a sense she was just as successful at having babies as she would've been at college.

As she always did after each appointment, Darcy and the kids headed to the mill to update Basil and say a quick 'hello' to him and her brother. She made a point of having her appointments mid-morning so she'd be done around their lunch break. Even if she was a little early or late, no one at the mill minded if Basil sneaked away for a few minutes to say "hi" and get an update. If anyone did, they sure knew better than to say anything about it. Darcy's father, Harlan was a manager on the floor for third shift.

Darcy wiped her boots on the large rubber mats in the office hallway and nudged the kids to do the same. Orion was already starting to whine about lunch, so Darcy knew she had to make it a quick stop. She waved to the foreman who noticed her and kids behind the glass. He nodded, confirming he'd send Basil out to her. Jackson opened the door and removed his earplugs. The smell of the chemicals swirled around his body and wafted to Darcy and the kids' noses. The kids cringed. Darcy hadn't cringed at that scent in years.

"Hey, Jack. Is Basil coming out?" Darcy said. She unbuttoned her coat.

"Jesus, you're showing more than the last time I saw you," Jackson said as he reached down for Cassie. "Hey, kid. Give Uncle Jack a hug." Cassie wrapped her arms around him and crinkled her nose more. Orion grabbed Darcy's leg. She shook him loose. "Hug Uncle Jack. Where you been anyway? You didn't come to Mom and Dad's for dinner the last two

Sundays and you were a no-show to help Basil with wood for Cecelia's place." Jackson kissed Cassie's cheeks and let her slide to the floor. He gave Orion a quick flick on the head, and the boy laughed. Darcy smiled. Orion adored Jackson. The flick on the head had become their thing.

"I was just busy, Sis. I got a life outside of helping your kids' sitter and hanging out at Mom and Dad's, you know?"

"Yeah, but you know she's going through a rough time with the divorce and all. She's all alone. And jeez, she's been my best friend for a decade." Darcy said. She tilted her head as Jackson averted his eyes, which matched hers. He also had her black hair, but he grew tall like their parents. Darcy was the only short one in the family.

"What? What are you looking away for?"

"Nothing," Jackson said as he lowered his head.

"Look at me. Dammit, Jackson. Look at me." Darcy said. She glanced around to see if anyone else was in the hallway. Jackson looked quickly then rolled his eyes at her.

"You messing with that stuff while you're working? Are you kidding me with this?" Darcy said. Her cheeks grew hot with anger.

"Whatever. I just took a few this morning to help get my ass up. I was out late with Jude and them guys. It's nothing. Stop acting like Mom." Jackson flicked Orion again.

"You can't get all fucked up in the morning then come work in here with that equipment. You're gonna get hurt, or worse yet, get my husband or someone else hurt. Jesus." Darcy said in a whisper through gritted teeth. Jackson exhaled and looked away from her. She was reaching for his collar when the door opened.

"Hey. Is everything all good?" Basil said while he pulled off his earplugs and wiped his forehead with his free hand. He reached down for Orion.

"Textbook. Just textbook." Darcy said. Basil gave her a quick peck on the cheek then kissed the top of Cassiopeia's head.

"Awesome. I gotta get back. I'll see you tonight."

"Yeah, me too. Bye, kids. I'll see you boogers Sunday at Grandma's." Jackson said as the two men put their earplugs back in. Darcy bit her bottom lip as she squinted at Jackson. He avoided eye contact and darted in front of Basil.

"I love you, Daddy," Cassie yelled as Basil looked back and blew a kiss to his family. The noise from the press and machines filled the room as they opened the door. Orion waved his tiny fingers at the men. Darcy leaned down and slid his mittens over his fingers. For the first time in her life, she looked into her son's eyes and thought the mill closing might be a good thing. There were better things for her son to be than a fourth-generation mill worker and, despite how much she loved her brother, there were better men for him to aspire to be than Jackson McElvaney.

# CHAPTER 3

Because of the sheer number of people who planned to attend, the town meeting about the mill was slated to be held in the high school gym. Cecelia agreed to watch the kids because she no longer had a stake in the mill. Since her husband left her months ago and disappeared to Canada with the wife of another couple from the trailer park, Cecelia didn't seem to have a stake in anything. She worked at the only full-service truck stop within a hundred miles of Winsockette and spent the rest of her time crying alone or on Darcy's shoulder. Darcy suspected Basil had grown annoyed with her moping around and constant need to talk to Darcy about it, but he was a compassionate enough man to understand Cecelia had nothing or no one else.

When Darcy and Basil made their way into the gym, she was flooded with the smell of the red rubber balls and basketballs. It instantly brought her back to their high school days. She realized the last time she was in that gym was her, Basil, and Jackson's graduation five years earlier. She was pregnant then, too. She was suddenly nauseous as she focused on that smell. Basil nudged her when he spotted Darcy's parents in the fourth row. Gemma was waving wildly and pointing at two empty metal chairs beside her. Basil shot his hand into the air to let her know they were coming. He led Darcy through the crowd, which mostly consisted of other people who were in the gym that very day five years ago. Even if a family didn't have a member graduating, almost the entire town turned out to see the other kids of Winsockette High School get their diplomas. The same was said for the prom. As each couple pulled into a parking spot in the lot in front of the school, townspeople lined the sidewalk and snapped pictures, oohs and awws following each couple into the school. This time there were no cameras snapping shots or laughter as people hugged and fawned over a handful of new graduates and soon to be mill workers and wives of mill workers. Grumbling, swearing, and lots of hand wringing by the ladies filled the gym.

Darcy wedged herself into the row of chairs. Gemma reached for her hand. Gemma's hair was higher and sprayed more than usual.

"You guys going out to dinner or something after?" Darcy said as she sat.

Gemma moved a few long wavy blond strands behind her shoulder. "No, honey. I just figured I needed to spruce up a bit for this. I'm a manager's wife, you know. Gotta look the part." Darcy nodded. She didn't bother to point out that her mom always looked the part, and if by chance she didn't, Gemma sure acted the part. Harlan reached over and tapped his daughter's leg. His belly rested on the top of his legs and overflowed from the sides of the metal chair. Darcy thought to herself how her father seemed to get bigger after each of her pregnancies.

"I hear your last appointment was good, huh?" He said over Gemma to Darcy and Basil.

"Yep, Dad. Textbook." She said as she squeezed his hand.

"Good. Keep it up."

"I plan to Dad," Darcy said with a laugh. The microphone set up in front of the chairs squealed and everyone sat up straighter. Harlan adjusted himself and cleared his throat.

"Let's get this show rolling," he said in a low voice. Gemma smoothed out her skirt and crossed her ankles as if a picture of her was going to be snapped at any moment. Darcy drew in a deep breath and took Basil's hand. The head of Great Northern Paper Mill, Mr. Wellington cleared his throat as he took the mic from the stand. Darcy had only seen him four times in her life. He came when nerves needed calmed, or layoffs needed justified. His company merged with Maine Quality Paper Mill when Darcy was in junior high. Without the merger and his ability to get the town on board, no one in the gym today would even have a job. His very presence commanded attention and respect. Darcy could tell Mr. Wellington had the weight of the town on his shoulders by the way his head hung low, only this time he didn't look as if he was ready to alleviate any of their fears. To her, he looked like the steam towers looked in her eyes right before the valves are turned to release the pressure.

He took notecards from his suit jacket pocket. He started to read statistics, numbers that made sense to Darcy. She arranged them in columns in her head. She saw them fall into line. Words such as 'digital revolution' 'recession' 'trade deals' 'high energy costs' floated above their heads. Darcy sensed the dread that seemed to hover above the gym. He wasn't alleviating fears, promising a future rebound. He wasn't even proposing any plans to keep Great Northern Paper Mill running even if it meant a slowdown. He was laying out the rationale for the one thing the town still refused to accept as fact—Great Northern was closing forever. Every shoulder slumped. Darcy looked up and expected to see bricks coming down around them. Everything they depended on, everything Winsockette was, was crumbling. Harlan shifted in his seat. Darcy glanced around. Everyone, everything looked smaller. Nausea set in. The smell of the red balls stuck in her nose. She glanced at Basil. He seemed smaller to her, too.

Mr. Wellington stopped talking. The words "I'm so sorry it's come this," ended his speech. He slid the mic back into the slot at the top of the stand. Darcy expected an eruption of voices, arguments, possibly even fists flying Mr. Wellington's way. There was nothing. Silence and the faint hum and hiss of the mill in the background. That too would be hushed in a matter of two months. 8 or 10 weeks at best. She'd still be pregnant. 75% through with her textbook pregnancy. The silence began to fill with low murmurs. Then the murmurs grew. Darcy heard a metal chair scoot away from behind her. She saw Harlan's co-manager, Denny Franklin, stand.

"Now hold up, Wellington. We've worked our asses off through the merger and the transition to digital readouts for the chem processing. Can't we streamline something? Production down to catalogs or newsprint only? Upgrade our energy output? Jesus, work out a better trade deal with Canada or something?" Denny huffed and drew in a long audible breath. "I mean, dammit, Wellington. There must be something in between running the mill full speed and closing it down entirely. Something, man. Something." Denny's hands hit the top of Darcy's chair. The rest of the gym started to echo Denny. Mr. Wellington shook his head and stepped back a few feet from the mic stand. He put his hands in his pockets.

"Listen, Denny, I know you worked your asses off to make the merger work. I know you all did. Great Northern is an incredible team. You guys all are. This isn't my call, well, not just *my* call. We're bleeding out. It's just the way it is. This isn't the only mill going under. I gotta tell ya, this breaks my heart. I feel for you guys. I really do. I'm losing my job, too." Shouts began to grow from the back as Mr. Wellington put up his hands. Gemma reached for Darcy's hand. Her manicured fingers were cold.

"Oh my. This isn't gonna end well. There's gotta be something we can do." Darcy squeezed her mother's hand back.

"What about a volunteer pay cut? I'll be the first to take a hit." Harlan shouted. He hoisted himself up from the chair. Other voices echoed his idea. Shouts of 'Me too' rippled from the back.

"I got a son and son-in-law who need the mill. Grandbabies who need insurance. Hell, I'll take early retirement. All us old guys will. Cut the work in half, save some dough, and keep these young guys working." A few cheers and whistles followed. Gemma whispered, "Jesus Christ, we can't afford early retirement." She let go of Darcy's hand and held her forehead.

Despite Harlan's pleas and the pleas of dozens of men after him, Mr. Wellington had no other response. Darcy saw the despair in his eyes and the exhaustion on his face. While others cursed him and hurled insults, Darcy realized he was there to close the mill, and he took no pleasure in it. The chairs scooted in and out as people began to file out the door. Mr. Wellington was still laying out numbers to justify the one thing no one in town wanted to be justified. She experienced a twinge and regretted drinking so much water before they entered the gym.

"Basil, let me out. I gotta pee," She said as she stood. Basil rose and leaned back. As Darcy straightened out her back, the twinge radiated across her stomach and downward. She hunched over and grabbed the top of the chair in front of her.

"Ouch. What the hell."

"What's wrong? What's happening?" Basil asked as he wrapped an arm around her. Gemma stood up and took her arm.

"Honey, what is it?"

Darcy shook her head and doubled over further. "I don't know. Just a cramp, I think. It's nothing really." She said as she contorted her face. Darcy realized everyone was looking at her. "I need some air."

"Give her space," Darcy's mom shouted as she slithered in-between the other chairs to get in front of Darcy. "We'll get you out of here," Gemma said in her distinctive and commanding southern drawl. "Harlan, move." Harlan scooted his chair and giant body back. Darcy overhead voices as she made her way from the gym.

"She does too much as it is." One voice said.

"It's her third in five years. Damn thing might slide right on out." Another said.

"Stop it, asshole. Make room." Yet another said. Darcy became dizzy as the air grew thicker. The murmurs echoed in her head. Her knuckles whitened as she squeezed her mother's arm. She needed out of there and free of all talk of the mill. She realized nothing about this night was reassuring and nothing would be for Winsockette again.

As the meeting attendees emptied into the parking lot, Darcy sat still in the passenger seat of the truck waiting for Basil. Gemma huffed and paced as the men found them. Once home, Basil helped Darcy up the four steps to the tiny front porch. The railing wavered under her hands. Basil vowed to fix it in the spring. Darcy didn't bother to mention they might not be able to afford the trailer past spring. Inside, Cecelia rushed to help her with her coat. Darcy had worn the same winter coat since her senior year of high school. She noticed it was harder to close.

"Gemma called, said you had cramps. I've been telling you to slow down. Cassie and O are in bed. How ya feeling?"

"I'm fine. Tired, but fine," Darcy said. She let Cecelia take her coat. Basil bent down to peel off her boots. Darcy sunk into the couch and swung her feet up on the coffee table in front of her. She leaned her head back and noticed the cobwebs on the ceiling fan. She vowed to clean it once she gave birth and it was safe to climb on the dining chair.

"I'll make tea," Basil said from the kitchen.

Cecelia sat next to her.

"What are we gonna do, Cec?" Darcy started to cry and lost the will to hide it. "There's nothing else for us. Three kids and soon no work, no money, no hope of anything else. What the hell are we gonna do?" Cecelia's long, skinny fingers coiled around Darcy's chubby hand. She caught a whiff of the peppermint tea as Basil sat it on the coffee table. He twisted open a beer for himself and one for Cecelia.

Darcy sipped tea, Cecelia and Basil swigged beer, they wrung their hands and lied to each other about how Darcy, Basil, the kids, and even Cecelia would all be fine. They lied in the subtle, natural way people do when they want to reassure those they love. The mill could be bought by another manufacturing company of some sort. A new industry could arrive. Tourism was booming in Maine. New inns and more bed and breakfasts would open, draw people in. Perhaps one of those big hiking and exploring companies would set up shop to take on Mount Katahdin. All those adventure instructors would need a place to stay and spend their riches. Wealthy tourists would flock to Winsockette to swallow up its quaintness before going on guided hikes and camping trips. The tech boom would eventually die down and people would want paper again. Love letters and postcards would be all the rage. The recession would end. They always did. But Darcy knew this was all talk. She knew they recognized it too. She knew the numbers. 75% of the town's revenue came from taxes from mill families. Every dime in the bank, every dollar spent at Bakers, every drop of gas pumped into trucks and mini-vans were all tied to the mill. There were three restaurants, four bars, two gas stations, one grocery store, one clinic, one gift shop, and two clothing stores if you counted the thrift store. There were two building and construction companies, and a handful of landlords who owned a few apartments above the bars and who owned the land the trailers were on. All of it, the very essence of Winsockette was tied to the mill. Mill money fed, clothed, and heated the town. The mill paid the mortgage, rent, health insurance premiums, and for the backpacks and school supplies of nearly every kid.

When the mill would fall silent in two months, so would everything else. The nearest town was 50 miles away and it had its own struggles because of the recession. It couldn't magically employ everyone from

Winsockette, feed its families, teach its kids, heal its sick. Winsockette wouldn't be the bustling town of her youth again. It wouldn't be filled with the latest cars, a bank bursting with pension plans with the backdrop of steam and acrid chemicals rising from smokestacks that billowed and hissed all day, every day. It would change in two months just as the world around it was changing. Other towns were sinking. The recession was hitting Maine harder than the rest of New England. Winsockette was no different just because it was hers.

As she sipped her tea and listened to the false promises of a better day, a renaissance period for northern Maine, she felt foolish and sick about bringing three children into this mess of a world. She realized Elara will never hear the mill. It won't be the soundtrack of her life like it had been theirs. Through all the surprises and moments of uncertainty in her life, Darcy counted on that one constant—the sound of the paper mill in the background. Once silent, she wondered what would replace it. What could replace it? What would Elara know as a constant? A wave of nausea overtook Darcy again as she finished her peppermint tea. *Basil was right*, she thought, *Winsockette was no place for dreamers and stargazers*. And soon it would be draped in silence.

# CHAPTER 4

A month after the meeting, Darcy was working extra hours at Bakers. Her ankles swelled after six hours, but that was a minor inconvenience compared to the restless nights worrying about the baby and just how they'd afford the rent and food soon. She never let Basil know where her mind wandered once everyone settled in bed for the night. She knew he worried about the same things as winter nights got more bearable. She usually looked forward to March and the little signs of spring to come, but now those signs of spring meant the mill's closure was right around the corner.

Darcy envied her parents who had fewer worries on their shoulders compared to the younger mill families. Gemma worked at the wellness clinic in town and Harlan had been a saver for much of his career. They'd be fine until her father got social security, even if he had to rely on a part-time job somewhere. But Jackson and Basil, and hundreds of other men their age in town were going to be left high and dry. Luckily, the mill was offering job training at the employment office and community college an hour away. Darcy held out hope each day that Basil would walk through the door and declare he was enrolling in anything anywhere to get another skill under his belt and ensure a future for them. She'd fantasize about him bursting through the door and telling them to pack up, they were moving to Augusta, Bangor, Lewiston, Portland, anywhere for

Darcy to start school immediately and save the family while he worked a high-paying job in the city. While Darcy believed she still had it in her to be an astronomer or any kind of scientist, she'd need a bachelor's degree to provide for their family. She didn't have four years. The kids didn't have four years to wait for adequate food and shelter. Basil certainly didn't have the patience to wait four years for anything either. Patience wasn't in his blood. Plus, the recession was worsening. There were no high-paying jobs in the cities or elsewhere, at least none they could turn to.

As the sun hung high on the first spring-like morning, Darcy packed up Orion and Cassie to drop off at Cecelia's so she could work a few hours at the grocery store. She rarely overlapped her work at Baker's with Basil's shift, but she took any available shift before her due date in June. Cassie whined as she slid off her boots at the door of Cecelia's trailer.

"I wanna stay home today. Why can't we just lay on the couch and watch a movie?" Cassie said as she let her thumb find her mouth. Even though Cassie was already portly like Darcy, she had Basil's blonde wavy hair and cool blue eyes, which meant she also resembled Gemma more than Darcy. Darcy accepted this was both a curse and a blessing. Cassie had Gemma's mannerisms and already loved to dabble in makeup. Darcy caught her eyeing up Gemma's crowns the last few times they had gone over for dinner. Gemma noticed her interest and Darcy realized her mom was encouraging it. Gemma rained down praise, love, and affection on Cassie the likes of which Darcy could never remember.

"Take your thumb out of your mouth. I already told you momma's gotta go to work for a bit. I'll be back before Daddy's done with work, so we'll cuddle then, okay beetle bum?"

"Okay." She lowered her head and dragged her blanket across the yellow linoleum of Cecelia's kitchen. Darcy lowered a sleepy Orion. He rubbed his eyes and wrapped his little arms around Darcy's legs. Cecelia reached down and scooped him up.

"Come on, sweetie. Let Mom head out," Cecelia said as she swooped Orion's black hair from his eyes. He unfurled his chubby baby fist and gave Darcy a slow wave as he rested his head on Cecelia's shoulder. She popped her hip out like a natural mother.

"Thanks again, Cec. I'll return the favor someday."

"Yeah, okay. Like I'm ever gonna get as lucky as you and have little munchkins." Cecelia said as she kissed Orion's forehead. Darcy stopped and turned around at the door.

"Yes, you will, Cec. I know it."

"Not if I stick around this town. Face it. There's nothing here for me to choose from anymore. Since Conner left me, ain't no one here looking my way. I'll die alone in this shitty trailer." She winced as she glanced at Cassie across the room. Cecelia mouthed 'sorry' to Darcy. Darcy shrugged.

"Oh, shut it. It's 2008 for God's sakes, not the 1800s where you're a washed-up old maid. Plus, you'll have me." Darcy said with a wink. "I gotta go. I'll be back by three."

"You and Basil, you guys aren't meant for this place. You know that. Someday you two will get out of here. Or least you will. I've always known you will someday."

"Not meant for this place? Hell, we aren't meant for anywhere else. And Cec, you know I had my way out and I blew it." Darcy shot a look over at Cassie before she closed the door behind her.

Darcy hesitated a minute in the driveway before backing out. She let the sun hit her pale, round face. She smiled. For a second, the gravity of what spring could mean for them all faded away. Darcy exhaled and thought about what Cecelia said about not being meant for that place. She remembered the bubbling desire to take off when she was a teenager. She couldn't wait to not belong to Winsockette, to peel its grip off her. She could almost taste the air on the other side of the mountain far from the hum of the mill. Now just a few short years later, she couldn't imagine going anywhere else. She thought about how it's funny that teenagers can't wait to leave, make a life away from their hometowns. Then, one day they look around and realize they don't want to leave their hometown, or more so, the people that make up those hometowns, people like Cecelia. She had no idea what type of world was even beyond that mountain anyway or if she would've made it on her own out there.

Darcy drove down the dirt winding road that led from the trailer park to town. As she crept to the stop sign, a familiar truck pulled into the trailer park. Darcy saw her brother in the driver's seat. She honked and rolled down her window. Jackson crawled to a stop, nearly passing her entirely.

"Hey, what're you doing here? I'm heading to Bakers if you're looking for me." She rested her elbow on the edge of the window. The sun bounced off her hand.

"Hey, Sis. I didn't expect to see you." Jackson said. He darted his eyes around.

"Then why are you here?"

"Where you going?" Jackson said.

"Huh? I just told you. I'm working a few hours today." Darcy said. She leaned out a little further. "Jackson. Look here. What are you doing here?" She squinted.

"I was heading up to see you. Yeah. But I guess if you're heading to work, I'll stop in and see Cec and the kids. She home with them?"

"Yeah, she's got the kids at her place. You okay? Shouldn't you be at work?" Darcy craned her head to get a little closer to her twin. Ever since they were children, when one would get upset, the other would put his or her forehead against the other. They hadn't done that in years, but for some reason, Darcy had the overwhelming urge to place her forehead against her brother's even though she couldn't reach him. She wanted to unbuckle herself, crawl out and grab his face, pull him towards her and make that connection she missed. But she didn't.

"Yeah. I'm good. Just bumming around. Took the day off. Well, I'll be heading up. You get to work." Jackson said. He started to roll up the window of his truck.

"Wait. Look here." Darcy said. Jackson averted his eyes.

"Goddammit, Jackson. Are you high? Are you?"

"No. Seriously, I ain't."

"Fucking liar. I know you better than anyone." She slapped the side of her Jeep.

"Jesus, Darcy. I'm good. Get the hell off my back."

"Don't go to Cec's and be around my kids like that. You hear me? I swear to God I'll tell mom and dad and Basil, too, if you keep this shit up." Darcy said. Her words got louder as her blood thumped in her temples. She knew he still smoked weed when he was alone at his place and with a few of his loser friends from school, minus Basil of course. But recently, she suspected he dabbled in something more just like so many others in town. She caught him with pills in his coat pocket at their parents' house at Thanksgiving. She confronted him. He leaned his forehead against hers and convinced her he only tried the pills every so often, maybe four times ever. If anyone could calm Darcy's fears and win her over as easily as Basil, it was Jackson. She loved him. He was part of her. Even if believing him didn't seem logical at the time, she had no choice when it came to Jackson. Darcy simply wanted to believe him. However, the more she forced herself to see the truth, the more she couldn't ignore it. He was taking pills more often than not. Part of her wanted to believe it was the stress of the mill closing and once everyone got back on their feet, he'd stop. Part of her knew Jackson might not. She debated telling their mom for weeks. As Jackson rolled up his window, Darcy vowed to call Gemma after work.

"I mean it. Don't go around my kids like that." Darcy bit her lip then exhaled as Jackson's truck crept away. She saw him looking back at her in his side-view mirror. She wanted to turn around and chase him down, force him to stay by her side until whatever he took was out of his system. But she rolled forward. She needed to get to Bakers. Darcy shook her head the entire drive as she tried to pinpoint when exactly Jackson would've started using whatever he was using. So many young people across the state, the country, were falling into drug addiction, and she just couldn't wrap her mind around why.

Her entire shift at Bakers was punctuated with thoughts of what she'd tell Gemma and Harlan. She didn't want her father to beat the hell out of Jackson. Then again, maybe that's what he needed. Darcy numbered the times she had seen her brother in the last few months. Fourteen, she thought. Then, while Gus Baker called her over the loudspeaker to help the produce department restock, she realized ten of those times involved her knowing something was off.

Once she left work with the fading sun behind her, she replayed what she'd say to Gemma, Harlan, and Basil about Jackson. Basil would want him to stay away from the kids completely. Darcy wasn't sure she would be on board with that extreme. As listless and unfocused as Jackson was in life, he was a good uncle. He was fun. He made the kids laugh and tired them out with his boundless energy.

After putting the Jeep in park, Darcy stepped onto Cec's tiny porch as Cec opened the door.

"Hey, girl. The kids are definitely ready. They've got cabin fever. If I thought you'd be later, I would've taken them for a short walk around the trailer park."

"Hey, thanks so much for keeping them. Did Jackson stop by here?"

"No. Why? Was he supposed to? I did see him drive by though," Cec said as she gathered Cassie's blanket from the floor and handed it to Darcy.

"Drive by? To where? The only place past yours is Mrs. Jeneau and he doesn't know her. Then, my place." Darcy said. She scooped up Orion as he held onto his pacifier. "Give me that bink, you baby." She said to Orion as he squealed.

"I think he did go to your place. I just figured you had him go get something for you or Basil. Didn't think anything of it. But he didn't stop here."

Darcy kissed the top of Cassie's head. "I'm just worried about him. You know what I found on Thanksgiving? In his pocket, remember?" Darcy said. Cec nodded and leaned down to zip Cassie's coat. "I think he's still doing it, or God knows what now."

Cecelia stood up and placed her hands on her pointy hips.

"What you gonna do? You gonna tell Basil or something." She folded her arms.

"I'm going to call mom when I get home."

"Let me know if I can help or anything," Cec said as she helped Darcy to the car. She squinted up at the sun. "Jeez. I guess spring is gonna come soon."

"Yeah, I guess it is." Darcy closed the door after they got both kids strapped in the back.

"Cec, I just feel like if I say something, I'm opening a big can of worms. And if I don't, I might lose my brother. He's given me no choice at this point."

"Well, I agree. Don't worry, sweetie. I got your back on this. Okay?" Cecelia said as she squinted. "Now go on home. Call me after you talk to Gemma."

Darcy nodded and scooted into the driver's seat. She watched Cecelia walk up the steps before she slowly backed out of the tiny, dirty snow-filled driveway. Darcy crept up the hill toward her white trailer with red shutters. Part of the skirting was rusty, right in the front. It always drew Darcy's eye. She hated that rusty section and couldn't wait for a warmer day to paint it. She hated the faded red of the shutters and door frame, too. But it was home, her only home. She wondered how much longer it would be. They had plans to buy a real home in the summer since their credit was great and Basil had a steady income. But since the closure was announced, she accepted they might have to leave the trailer under a whole different set of circumstances, or worse, stay in it forever. Darcy had a theory about trailers. Since there wasn't a foundation, no real anchor to the Earth, it was impossible to be centered, grounded while living in a trailer. Basil would laugh every time she said that out loud. Despite his laughter, Darcy knew he gave a certain level of credence to her theories. After all, he'd say, she was the scientist in the family.

She settled the Jeep into its spot and turned the key. Darcy looked up past the tiny porch to see the red storm door swaying. It only swayed when it wasn't shut right, a skill she and Basil mastered after the first time the wind roared through Winsockette and ripped it right off the frame their first winter there.

"Huh? I know I shut it right." Darcy knew Basil wasn't home yet so he didn't leave the door ajar. Darcy left the kids in their seats and closed her door. "You guys stay there a sec. Momma's going to get the door for us first. The wind is wicked awful." Darcy said as she stepped away from the car. She walked up the steps of the porch. An eerie and inexplicable sense of dread rolled over her as she reached for the door. For a moment, she considered driving back to Cecelia's and waiting for Basil before she entered. Then, she instantly thought she was being silly. She probably forgot to close it right due to being scattered this morning trying to get the kids ready. Darcy slid her house key in the lock as she held the storm door open. She turned the knob and realized it was unlocked. Her heart began to beat against her chest to the point it hurt. Darcy cautiously opened the door.

"Oh my God." She sensed in her gut someone had been in her house. Her chest seized and she had trouble expelling air. Darcy was dizzy and a queasiness roared from her pregnant belly. She darted down the narrow hallway to her bedroom. She bounced from side to side like a ball in a pinball machine. She had to get to the nightstand. Inside was a small cedar chest with a pinhole lock. She had gotten it as a teenager to hold love letters from Basil. Now it held over $5000 in cash. It was all they had. She repeatedly told Basil it was stupid, paranoid, and irresponsible to keep it in the trailer and not in the bank. He swore once they got a little more, they'd deposit the cash.

The recession news had scared him as much as the mill closing. All he envisioned were bank lines like those during the crash of 1929. Darcy would tease him that those pictures were the only ones he even looked at in his American history book. He'd laugh and tell her she was right. The absurdity of it didn't stop Basil from adding cash to the tiny wooden box each week. He grew up hiding anything he ever valued, so she dropped her insistence of putting it in the bank. He needed to be able to touch it, smell it, and see what they had saved.

She scurried around the bed, knocking over a basket of clean clothes that teetered on the edge. Darcy got on her knees and opened the door of the oak nightstand that had been her parents, like the rest of their bedroom furniture. She inhaled as she opened the door with shaking hands. The box was still where she left it. She whispered a few thank you's to God. Then she spotted the key on the carpet by her knee. She always kept in the drawer above. Darcy picked it up and tried to will her hands to stop shaking. She put it in the lock and turned it as she prayed this was all related to pregnancy brain, and she had simply dropped it and left the door unlatched. Darcy lifted the top. The box was empty except for a few letters with faded blue lines. Darcy grabbed her chest. Tears scrambled to escape her eyes as disbelief washed over her.

"No, no, no, no," she said. She closed the lid and opened it again. It was still gone, all of it. Everything they had saved was gone. Her dream of a little house and two acres in the country, a small herb garden to tend with Cassie, a basketball hoop for Orion at the end of a winding driveway, windowsills filled with antique glass bottles she had collected since she was a kid, all of it gone. Gone was all they had saved for added protection after the shutdown. There was enough saved for rent, food, gas, and anything else if they needed it once unemployment would run out. Gone was their security, their plan, their hard work and diligence, their reward for doing the right thing. Gone was the last shred of hope Darcy had that everything would be okay before Elara was due to arrive.

Darcy sat back on her swollen ankles and wiped her eyes with the backs of her hands. The last slivers of sunlight crept across the old, musty tan carpet of her bedroom. She shook her head a dozen times in hopes the money would reappear. "It had to be Jackson," she whispered. "It had to be." As much as that realization filled her with anger and a quicksand pit of betrayal and hopelessness, it also gave her a slight spark of relief. If he took it, chances are he still had it. He made a mistake. He'd give it back. Having her life savings in the hands of her twin brother had to be better than in the hands of a stranger. She reasoned, he was probably on his way back with it, along with crushing guilt and endless apologies. Once he'd hand the money back over, she'd help him get the help he desperately needed.

Darcy picked herself up off the floor of the bedroom and ran her hand along the cheap wood paneling that graced the hallway. Darcy stepped back into the cold and wind to get the children from their car seats. Orion was crying and Cassie was kicking wildly as Darcy opened the door.

"You forgot us, Momma!" she screeched.

"No, Momma didn't forget you, beetle bum. I had to check the house first. Make sure it was warm." Darcy unstrapped and lowered Cassie to the gravel of their tiny driveway. "Stay put a second while I grab your brother." Darcy unstrapped and hoisted Orion on her hip as she reached for Cassie's hand and led her to the porch. She glanced behind her in hopes Jackson was coming up the road. No one was driving toward her trailer or any of the trailers below. As she got the children inside, her rationale for believing he would come back was once again replaced by anger. Darcy placed Orion on the couch and walked to the kitchen. She grabbed the phone from the kitchen wall and dialed Gemma.

"Mom, have you seen Jackson today?"

"No, baby. Why is my baby boy crying? Everything okay over there?" Gemma's honey voice usually soothed her. Now it only irritated her further. "So, you haven't seen him at all?"

"No, I haven't. Why?" Darcy hung up and dialed Jackson. It went to voicemail. She dialed again. "Dammit. Jackson. Answer the fucking phone! We need that money. What the hell were you thinking?" She said. Darcy hung up, dialed again and again. She texted even though texts rarely went through when sent from the trailer. Darcy gave both kids a package of cheese snacks. She knew it was time to call Basil. She had no choice. Gemma called her back before she had a chance.

"Darcy, baby, what's going on? You okay?"

"Yes, Mom. The kids and I are fine. Listen, I gotta tell you something." Darcy exhaled and tossed her head back. "Jackson's been doing pills and stuff lately. I caught him with some at Thanksgiving and I know he's using whatever the hell he had then." She paused as her mother gasped.

"What? Honey, you've got to be mistaken. He works too damn hard to be mixed up with anything like that. Now I know he likes to party it up on the weekends with those boys from school, but he ain't mixed up in anything bad like those boys on the news last week. You saw that right? That big 'ole group driving up from Mass and selling stuff up this way. That ain't my Jackson. You hear me?"

"Well, Mom, that is your Jackson."

"If so, why wouldn't you say something to me right away? You say Thanksgiving? That was over what? Three months ago?"

"Yeah. I should've said something then. Trust me, I wish I had cause it gets worse." Darcy paused again suspecting her mother was making that 'I'm a southern bell about to faint' motion she always did when heavy and unwanted news of her children came out of thin air, like when Darcy told her she was pregnant with Cassie, and Orion, and this little one too. Darcy rubbed her belly as she paced the bubbling linoleum.

"I just got home from Bakers and someone broke into the house."

"Dear God. Did you call the police? Darcy, get over here with those babies. Did you call Basil?" Gemma said in a flash.

"I'm calling Basil next. Jackson did it, Mom. He took all the money we had hidden in the back bedroom. He did it, Mom."

Darcy could practically see Gemma shaking her head and holding her hand over her mouth. The muffled 'no's confirmed it.

"Mom, he came here today while I was at work. He was the only one who knew where the key and money was. He is the only one who could've done it."

"Oh my God, Darcy, are you sure? Like 100 percent sure? Honey, he loves you, and Basil, and those babies. He loves all of us. Jackson ain't never hurt a fly."

"I know, Mom. But whatever he's on must've made him do it. Made him not think or care who he's hurting. Mom, I need that money back. We need it. It's all we had, and Jackson knows it." Darcy got choked up out of the blue. She swallowed and looked up at the light to try and stop the tears. "I know he loves me. I love him. He's my brother for God's sake. I gotta find him. I'm scared for him like I'm scared for myself and Basil."

"Darcy, hon, please don't cry. We'll figure this out. I'll get your dad. You call Basil and we'll find him. I'll call those boys moms, the ones in Madison he's been running around with. Dammit, how did this happen, honey? How did Jackson get this mixed up this fast?"

"Good question, Mom. I should've said something in November, or at Christmas, too. I should've done more but I didn't think he'd ever in a million years do something like this. I should've grabbed him by the damn arm and made him tell me everything and dragged him to get help. I should've."

"We'll get this sorted out, okay? This is family business. We'll deal with this together. How much money, sweetie?" Gemma said.

"Almost $5000." She heard Gemma gasp and Darcy understood what she meant by family business. In Winsockette, everyone deals with things on their own. There's no need to call the police, authorities of any kind for family matters. Each family handles their own justice, own problems, own missteps. Unless someone else gets hurt, a family takes care of it on their own. That's how it worked in northern Maine, all of Maine for that matter. You minded your own business and in return, everyone else stayed out of yours. That was the Maine way.

Darcy paced with Orion on her hip while he wiped his cheese curl stained hands on her shoulder. She glanced down around her belly. Her ankles looked as if they'd burst any second. Cassie fiddled with the remote, already aware of which buttons to push to find cartoons or music. Darcy looked at them both and tried to remember when she and Jackson were those ages. They were inseparable their entire childhoods. They held hands throughout kindergarten and grade school. They swung together on the playground. They sat together for lunch, snacks, and naptime. They cried for the other when one was hurt or in the school bathroom sick. They pressed their heads together whenever one was sad, angry, or in need of protection and affection. They were twins, formed together, born together. Darcy grew up believing there would never be another man on earth who could replace Jackson as a friend, protector, or soulmate. It wasn't until late junior high and high school that they eventually gravitated towards other friends, letting go of each other's hands, finding a sense of themselves as individuals. While they freed themselves as adolescents, they never split. They never turned on each other. It was protect Jackson at all cost, and the same for him with her. The only reason Darcy and Basil started to date was that Jackson gave his blessing. He knew Basil was good, pure, and despite his family problems, he'd protect Darcy from the harshness of the world almost as fiercely as Jackson had since birth.

Darcy stopped pacing as the weight of what Jackson had done pressed down on her thick, rounded shoulders. *How could he do this?* She thought. Darcy pictured Jackson in a hundred different scenarios where he'd hurt something or choose wrong, leaving someone hurt or disappointed afterward. But never her. Never would he hurt her. Yet, there was no other way to see it. He had. Her other half in this life, her Gemini, had chosen her to hurt.

She remembered the first pierce of the tattoo needle when they got matching Gemini tattoos at 18. Gemma nearly had a heart attack. Darcy first showed Jackson how to find it in the sky when they were ten and she started her love affair with the stars. It was just overhead in January and into May. She and Jackson started to secretly call themselves Castor and Pollux, the Greek mythological names of the twins in the heavens. One couldn't live without the other and that was why Pollux couldn't accept the death of the mortal Castor. He begged Zeus, to make Castor immortal so they could spend eternity in the heavens together. It was like a secret language twins have. Between their mythical names and touching foreheads, Gemma used to tease that they were one mind meshed together, a yin to the other's yang. In reality, they truly were the male and female versions of the same person, until they got older and broke off into individual lives. However, despite that natural breakage between twins, between brother and sister, there was always a connection and a need to guard the other as one would guard themselves. That was until now. Jackson had stolen from her, her family, her children. He broke something inside of her when she opened that cedar box to find nothing but old letters. Tears streamed down her face when she realized she would've known it was Jackson even if she hadn't have seen him earlier coming up their lane. She knew it was him without a doubt. She felt it just like she felt his pain, his sorrow, his joy, his struggles lately. Yet despite knowing what he did, part of her, that shared soul, wanted to find and protect him.

# CHAPTER 5

After Darcy called Basil with a quick version of the day's event, he rushed to the trailer. Right as he pulled in and leaped up the porch steps, Darcy opened the door. She hadn't stopped crying since she hung up with Gemma. He wrapped his arms around her.

"I'll kill him. I swear." Basil said as his lips touched the top of her head.

"Kill who, Daddy?" Cassie asked as she tugged at him.

"No one, beetle bug," Basil scooped her up. Orion reached for him also. His cheeks were on fire, and he had started to sweat. Darcy knew that meant he was beyond angry.

"Mom's coming over. We gotta find him, Basil. Maybe he still has it all and he'll come to his senses."

"Yeah, I'm gonna find him alright. I already texted a few of those losers he's been running with from third shift. One guy said he might be in Great Pines at this one bar they've been going to." Basil said. He made his way to the couch with the two kids attached to him. "And I made it damn clear that this was family business and if anyone tips him off that I'm looking for him before I find him, they're gonna pay too." Darcy placed her hands on the small of her back as she looked at the ceiling.

"I know he's gonna give it all back. He needs help. Dammit. I should've made sure he got help when I first found pills in his coat months ago. I figured he'd just snap out of it. Jesus. I should've done more then."

"No, don't do that to yourself. You aren't his keeper. I know you guys are twins and all. I get you have a connection I can't relate to but that ain't no reason to blame yourself for whatever the hell he's done. Listen, I saw stuff at the mill, too. I knew he was running with the wrong guys. I suspected shit a few times. I'm sure your Dad did too. But, I'm not his keeper. None of us are. Not you, your mom, Harlan, no one. He did this on his own and I'm gonna fix it. We worked hard for that money. We need it. It's all we're gonna have here and we've got a third kid coming. He's gonna hand that money back."

"Basil, I'm scared," Darcy said as she rubbed her belly. Her cheeks were hot and she spoke through gritted teeth. Her hands shook like they did when she was waiting for a ride at the fair to begin or a scary part of a horror movie.

"Sit. You know you're supposed to relax and not get stressed."

"Not get stressed." She said. "That's kind of impossible now."

They both turned their heads toward the door as they heard a car door slam shut. Darcy exhaled as she said, "Mom."

Gemma opened the door as a cold wind raced behind her and swirled through her coifed hair. The howling stopped once she leaned her entire body on the back of the front door. "That air is wicked." She said as she unbuttoned her black wool coat. Gemma ran her fingers through her hair as her grandkids raced into her thin legs. "Hey, babies. G-Ma misses you bunches. Beetle Bug, help G-Ma take off her boots, would you please?" Gemma threw her head back as Cassie pulled one then the other. Gemma put her manicured hands loaded with silver and turquoise rings on her hip and blew a blonde strand from her eyes. "Now Harlan thinks he's in Madison. He called off tonight. He's coming over here to get you and take you to find him." She nodded at Basil.

"Okay. He's not answering when you call either?" Basil said.

"Nope. That's how I know he done it. That, and he won't answer his sissy. If he ain't answer Sissy, he ain't answering no one." Gemma made her way to Darcy. "Come on, baby. Sit down. I'm gonna fix y'all dinner while these guys go and take care of family business." Headlights hit the ceiling and beep came from the driveway. Basil dashed for the door and slid into his boots.

"Bay, honey. Please be careful. And please, please don't hurt him. He doesn't know what he's doing right now." Darcy said through a new stream of tears.

"You relax and let Gemma help here. Harlan and I are gonna fix this and then we'll make sure he gets help. I promise." Basil said. He darted back over to Darcy and kissed her forehead. "You just worry about yourself and this little one." Basil placed his hand on her belly. Darcy ran her hands up his arms and stood on her tiptoes. She kissed him.

"I love you, Basil Sullivan." She whispered. He patted the tops of both kids' heads and walked out the door into the night.

There was an ache in Darcy's heart she hadn't felt since the time Jackson got trapped in the woods behind their house. He had jumped from the tree they used to climb and rolled into the ditch that led to a small creek. His leg broke through the ice and he couldn't get it free once the boot filled up with cold, rushing water. All she heard was his screams for help. He sounded so far away, farther away than they had ever been from each other. They were only 8 years old and told to stay close after dinner because of how quickly night blanketed the woods. Darcy screamed back for him to let him know she realized he was trouble. She tried to follow his shouts. While it was only two or three minutes of yelling back and forth before she got close enough to see his hood peeking out from the ditch and creek, it seemed like a lifetime. She felt like Pullox trying to find Castor in the sky so they'd never be apart again. Once she found him and pulled his leg free, Darcy smacked the top of her brother's head. She remembered telling him to never scare her again like that. Together, the two of them snuck back into the house and casually put his boots in front of the woodstove to conceal what happened. Darcy saved him, protected him, covered for him. This time, it was out of her hands, and that made her heart ache and her stomach flip. She had to surrender her urge to save and protect him and hope Basil and Harlan did it for her. However, she swore to still smack him for doing this to her once she saw him again.

Gemma fawned over the kids, fixed dinner, cleaned up dinner, and re-fluffed Darcy's five-dollar couch pillows. She smiled her pearly, disarming smile the whole time. That was her gift to them, Winsockette, and the world. Gemma brought light, calm, and oozed a clueless kind of tranquility. Part of it was because of her upbringing as an only child and beauty queen from a well-to-do Charleston, South Carolina family. Part of it was also due to Harlan. He adored and sheltered Gemma. He was the filter that kept everything dirty, ugly, or unsafe from her home and life with him. He wanted her to be as glamorous and carefree as the day they met at the foot of Mount Katahdin. Gemma's family had been vacationing in Maine as they did each summer. They had a summer home in Bar Harbor and ventured away from the tourist traps once in a while. Harlan McElvaney was a mill worker who loved to hike on his days off. He worked hard and played hard. Once he saw Gemma, he knew he'd love hard, too. Gemma was the most beautiful creature he'd ever seen, or anyone else in Winsockette had ever seen either. Her smile, dainty walk, and unabashed confidence engulfed him. She owned him after the first slow southern buttery 'hello'. He was sure of it and didn't mind at all. Her family wasn't too keen on her toying with the idea of marrying a paper mill worker from northern Maine instead of heading to college and getting her MRS. Degree, but Gemma did what Gemma wanted. And she wanted Harlan as much as he wanted her. Within three months of writing back and forth, a visit at Christmas, and a few more months of love letters, Gemma had her bags packed and was headed on the train north before the last of the snow melted off Mount Katahdin. It was a whirlwind romance, but everything was a whirlwind when Gemma flitted by. The entire town became enraptured with her. She was even so bold as enter the Ms. Maine contest and compete weeks before her wedding. She won, of course, and solidified her place as a true Mainer, the most beautiful Mainer—at least for the year 1980. She was also the only woman to have a Miss Maine crown and a Miss South Carolina crown, too from the previous year.

Darcy waddled into the kitchen to make tea. Gemma brushed past her. "Now, you heard Basil. Sit right down and I'll get it."

"I can't just sit, Mom. Aren't you worried?" Darcy said.

"I am. I am" Gemma said as she put a mug of water in the microwave. "But honey, we just need to sit tight and hope for the best. We gotta believe they'll find him, get your money back, and he'll agree to get whatever help he needs so this never happens again. I'm sure wherever he is, whatever he's doing, Jackson is torn up with guilt and shame having done this to you two." She bobbed a teabag as Darcy shifted to the comfortable spot on the couch. "You know your Daddy is going to make sure this all works out. He loves you kids so much. He'll fix this. He can fix anything."

"I know he can, Mom. I just can't wrap my head around Jackson doing this no matter what he's on or doing out there."

"Hey, Cassie and O, come on guys. Let's get you to bed." Gemma scooped up Orion and took Cassie's hand. She led them down the skinny dark hallway where hours earlier Darcy had bounced against in a panic. Darcy sat alone on the couch. Despite Gemma's assurances and Basil's too, she knew in her gut things wouldn't end so neatly tonight. She knew if they found Jackson, it would get messy, painful for her brother. She also understood if they didn't find him and get back what he took, it would get more than messy. Something in her and Jackson might be irreparably broken. They'd fall apart from each other in the sky. One's hand would slip from the grasp of the other and their stars would drift, never to be reunited above the world again. Darcy was sure that outcome would be more than her heart could bear. She didn't know who she was without Jackson nearby, without his forehead pressing against hers when she needed grounding.

It was well after midnight when Darcy fell asleep on the couch with her head in her mother's lap. Gemma always lulled her to sleep by running her fingers through Darcy's short black hair, tickling her scalp. It settled Darcy's mind and stomach to just let herself go, fall asleep pretending nothing was going on in her family. Everyone was fine, tucked in, warm, and at peace. She was floating in a dream when the sound of a car door brought the real world roaring back. Darcy sat up and grabbed her phone. Her mother hushed her as a last attempt to soothe Darcy before the night's events would unfold before them. There were no calls or texts from Basil, Harlan, or Jackson. She shook her head as the front door opened. Harlan stepped in. He looked heavy, worn. Gemma dashed to him. Darcy rubbed her puffy eyes.

"Where're the boys?" Gemma asked as she took Harlan's giant coat. Darcy scooted to the edge of the couch and used the arm to push herself up. She couldn't get over how quickly this pregnancy was making everyday tasks difficult for her once-tiny body. She didn't remember having this much trouble getting up from the couch until close to the end of her third trimester. Yet now in her second trimester, she was a bloated blob of her former self. When Darcy stood straight and tried to arch her back, the door cracked open again. She saw Basil's curly blonde locks sprout from a bloodied face. Darcy grabbed her belly. Gemma let out a shriek at the sight.

"Oh my God, Basil. What happened?" Darcy said. Her voice cracked as she shuffled closer to her husband. Gemma reached for his chin as he pulled away. Harlan took her hands.

"He's hurt, but nothing's broken. Let him go get cleaned up, will ya?" Harlan commanded. Darcy's chin trembled as her husband cringed.

"I'm gonna be ok. It's worse than it looks." He said through a bloodied lip. "The cut on my forehead is what bled the most. I'll be alright." He reached up and blotted his oozing lips with his sleeve.

Darcy was scared to touch him. Basil had only ever looked that brittle to her and her parents one other time since he had been part of their lives. It was the night of his 17th birthday six years earlier. Basil was supposed to come to Gemma and Harlan's for ice cream and cake after dinner with his dad, Ed. Everyone knew Ed was the town drunk, unable to hold down a job even at the mill where every other town drunk still managed to show up on time and be semi-capable of running the equipment without getting anyone killed. Gemma instantly had a soft spot for Basil because she too understood what it was like to live with the town drunk. The only difference with her father was he was filthy rich. This makes the town drunk more eccentric and certainly more acceptable.

That night six years ago, Basil was late. Darcy had called his house a few times to no avail. Then, Ed answered on the sixth call as the sun set on a summer night. He was slurring, which wasn't unusual. But Darcy noticed he was more agitated than usual. He was angry, bitter, and vile. Darcy winced and could almost feel the spittle come through the receiver. Just as she was convincing Harlan and Jackson to find Basil, there was a knock on the door. Basil was standing there alone, sunken shoulders, tear-stained face, and blood through his shirt. Gemma walked him in and lifted it to see a gash about four inches long from his belly button to his side. She gasped then too. Gemma cleaned him up while Basil made excuse after excuse for why the McElvaney family shouldn't call the police. Ed Sullivan was already shunned by most. The scars from cigarette burns on Basil's arms told them the abuse had been going on for years, ever since Basil's mom left. Gemma and Harlan agreed not to call the police, or kick Ed's ass if Basil moved in and finished his senior year of school. He did. He also healed. They absorbed Basil Sullivan into their family that night.

Basil's dad would show up from time to time, mostly to get into Basil's good graces or borrow money. Then he'd turn belligerent, yell, scowl, and disappear leaving Basil cast aside again. While Gemma never experienced the same type of abuse, she recalled the humiliation of a drunk dad making his kid feel like shit. Her tenderness for Basil that night was the same as she approached him now. Despite Harlan's orders, she reached for him again. Basil let her. She was the closest thing to a mother he had.

Darcy tried to regain her composure as Basil tried to project a smile to ease her fear. Gemma stood on her tippy toes to touch his nose, move it slightly from side to side.

"You're right. Nothing's broken. Let's go to the bathroom and clean you up." She said as she rubbed his arm and then took his hand. She stopped as they approached the hall and turned back to Harlan. "And Jackson? Where's he at?" She bit her bottom lip. Darcy recognized that look. She was trying to be the calm one, trying to not cry as her own son's name crossed her lips. Harlan exhaled.

"We dropped him off at home. He's got cleaning up to do, too. They gave it to each other pretty good. He'll be okay too, Momma." He said. Gemma nodded and took Basil down the hall. Silence fell over the living room as Darcy stared at her towering father, the man who kept them safe her whole life, who protected Gemma and her from any pain.

"Where was he, Dad? Did you get the money back?" He motioned for her to sit back on the couch. She shuffled over and let her tired body sink into the thrift store find that held her family for almost five years. Even though it was as musty as the carpet, oddly enough it smelled like home. Harlan sat beside her. His giant body meshed into the couch deeper than hers.

"Well, kid, he was in a bar in Great Pines, right where Basil thought he'd be. He was out of it and with those guys he's been running with. None of those assholes tried to interfere. They knew it was family business. We dragged him outta there to the parking lot, and that's when Basil laid into him and demanded to know where his money was." Harlan took in another deep breath. He patted Darcy's knee. "Jack says he gave it to these guys from Lewiston he owed for drugs. He was in deep, kid. Deep. Guess he owed them a few grand."

"My few grand, Dad? That's money Basil and I have been saving for a few years. Money we need back."

"Honey, I'm afraid we might not get it back. But don't you worry. Your mom and me, we'll make sure you kids are alright." He squeezed her knee. "This is family business, and we'll take care of it. That's what family does."

Darcy's cheeks grew red and her heart started to beat through her chest. "No Dad. Covering this up for Jackson isn't what a family does. He needs help, and we need our money back."

"Listen, we'll take care of this, Darcy, like I said. Your mom and me got a few bucks saved. We'll help you kids out. We'll make sure Jack stops this nonsense."

"No, Dad." She said again. Darcy wasn't sure she had ever told her dad 'no' about anything. "You can't just help us out. We aren't kids. We're adults with a third kid on the way. We did the right thing, years ago and now. I know we let you down when I got pregnant, but we did the right thing. We proved to you guys, to everyone that we could step up. Then, we not only got our own place, but we've also fed, clothed, and taken care of ourselves and our kids all on our own. On our own dime. We saved." Darcy's voice cracked. "We got all of this ourselves. You can't think you can just swoop in and fix this, and fix Jackson. His problem is much worse than you telling him to stop and giving me money to make up for what he did. Don't you get that?" Her pulse quickened more. Darcy's knees started to shake. Harlan huffed and patted her again.

"I know it's bad, Honey. I know. But we're family. We'll get through this."

His words lingered in front of her. The word 'family' suddenly seemed foreign. Darcy was sick to her stomach. Time stopped, and her ears rang. Her bloodied husband was getting cleaned up by Gemma down the hall. Her babies were sleeping mere feet from the scene. Jackson was alone in his apartment above the restaurant in town. He was surely downing a few beers while dabbing his and Basil's blood from his face and knuckles. Harlan was doing what Harlan always did, trying to take control and set the course for them all, trying to keep the dirt, grime, and grit of the real world from touching the family he loved.

Darcy touched her belly and thought of Elara inside, swimming in the blissful ignorance of amniotic fluid and protected from the outside world while the men Darcy loved most in this world, needed the most, had beaten each other to a pulp. Her twin, her star-embedded other half had betrayed her and his own best friend at the same time. He had detached from her and drifted to a place unreachable. She wanted to hate him, wanted to banish him to eternal separation in the night sky, to drift alone without her love. She wanted to but couldn't. The thought of banishing Jackson from her life seemed no different than ripping off her right arm. He was part of her. They were celestially linked forever, doomed to exist as one despite anything else. Darcy's gut tightened. Hating Jackson even for an instant was like hating herself. She let a few more tears fall.

"Dad," she said through lips she tried to stop trembling. "Why did he do this to me? I never thought Jackson would hurt me in a million years. Why us? He could've stolen from anyone but us, but me." Her shoulders sunk and breath escaped. She didn't need an answer from Harlan to know. But he sighed and gave her one anyway.

"He knew you'd forgive him. You're the one person who will always forgive him, and always love him." Harlan said. He draped his hefty arm around her shoulder and drew his only daughter in close. She sobbed into his chest, something she hadn't done since the night she sat him and her mom down to tell them she was pregnant. Darcy drew in his rugged scent, unchanged from when she was a girl'. Despite his fullness and the fullness which consumed her own belly, she felt empty and wondered how much more she and Basil could afford to lose. Then Elara moved. Hope started to creep back in and the mill, the uncertainty, and the betrayal by Jackson seemed to fade a bit. There was something tangible to look forward to, to celebrate, to anticipate, someone still untouched by the tarnished world around her.

# CHAPTER 6

Darcy rose with the sun and let Basil catch up on sleep. His body needed to recover. Everyone needed to recover. Darcy played with Orion and Cassie. After filling their bellies, she cleaned the kitchen and tackled the basket of towels next to the couch. It was beginning to seem like any other weekday she had off until she looked up to see Basil in the hallway watching his family. She smiled at him from behind the stack of towels and socks.

"How you are feeling?" Darcy asked.

The kids ran to his legs when they realized he was awake. "Easy guys. Daddy got hurt at work."

Basil reached down and scooped up Orion as he patted Cassie's blonde ponytail. "How's my big guy doing?" He said as he kissed Orion's forehead. He cringed. Darcy knew it was his ribs. "And beetle bug?" Cassie blew him a kiss and meandered back to her dolls and cars. "I'm okay," Basil said. He slumped into the chair closest to the front door. "I gotta fix that draft." He looked at his watch. "I gotta call work."

"Dad said he took care of it. They don't expect you till Monday." Darcy said.

"Yeah, but we've only got a few weeks pay left and we can't afford to miss a penny, especially now," Basil rubbed his head. "I gotta make some calls about interviews, too." He slid his boots on, grabbed the phone and his cigarettes. Basil smoked and talked on the front step. She heard him say, "I understand" a few times.

The weight of his words filled the space between them and slowly flowed across the hall and engulfed every room of the trailer. She swallowed a lump in her throat. He stepped back in and slid off his work boots.

"I feel, I feel like this is my fault. I never should've told him where that money was. I just. I just—"

"No, you don't get to blame yourself for what he did. You always do that when Jackson fucks up. You only told him in case of an emergency after I got hurt last year. He did this. Not you. Him."

"But he's my brother. My twin, for god's sake. I just can't help but think if I said something sooner, about the drugs, this might not have happened. You know?" Her words trailed off into tears. She was so tired of crying over Jackson, over money, over the mill, the town, over everything. She told herself it was hormonal from being pregnant. But Darcy accepted their circumstances and the downward spiral that was becoming their new reality in Winsockette was to blame despite the flashes of hope she clung to in quiet moments like last night in her father's arms. And Jackson. Jackson was to blame. Basil walked over and nestled in beside Darcy and the armrest of the worn-out couch.

"It's going to be okay. I promise." He reached his arm around her as she collapsed her head into his chest. Cassie tugged at her arm as Orion tried to crawl into her lap. Her tiny family was folded into her, around her. She inhaled their scents, their collective warmth. Darcy nodded yes as the smell of Basil's cigarettes and sweat combined with the smell of cheese snacks and apple juice, and freshly washed baby hair. As comforted as Darcy was with their closeness and the unshakable protection of her husband, she sensed his anger and fear. They were both angry and fearful of what their future would bring. Her babies were free of the worry that consumed her and Basil. She wondered if her parents had ever experienced this level of fear and uncertainty when she and Jackson were little. *No,* she thought, *Mom was always sheltered from fear, from everything.*

Basil spent the rest of his day making calls and answering texts. The news kept getting worse as the days wore on. Interviews never materialized and bills that usually got paid right away were now being prioritized and stacked. Jackson had texted and called with apologies that always left Darcy in tears and Basil with a vein bulging from his forehead and neck. The calendar showed two more paychecks. While unemployment would kick in and there were job and trade training opportunities dangled in front of them and the rest of the mill workers, there was a sense of doom settling over the skyline. Everyone knew the mill would grind to a halt, the smoke would dissipate, the smell of the chemicals and paper reams would fade, and silence would replace the heartbeat that kept Winsockette alive for over a century. Despite the paperwork and promises which came in the mail regarding health benefits, 401Ks, shares and dividends for retirees, and plans for the mill space, everything Darcy, Basil, and their families knew was slipping away.

Darcy found herself obsessively rubbing her belly like it was a magic orb and this new little girl was going to come out with the answers they all needed. She began to think of Elara as a solution as if a moon of Jupiter held all their hopes and dreams and would somehow pass through her round body and into the world around them. She had dreams of labor and Elara being crowned as a messiah sent to save the town, with a crown of thorns and glowing lights. She had dreams where Elara passed through her and was lifted for her first breath just as the pressure valves were turned again and the steam billowed above their tiny town, their kingdom.

As Darcy searched for signs, analyzed her dreams, and scanned the night sky looking for proof the seasons would change and somehow nothing else would, Basil grew darker, less hopeful. The strain of her parents demanding forgiveness as Jackson went to an out-patient program paid for with her parents' retirement savings and the strain of no real prospects of a new career were taking its toll on the proud young father and husband who had always provided a predictable life for his family. Darcy saw it in his eyes. He also drank more at night. Darcy had never looked at him with a beer and thought he looked like his father, until now. She hated the thought that any part of his dad was in Basil. She knew Basil did, too. From the night she met him, Darcy understood Basil was determined to be the man his father wasn't. As he tipped back beer after beer as she scurried the kids off to bed, Darcy strained her eyes to see the boy he was that night at the dance when he first kissed her. Darcy would also envision the man he was destined to grow into, a man who would always protect her and the kids. But this Basil, the in-between Basil worried her. She couldn't lose him to drink and Jackson to drugs. Darcy couldn't lose either of them.

Whenever Gemma and Harlan would visit and show up with a few extra groceries and goodies for the kids, Basil would retreat into himself. He was accepting but not warm anymore. He understood their need to help Jackson as much as he understood Darcy's need to check in on her brother, but Darcy knew he was betrayed in a way that went beyond family strife. Basil was robbed of the chance to do right by Darcy and the kids. Darcy could see him sinking. As the night shift was sent home for the last time and the mill would only run daylight shifts for 12 more days, Darcy realized they were all sinking. No amount of blooms, or buds of spring, or growing hope in her belly would change it. Winsockette would sink, too.

The last day Basil worked at the mill was the first day nice enough for Darcy to take the children on a long walk to town and back. The sun was high and warmed her pale face. The kids squinted in the stroller as she and Cecelia walked and talked.

"I know something will come up. Something great will come our way. I can feel it." Darcy said as Cecelia took over pushing as they approached the hill back to the trailer park.

"Ever since Conner left me, I thought the same thing. Something will come up, something or someone will knock on my door and make everything great. But that's all just bullshit."

"Oh, Cec. It will. Someone will." Darcy said while she followed her up the hill to the trailer park.

"No, it won't. Not if I stay here. Face it, Darcy, there's nothing here for me. I've been thinking of leaving for a few months now. If I can get out of the lease for my trailer, I'm gonna. I think I'll head to Mass to stay with my aunt for a bit and figure things out. Maybe wait till summer." Cecelia said.

"What? You can't leave me. I've got a new kid coming. I need you. We need you. I can't imagine my life without you within earshot. Dammit, Cec. Things will get better."

"No. they won't. Not here. You know that. Hell, with the mill closing, there isn't even a chance of picking up a new guy that has any promise much less making it on my own here. I can't get by working at the truck stop forever. Conner left almost a year ago. He's not coming back. There's nothing here for me. And, what happened to Jackson is just gonna happen to more and more guys in this town. You know that."

"But-"

"Face it, Darcy, Winsockette has chewed us up and it's gonna spit us out." Cecelia said. She blew her hair from her face as she pushed the stroller up the hill.

Darcy looked at the ground. She tried to hide that she was having trouble keeping up on their walk. She couldn't picture a day without having Cecelia around if she needed her. Then again, weeks ago she couldn't picture a day without having Jackson if she needed him.

Once they parted ways at Cecelia's trailer, Darcy pushed the stroller up the rest of the hill. Her belly was getting in the way more with each passing day. After she unbuckled the kids and corralled them into the house, Darcy saw Basil sitting on the couch holding his head in his hands.

"Well, that's it." He said into nothingness. "Today was my last day. We thought we had another few days left, but nope. Today was it. After second shift gets off, everything will turn off for good." Basil said while looking through her.

Darcy understood this moment in their existence in this little corner of the earth would come. She feared the silence was looming in the background and it would consume them once the mill stopped. She had dates, times, hours, but it didn't seem real until Basil said so. Her dad, who was undoubtedly eating and getting ready for work would show up and be told he had about four more hours doing the only job he had ever known. Nearly every man and some women in town would punch out and walk away from the machines, valves, reams, vats of chemicals that had been a part of their days, their parents' and grandparents' days. They'd all leave and walk back to a community that was collectively lost.

The air was being sucked out of her chest. She held her belly as Elara pushed from one side to the other, with a few kicks as if she wanted to crawl out early and comfort them all. Darcy suddenly became fearful of the silence that was sure to fall. She wanted to open the kitchen window and force the kids to listen, to remember a sound they'd probably never hear again. Just as a wave of despair started to bubble up in her gut, Basil sat straight up as his eyes grew wide. He took a swig of beer and set the bottle down on the end table without looking away.

"Darcy, come here. Look at this." He said with his eyes fixated on the tv that sat on top an old entertainment center Gemma gave them. She sat next to him, annoyed he was already drinking. It was the news.

"What happened?" She asked.

"Shh. Just listen." Basil said as he turned up the volume. Darcy let her eyes absorb the destruction pictured in front of them. A newscaster spoke in a frightened voice.

"As you can see, the damage is far beyond what forecasters expected. Residents only had one minute from the sound of the tornado siren until the twister touched down. From what we know, there are dozens trapped in an elementary school. The front face of a clinic is rubble. And if you can pan over to the right, Bob, you'll see what's left of a strip mall where shoppers filled each parking spot when it touched down." Her words trailed off as Basil and Darcy became engrossed in the tragedy that was still unfolding. Even though streaks of sun broke through the clouds, debris filled the screen. As they watched over a thousand miles away in a mill town in Maine, people who looked exactly like them were running, digging, crying and frantically calling and searching for loved ones. Darcy wanted to pull Cassie onto her lap as Basil picked up Orion. She wanted her parents and Jackson with her. She wanted to be surrounded by the warmth and safety of her family as she watched live as families in Nebraska were stripped of everything and possibly everyone they loved.

"Jesus. Look at that." Basil said in a low and hushed voice. He reached for his beer. It was as if the people and places on the tv were brittle and more buildings would fall if they spoke too loudly. Darcy was instantly transported back to school the day they watched the terror attacks of 9/11 unfold live in study hall. A fire chief and police officer stood at a group of microphones and rattled off more facts and figures about wind speed, unpredictable paths, F5 ratings, which buildings were a total loss and where to go for help. Her tiny trailer seemed like the safest place in the world as they watched the horror unfold over a thousand miles away. A baby was pulled from his mother's arm as they hid in a tub. A toddler who was lucky enough to have someone slip a football helmet on him was found wandering in a field, alive but lost. Nursing home residents were trapped. Families grocery shopping were pinned under rubble. A high school bus filled with kids on a field trip was tumbled and crumpled as it blew off an overpass. A state of emergency was declared. Lives were ruined. Families separated. Belongings scattered. The only church was left wide open without a stitch of the roof. A passerby stopped by a news reporter and asked, "Where was God?" It seemed all of Nebraska was asking "Where was God?"

Darcy and Basil held hands as the kids climbed over and under them. Basil only moved to grab more beer. The news replayed the same footage with a few gruesome updates scattered here and there. A young pregnant woman who looked not a day older than Darcy made her way to the microphone of a reporter. "The noise was torture. Now the silence is. It's too quiet. Nothing but quiet." She said as her bottom lip trembled. She rubbed her belly just as Darcy did 1700 miles away. Darcy gasped and Basil squeezed her hand tighter. "Please, send help. We need help." The woman muttered as the reporter took back the microphone.

"My God, Basil. Those poor people." Basil nodded in stunned agreement. Darcy rose to make dinner in the kitchen and go about the business of taking care of the family, thankful for the drafty door and leaking roof they had. She needed to look away, however, Basil stayed and absorbed more.

After the kids were put to bed and the kitchen cleaned, Darcy stared out the window at the smokestacks. Night had fallen and she knew the sound would soon fade. She cracked the tiny kitchen window. As the cold spring air trickled in and up her neck and face, she let the noise surround her, protect her. She pictured that poor woman, alone, pregnant, in silence.

"That's it. I've got it." Basil said from the couch as he put down another bottle. Darcy looked over her shoulder to see he was still watching the news coverage.

"Basil find something else to watch, please. I can't take hearing any more of those people's stories. And seeing that town, the school and church, it's just too much." Darcy said.

"Come here. Just listen." He sat alone with the tv glow all around him.

Darcy slid the window down and left the view of the mill. She sat next to Basil.

"God did that. God took everything from those people." He said as he pointed at the screen.

"Basil, that's awful. Don't talk like that." Darcy said. While not overly religious, she was superstitious. Talking ill of God had to bring bad luck and they couldn't afford any more of that.

"No, listen. God took from them just like man took from us." Basil said. He beat his chest with his fist.

"What are you talking about?" She wished she had paid attention to how many beers he had already. She wasn't up for arguing with a drunk Basil.

Basil jumped up and stood in front of the glow of the tv. "Man, greed, and technology took everything we had. The mill, no more need for paper, this damn recession caused by rich Wall Street bastards, all of it. Everything bad that's happened to us, even with your brother and the pills. Man did it all. Man-made drugs swallowed your brother whole. Man-made phones and shit took away our mill." He threw his hands in the air. He grabbed his cell phone from the coffee table and lobed it on the chair by the door. "Man-made greed caused the market to plummet which is why there isn't shit for opportunities here now. Man!" Darcy shuddered as he paced. She was afraid he'd wake the kids. "Man took it all away even though we've always done the right thing. You see what I mean?" He paced back and forth as Darcy followed him with her eyes. "Me and you, Darcy. We've always done right and we're getting screwed!"

"I...I guess. Sure. The tech boom and recession bullshit has hit us hardest. I get that. But what's that got to do with Nebraska?" She glanced at the tv and wondered why Basil thought they had any reason to complain.

Basil stopped right in front of her. He put his hands up to the ceiling as if amazed Darcy wasn't making the connection. He drew in a deep breath and rolled his icy blue eyes at her. The light of the tv made a glow behind his long, lanky body.

"God. Man took from us. God and his wrath. His storm," He pointed up to the heavens, the stars right outside their picture window. "God took everything from these poor folks down there. For no reason. None of it was their fault like none of this was our fault." He paused as if she should understand. "God did it to save us, save me and you." Basil raised his hands high again and looked at Darcy with confused and wild eyes. He looked stunned that she wasn't following his grand revelation.

"Wha—Basil, those poor people didn't deserve that. How does their pain save us? What the hell are you babbling about?"

"I know they didn't deserve it. Just like we didn't. But listen. God's wrath will be our salvation." He leaned down in front of her and banged his hands on the coffee table. "We will go and follow his wrath and rebuild. We'll get by, make a living, by rebuilding what God destroys. You see?"

"Honey. That's crazy. You sound like a crazed tv preacher. You've been glued to that tv for too long tonight. You've had a few too many. I hardly think it's right to talk about making a living off the destruction of everything those poor people had."

"Why not? Someone is profiting from our destruction. The mill closing, the tech boom, it's a moneymaker for someone. And that someone ain't us, Darcy. The recession. All those rich Wall Street bastards made a killing, a fortune like we'll never know, and they made it all off our backs. They'll get a bailout while we get shit. We're paying the price for their greed. We've lost everything because of them, and God is showing me a way to get it all back, to take care of you and the kids." Basil said. He grabbed his drink and swigged more. He paced faster and faster in front of the tv.

"But…but how are we gonna help a town across the country rebuild? Sit, please. You're making me dizzy." Darcy rested her head in her hands. It seemed so much later than it was.

"We're gonna follow God's wrath like I said." Basil got on his knees in front of Darcy. His words quickened. "We're gonna move to Nebraska and follow tornadoes. We're gonna rebuild houses, churches, whatever we can, and that's how we're gonna save ourselves." He darted his eyes to meet hers.

"We can't just move to the middle of nowhere and rebuild tornado-damaged towns. Basil, that's just…just crazy." Darcy felt short of breath. He was sucking the air out of the room.

"It's not crazy. It's God's plan. We'll follow God's wrath. It's perfect."

"Perfect? No, it makes no sense. Stop it. You're scaring me. You don't even believe in that shit that much. God's plan? God's plan is we find other jobs and make money to replace what my brother stole and buy a small house with a yard, and enough room for these three kids. You remember that, don't you?" Darcy fought the urge to yell and shake her husband by the shoulders. She couldn't believe she was having this conversation with the love of her life. "We're about to have a third kid. I'm in no condition to chase tornadoes!" Darcy stood. Her voice rose higher than it had since Jackson stole their money. She threw her arms up then wrapped them around her belly. "I'm due in two months! We aren't moving anywhere, and we aren't chasing any damn storms! Do you want to get us killed? Orion, Cassie, me, this baby? Do you? What the hell are you thinking? God's plan? Dammit, I love you Basil, but I'm going to bed, and we'll figure it out tomorrow." She drew in another deep breath and tossed her head back. "I might not know too much about what we're gonna do now that the mill is stopping, but I sure as hell know God's plan for us doesn't involve me and you and the kids chasing any damn tornadoes."

Darcy stomped down the hall. She huffed as she closed the bathroom door and turned on the water to wash her face. Her heart was racing and, and her temples throbbed again. She looked in the mirror and saw streaks from tears she didn't know she shed. Eyeliner was smudged everywhere. Her eyes were swollen from being tired and lost. She cried quietly and washed away her make-up. Her face was puffier than it had ever been.

As she settled into the full-size bed and pulled up the quilt she got as a wedding gift from her mother, Darcy heard the faint hum and voices from the tv in the living room. She knew Basil was still watching storm footage. She realized he wouldn't come to bed anytime soon. She heard him crack another beer, then another. She sat up and scooted to the edge of the bed. Darcy stood and took two steps to the window. She peeled back the yellow curtain and saw the lights of the mill. They were going off, one by one. Darcy lifted the window enough to hear but not alert Basil that she was still awake. She heard the sound she had always heard her entire life, a few hisses and groans. Then, the steam and smoke turned to a single streak in the moonlit sky above Winsockette. A few more hisses unleashed the last remnants of life in the mill. Then, silence. The Great Northern Paper Mill groaned as it took its last breath and expelled the lingering air towards the stars. A few lights flickered as she saw headlights come on in the parking lot. The mill workers, including her father, were leaving for the last time. A moment of panic, an overwhelming need to run to the mill and turn everything back on bubbled up in Darcy. The silence was choking. *How had this happened?* She thought. *God's plan? How could any of this be God's plan for us?* Darcy crawled back into bed and pulled the quilt up to her chin. She didn't close the window. The cold air swirled around her and the silence covered her. It was as if her entire world was new, unrecognizable. Even though she was in the same bed she had shared with the man she loved for five years and he was in the next room, she felt alone. She was tumbling and despite the baby she carried, there was nothing certain or steadfast in her life anymore. There was nothing but the night sky and quiet.

# CHAPTER 7

All hopes of Basil's crazy idea fading and a new plan coming into view were dashed for Darcy in the morning and in the days after the F5 tornado destroyed parts of Franklin, Nebraska. As Darcy muddled through the motions of loading up the kids and keeping them entertained at the employment office and keeping them out of Basil's hair as he made appointments for job training and employment counseling, she noticed he spent every spare moment watching news footage or talking about the force of tornadoes. He was like a kid who recently learned about a subject or phenomenon and couldn't talk or think about anything else. Darcy shrugged her shoulders behind him as he rambled on to Harlan and Gemma about the amount of damage, numbers of dead and missing, and the extent of insurance claims for rebuilding efforts.

He told anyone who would listen that they planned to move. As she fiddled with dollars and crossed out unnecessary items on her grocery list, she had to tug at his arm as he told the manager at Bakers that Darcy might not be working there much longer. Darcy made a point of ducking back down an aisle to tell the manager to give her as many hours he could until Basil found something else. Any talk of them moving was just talk, she explained. Darcy found out through co-workers at Bakers that word had spread of Basil's plan to move them to Nebraska. This plan that came to him in a drip and was now a full-fledged faucet flooding their lives. The more Darcy tried to forget it or divert the looks and questions from others, the more the plan was coming to life for Basil, the more people who grew exponentially concerned. Within a week of the storm and the mill closing, Darcy was worried Basil was having a breakdown.

As she returned home from Bakers after working an entire Saturday, Darcy saw her parents' truck in her driveway. She exhaled and hobbled up the porch steps holding her belly. She glanced over beyond the hill at the empty mill. Darcy was still startled by the silence. Inside, she found Basil standing at the kitchen sink and Gemma, Harlan, and Jackson sitting on the couch. She hadn't seen Jackson since the fight despite never-ending texts from him asking her forgiveness. Jackson stood and slid his hands into his pockets. Darcy furled her lips as Cassie and Orion ran to her.

"Hey. What are you doing here?"

"He's come to apologize in person," Basil said from across the trailer. He opened the fridge and grabbed a beer.

"A little early, ain't it, Basil?" Gemma said. Basil rolled his eyes. Darcy's pulse quickened. She hated it when he did that, even if Gemma deserved it at other times.

Darcy leaned down and kissed her kids as she slid off her shoes and pulled her shirt down over her belly. Every time she bent down and back up, her shirt was sliding up more and more, revealing the lively bump underneath. Jackson took a few steps towards her. Darcy looked down at the carpet.

"I don't expect forgiveness, but I need you to know I'd change what I did if I could. I know what I took from you guys. I hate myself for what I did, and I know with the mill closing, I'm to blame for this being harder for you guys. Darcy, you're my twin, and you, Basil, and these kids mean more to me than anything." Jackson said as he stepped closer.

"I know, Jackson. I know. I just——"

"It's ok. I honestly don't expect you to say anything. I just need you two to know I'm going to make it up to you somehow, and I'll spend the rest of my life earning your trust back. I love you too much to lose you guys."

Gemma held her hand up to her mouth as she fought tears. Darcy knew Gemma had been with Jackson every day since that night. He had moved back in with them, and she made sure he attended meetings, drug testing, and stuck to a plan. It had become Gemma's latest job. Darcy sensed it also took her mind off the mill and what she and Harlan would do once their savings ran out, what savings they had left.

"We're gonna be okay, Jackson. Hasn't Darcy told you guys about our plan?" Basil said from the archway from the kitchen to the living room. Gemma rolled her eyes then widened them as she looked at Darcy as if to say 'get your husband under control, darling.' Harlan stood up from the sunken couch.

"Yes, Basil. We've heard the plan that wasn't. Give it a rest already." Harlan said. "You've got serious plans to focus on."

"Give it a rest? Harlan, I don't think you understand. I'm serious. God wants us to go. There's nothing left for us here anyway." Basil said. The air in the musty and now crowded trailer thickened. She wanted them all to disappear, except the children.

"Honey, y'all have us, family. You aren't taking those babies to some hick corn town in Nebraska and rebuilding jack shit. It ain't gonna happen." Gemma said from the couch with her eyes rolling even more wildly.

"Everyone stop. I just got home. I worked for ten hours on my feet. The store was busy as hell and I really don't wanna listen to any of you argue. I just want to sit down, eat dinner, and relax with my kids and husband." Darcy said. She waddled past Jackson and took a seat next to her mother. Basil ducked back in the kitchen to get her a plate.

"Alright, alright. Relax, honey." Gemma said. Jackson turned to face her.

"I'm already working to pay you guys back. I promise. Just know that. And I've been clean since that night. Ask Mom."

"I know you've been. Mom has told me constantly. And I believe you're sorry. And I know I should've done more when I first found those pills on you. I'm too exhausted to give you the forgiveness you need right now. Someday, yes, but not right now. I can't deal with this all right now." Darcy rubbed her belly as Basil handed her a plate of homemade chicken potpie. It was his specialty. Gemma smiled up at him. Despite the overwhelming stress and tension her family was filling the room with,

Darcy knew they loved each other and her. For a moment, Darcy let that be all she needed, that and the chicken potpie.

She ate a few bites as the conversation once again turned to Basil's plan. Harlan's face grew red as Basil droned on about May being peak tornado season. Jackson tried to calm Harlan and Gemma tried to calm Jackson. Voices gradually rose as the kids ran from adult to adult to be held, kissed, and sent along to play. Just as Darcy took the last bite and noticed her feet were a little less swollen, Harlan yelled out.

"Dammit, boy. You don't know nothing about building or rebuilding. You're just a god-damned paper mill worker. That's all you know!" Darcy's shoulders rose and the children cringed. Gemma did that twisty mouth move when words were unleashed, and she was unsure how'd they land.

"I know that! Don't you think I know that? But guess what, old man. You're nothing but a mill worker too. And you too, Jackson. Now here's the real kick in the ass. There's no more mill! Jesus, Harlan, you sound like my Dad sometimes." Basil shouted louder than anyone had ever heard him shout. The room shook. The silence of the mill was replaced for a moment. Darcy wondered how much of this plan was a way to escape his dad and avoid becoming him, jobless, stuck in Winsockette forever, a drunk. "I've got no choice but to leave. You guys can stay here and rot, eat the scraps left behind by Great Northern. But, me, I've got babies to feed and a wife to care for. We're going. We're chasing something. We're chasing a future whether you want to believe in it or not." Basil said in his normal voice. "I'll learn to build just like I learned to work the mill. End of story. I'm not gonna stay here and sit on my ass."

Silence returned to the room. Basil had a determination in his eyes Darcy hadn't seen before, but also a spark of fear.

"I believe it's God's plan for us to follow those storms and rebuild what's lost. I think it's God's work. Are you gonna stand here in my house and tell me it *isn't*? Anyone? Those people lost everything. I intend to do what I can to help them recover. Now, you know I worked a few summers roofing. Remember that, Jackson? We both did. In high school."

"Yep. You were good at it, no doubt. But summers roofing and repairing tornado damage are two different things." Jackson said.

"True. But there's nothing here for me anymore. For us." He nodded toward Darcy and Orion who had climbed onto her lap as she balanced her empty plate. "This is a way for me to do what's right and provide for my family. I did the unemployment bullshit and training class. I went to the welfare office to watch Darcy sign us up. That didn't sit right with me. None of it did. Man, this recession, all that greed out there took everything from us and I'm gonna get some of it back, without any damn welfare check."

"Now come on, there's no shame in taking help when you need it. You worked hard for those benefits just like everyone else in town." Harlan said in a tone that told Darcy and Gemma his blood pressure had lowered.

"I know. Harlan. I'm not saying anything against you guys and everyone else who needs that help until something else opens up here. But for me, for me and Darcy, I know there's something more. I can't explain how or why, or what, but I just know it. I know taking us to Nebraska and doing this work, cleaning up after God's wrath, is what I'm supposed to do." Basil said. The air grew heavy again. Darcy knew her family was shell-shocked and resigned to the fact that Basil meant every word. Whether he was right or not, whether leaving was the best thing or not, none of that mattered. It was the right thing in Basil's mind, and no one was going to change that. Harlan's face sunk. Gemma wrung her manicured hands and twisted her red lips again.

"But, what about my babies? What about family?" Gemma said. Her voiced cracked. Darcy ached for her, but not enough to object to the plan. "Basil, honey, you aren't your dad and staying here won't turn ya into him. We all know that."

"You're just gonna have to trust me. Trust that I'll take good care of Darcy and the babies. Hell, you guys can come with us if you want." Basil said. His voice always softened when he spoke to Gemma. She had that effect on everyone, even if eye rolls were involved.

"When exactly do you plan to go? I mean like next year or something? When? The summer to help repair stuff?" Harlan said. His words trailed off, which Darcy knew meant he didn't want an answer.

"Next week or so. It's April. May is the start of peak tornado season." Basil said. Darcy glanced around.

"Is that right, Darcy? You think you can all just up and move in a week or so? Jesus girl, you're due in June. You gonna have my third grandbaby while out and about chasing a tornado through a cornfield? Really?" Gemma said. She stood up and crossed her arms. "Nope. That's not gonna happen. Now here's a better plan. Basil, you go off and chase that dream, or God's plan or whatever. Darcy and the babies will move in with us. You earn that storm money and come home, take care of them here. That's a better plan."

"Darcy and I are a team. I'm not leaving her or my kids. We're going, and we're going as a family. That's all there is to it."

"Man, mom's right. She's due in less than three months. You can't move them now. I'll get your money back as quickly as possible. You get by here until next year. Then go. Or go alone like mom said." Jackson said. "Jesus. You can't do this."

"Jackson, even if you handed me that money right now, it wouldn't be enough for us to get by until next year. I know you can't understand this, but this isn't up for debate. It's a calling. I saw it that night. I don't know. Kinda like God talking to Noah about building that ark. I heard it. I felt it. I'm supposed to go and fix it. I just know it." Basil said. "My uncle still lives in Kansas, right by the border. He's already trying to hook me up with work. I talked to him last week. And like I said, it's a calling. I feel it."

Everyone exchanged glances as if they were looking to the others to come up with another reason or anything to refute Basil's determination or insanity.

"Jesus H. Christ. Now it's a calling like God telling Noah to build a goddamned ark? Dammit, Basil Sullivan. You've gone and lost your damn mind." Harlan said. "I've heard enough. Come on, Gemma, Jackson, come on."

"Wait, Dad." Darcy said before she thought of what would follow.

Harlan grabbed his coat and handed Gemma hers. He huffed about Basil losing his mind and they'd all talk about this later. Jackson slouched his shoulders and followed his parents. Gemma fought tears, which made Darcy's heart ache more. But Darcy didn't budge. She didn't know how to fix any of this, how to make sense of it. Ever since the mill fell silent, chaos had seeped in. She couldn't see through it, hear the right answers, or even think clearly. It was all muddied, thick, and weighing down on her. Darcy wasn't sure which end was up or even who was right. Everyone she loved was drifting from each other, pulling away. She wondered if this was what it was like for the sun, to hold it all in orbit, keep everyone circling and close, in order, stable. *What an awful job. Being the sun of the family,* she thought. Panic seemed to set in everyone's heart, panic mixed with despair. Regardless of what the answer was, staying and finding another job or skill, or running off to another part of the country, Darcy sensed the entire family and town was suffering a type of growing pains that had no end in sight. Her twin was being peeled from her side. The thousands of little invisible strings that connected them were being severed one by one. For Darcy, there was a physical pain of not being close to him anymore, not being able to see inside of him and know him as she knew herself. She missed his forehead pressed against hers. Darcy believed Basil was slipping from her, too. Darcy wanted to transport them all back when they were in high school, flirting over afternoon snacks, inseparable, no worries of the mill closing, no unplanned pregnancies, not even worries over the drafty door or leaking roof.

After night swallowed up the town, the trailer, Darcy made a cup of tea and sat next to Basil. He was scrolling through the channels.

"Hey, we gotta talk about all this," Darcy said into the glow of the tv.

"I know we do." Basil said. He lowered a bottle.

"The drinking, too, Bay." She wanted to reach back and grab the words from the air. She didn't really want to talk about the drinking. He exhaled.

"It's fine. I'm not turning into my dad. It's just a stressful time. You know that. Don't make this bigger than it is." He took another sip.

"Cec said you saw him the other day. He came here?"

"Yeah. Just for a bit. He wanted to ask about the kids, the pregnancy. I think he heard about the fight with Jackson in town, wanted the scoop."

"And?" Darcy said.

"And, yeah. He asked for money. That's when I told him we got none, which is why I had to kick Jackson's ass. That put an end to that." Basil smirked. "He left, just like he always does." He pushed himself up off the couch. As he walked into the kitchen, he turned back to Darcy. He stretched his arms over his head and swiped the tips of his fingers across the popcorn ceiling. "Listen, things are gonna be okay. Okay?" He cocked his head to the side in the way that he knew got to her anytime they fought. Darcy let a slight smile slide across her face. Amid worry, doubt, and fear, she still got butterflies when the world was quiet, and she was looking up at Basil.

She watched him as he stepped out onto the porch to smoke. He stared up at the sky above Winsocektte. Darcy scooted into her slippers, grabbed her blanket off the couch, and stepped outside next to him. It was colder than she expected. She could see her breath even though it was April. Darcy wondered when spring would come. She nudged his elbow as he leaned on the railing.

"What's that one? That group? That's Orion, right?" Basil said as smoke swirled above his head. He pointed with the end of the cigarette like it was a flashlight.

"Yep. That's it."

"I swear, Darcy, one day I'll buy us a telescope that's strong enough to see the whole universe. I will."

"I know you will." She rubbed her belly as a chill slithered down her back. The hair rose on her pale arms.

"We're gonna be okay," Basil said, still looking up at the stars. "I just know it. We need to go help those people, and everything will fall into place."

"Basil, I don't think going to Nebraska is what's meant for us. I just—"

"I do. I'm not trying to escape my dad and all that bullshit you and your family think. I'm not. And I'm not crazy."

"Are you sure, honey? Cause look at you. Drinking away every night right now, talking about Noah's ark and some crazy plan, a calling from God. I don't know if half of this is because your dad keeps popping up around here, or the mill closing, or desperation to get away from here. I just…I just don't know what you're thinking. Why the hell do you think packing up these kids and leaving here is what we gotta do?"

"Darcy, staying isn't an option," Basil said. He flicked his cigarette. "I see it. I see what my life, our life will be if we stay. I can't do it. I can't live that life."

"Since when? We were fine living this life until you saw that storm on the news. We were gonna make it work here somehow. I know the mill closing throws a few wrenches into our plans, but it did for everyone here. We have family, a home, I have a job, a best friend two trailers down. We still have everything we always planned to have." Darcy tugged at his sleeve. "What's so wrong with Winsockette and our life here? I feel like…like your rejecting all we've built. It's like you want to run away from not just here, but me. Run from us."

"No. Dammit, Darcy. That's not it. And you wanted to leave here when we first met anyways. Remember? You had that scholarship. You were gonna get the hell out of here five years ago and never look back until we found out about Cassie. Now that I'm ready to leave, you want to stay?"

"That was different. I had a plan, college. I didn't want to take off for Nebraska and chase tornadoes. I had goals, not a whim or a so-called vision or whatever after watching the news one night." Her temples throbbed as her words got louder. The tension between them, the pent-up anger against the world and all it had dealt them was building, filling the space between them on their front porch.

"This is my plan. You gotta trust me on this."

"It's not that I don't trust you. I don't trust the world and what it can do to us. The kids, me, and you. We're safe here. Poor, sure, but safe. This is home."

"Home is wherever you, me, and the kids are," Basil said still looking up at the stars. "We're never gonna be more than what we are now if we stay. Face it, Darcy. No one is coming to pump life into this town."

Darcy drew in a deep, cold breath. "What's wrong with what we are now, here?" She shrugged her shoulders, even though she too wanted more from life than what Winsockette had to offer. She wanted to experience what was beyond that mountain. Darcy wasn't sure she wanted to find out this soon. Darcy slid back inside as Basil lit another cigarette. She tossed her blanket on the couch and shuffled down the hall. Darcy couldn't talk anymore tonight. As she undressed for bed and noticed her swelling belly and stretch marks in the mirror, Darcy realized she was as big as she felt. *Perfect size for being the sun in the family,* she thought.

Darcy understood Winsockette haunted Basil in ways that it didn't her. Seeing Ed Sullivan randomly in town or when he'd show up drunk outside their trailer reopened wounds that would never heal if they stayed. Every time they saw his dad, or the two men fought in the driveway, Darcy saw Basil change. Those scattered incidents ingrained pieces of Basil's father in him, his blood, his bones. After each encounter, it was harder to get back the husband and father she knew he could be. Within minutes of telling his dad to leave their driveway, he would snap at the kids, drink more, even snap at her a time or two. Maybe Basil couldn't become the man she knew he was meant to be if they stayed? She exhaled and was sure deep in her gut she was going to follow him. She needed to. If he was falling apart, Darcy whole-heartedly believed it was her job to be there to pick up the pieces. Just as the heavens and stars that were out of reach had always fascinated her, called to her, she couldn't resist going into the unknown with the only man she loved. If Basil and his plan meant they'd crash and burn across the universe like a shooting star, then Darcy would be right there falling from the sky with him.

# PART II

# CHAPTER 8

Darcy had never packed for a journey across the country, only for a hospital stay when the babies were born or camping with friends. If she thought too much about it, Darcy's heart would race and panic would spread throughout her body like an electrical current. She kept stopping to ask herself if Basil might've truly lost his mind, and if blindly going along was a huge mistake. Her certainty that the last five years wasn't one giant list of mistakes was fading.

The sound of the trailer door opening and Cassie squealing "Gamma G" woke her from her daydreaming while packing clothes in her suitcase. Darcy waddled down the hall to find her mother hugging and kissing Cassiopeia.

"Shh. You'll wake Orion," Darcy warned as she passed her mother and headed toward the kitchen. "Tea, Mom?" she asked.

"Yes, please. It's colder than a witch's tit out there this morning. Spring my ass." Gemma said as she slid off her coat and tossed it on the couch.

"Mom. I told you about saying stuff like that in front of her."

"What's a witch tit, Momma?" Cassiopeia asked as she followed Gemma into the kitchen. Darcy rolled her eyes at her mother. Gemma shrugged.

"Nothing, beetle bug," Darcy said. She filled mugs with water. "What brings you by right now? Basil and I'll be at the house tomorrow for dinner before we head out."

"I know. I just wanted to talk to you alone before y'all headed out. I knew Basil was with your dad renting the trailer and all, so I figured this might be my only chance."

"If you're here to talk us out of going, it's pointless, Mom. Basil is hell-bent on this idea and nothing is stopping him. And I'm not staying behind. I think we already made that clear. It's bad enough his dad is calling us crazy all over town and still showing up here at ungodly hours looking for money, booze, forgiveness, or whatever." Darcy slid a mug to her mother. "Basil already talked to his Uncle Quincy who's planning to meet up with us. And listen, his dad has no idea Uncle Quincy is gonna help us, so don't go talking about that in town. You hear me, Mom? Just don't make today harder with lecturing me on why I need to stay in—"

"Stop Darcy. I'm not here to talk you out of it or call you crazy or anything like that. And I sure as hell won't let that useless piece of shit know anything about where you're going or who's gonna help," Gemma said. She scooted onto a stool at the counter and fluffed her perfect hair. Darcy glanced at her as she bobbed the teabag. Her shiny red nails were perfect as always as she squeezed the bag with a spoon. She couldn't help but think Gemma would still win any beauty pageant she entered. While she didn't look as fresh and vibrant as she did as a young pageant winner, there was no denying that Gemma was still the prettiest woman in northern Maine, probably all of New England. For a moment, Darcy thought it might be nice to finally get from underneath that blonde perfectly coifed shadow and move somewhere where no one had ever heard of Gemma McElvaney. Gemma scooped sugar into her cup and slowly stirred. She exuded grace, a deliberate hypnotic slowness and enraptured the world around her. Sometimes, Darcy thought Gemma's presence gave her vertigo and threw her so off-balance, she didn't know which end was up. Cassie climbed onto the stool next to her grandmother. She swung from side to side. Darcy realized at that moment Cassie looked more like Gemma than Darcy more than she realized before. Cassie also inherited her grace. Darcy was beginning to think she'd never be out from under Gemma's shadow.

"Honey, I just want you to know I get it. I get the idea of going on this adventure. I know the draw of somewhere new to start over, to find a new life, a new way. I remember my family's reaction when I left South Carolina to stay forever in Maine with your father. Even though your grandparents loved him and were fine with it, the rest of my family thought I was nuts. And even though I was in love and was a front-runner for Miss Maine, and I might add, the only person to also be Miss South Carolina and Miss Maine, I was scared to death and had no idea what to expect. I didn't know who to be up here. Sometimes I didn't know if I ever learned to fit in."

Darcy didn't want to tell Gemma she didn't fit into Winsockette. She would always stick out like the first buds of spring flowers when the trees are still encased in dirty ice.

"Well, this is a little different, you know. I'm not going alone and it's not forever. We'll be back…someday." Darcy paused and sipped her tea. She realized she and Basil never talked about that part. Convincing her to go was the sole subject of their recent conversations. "And I won't be totally out of my element. We're going to Nebraska, not overseas or anything. It's not a whole new world, Mom."

"True, but no matter if it's moving from South Carolina to Maine or Maine to Nebraska, you'll be out of your element, and I just want you to be prepared for that. That isn't always a good feeling. In fact, I've rarely found it to be." Gemma sipped and looked down at the counter.

Darcy reached over and patted her mother's hand. "I know it's going to be an adjustment. I expect that. There's uncertainty. I'm pregnant. We're broke. There's so much standing in our way. And Basil's plan might just be insane after all, and Jackson, well, Jackson—"

"I know. What Jackson did was horrible. Trust me, I haven't forgiven him either. But I hope that's not going to drive you and my grandbabies away forever. My heart can't take that." Gemma started to tear up. An ache filled Darcy's gut.

"Mom don't cry. Please."

"I won't. But I will tomorrow, no doubt. Listen, I have something for you." Gemma reached down for her purse. She pulled out an envelope.

"What's that?"

"Your insurance, my insurance that you can get back home if you need to." Gemma handed her the package. Darcy peered inside the thick padded envelope. Her eyes grew wide.

"Mom? Where'd you get this?"

"I've been saving up for a while. Your dad doesn't know about it. No one does. Not Jackson either."

"I'm not taking your money," Darcy said. She slid the envelope back to her mother.

"I want you to take it. Just in case."

"In case what? Basil and I have saved his last paycheck, his unemployment. We've got the rent and our bills paid up and have enough for this trip and getting settled. We're fine. His uncle even has a lead on a house for us to rent on the cheap."

"This isn't for you both. This is for you."

"What do you mean?"

"If things go sour, if you find you can no longer follow him, if you decide this isn't going to work and Basil won't listen to reason, this is yours and yours only. It's not for gas, a hotel, groceries, or anything you guys need like that. It's for a plane ticket or bus ticket for you, Cassie, Orion, and Elara if she comes along at that time." Gemma slid the money back to her only daughter. The look on her face told Darcy not to dare slide it back. "I need to know you have a way out of this journey, this calling, or God's plan or whatever the hell Basil calls it now if it doesn't pan out. I won't be able to sleep at night without knowing you have a way back." Gemma exhaled, and took a long slow sip. "I know you've been worried about Basil and I know the kind of anger and rage that can bubble up in a man raised like him. You know I love Basil like my own and would change his entire childhood if I could, but I can't. Like I said, if things get dicey along the way or out there, I need to know you and my grandbabies have a way out."

"Mom, none of that's going to happen. Basil and I will be okay. Basil will be okay, believe me."

"I know. I know. Like I said, it's insurance. You only use it if you need it." Gemma looked her sternly in the eyes. "Darcy, I'm your mother. You're taking that money, stashing it away, and using it if you need to. If you don't need it, God will tell you what to do with it. There's a little over

$3000 in there. Insurance." Gemma nodded and raised her eyebrows. She slid off the stool, kissed Cassie, and scooped up her jacket. Gemma dashed to the door. She opened it and turned to Darcy. "You'll know when to use it, and I'll sleep better at night. End of story." Gemma disappeared before Darcy spoke.

Darcy stood there with the envelope in front of her, clothes piled up half-packed, cupboards bare after giving most items to Cecelia, and a toddler crying awake in the other room as a baby kicked her bladder. Cassie slid down from the stool and grabbed her baby doll. She held the money to her chest then put it in her overnight bag on the coffee table.

Darcy realized they only had roughly 24 hours left in the only home they've shared. She stared at every corner, the faded flowers on the kitchen curtain, the countertops that still had a trace of a circular beet stain from her attempt at canning. She looked at the living room with the musty carpet, the sunken couch where she spent countless hours in Basil's arm watching tv and holding her babies. She remembered three years earlier when she and Cassie both had the flu and practically lived on that couch for a week. Darcy looked at the dark wood-paneled wall behind the tv where family portraits hung before she packed them in boxes a few days ago. She looked at the ceiling fan which wobbled and provided little relief when the rare heat spell devoured Winsockette last August. Darcy absorbed the laughter, tears, screaming matches with Basil, giggles of the kids when she spent hours on the floor playing 'restaurant' with them. She wanted each moment of their time there to seep into her bloodstream and become part of her forever.

While she believed she and Basil would come back someday when Winsockette, the trees, and land, could once again give their family hope, she knew the trailer wasn't going to be their home ever again. Darcy smirked as she thought how desperate she had been for them to buy another home once she got pregnant with Elara. As desperate as she had been to leave that little plot perched above the others and in plain view of the mill, Darcy never thought it would be under these circumstances. She had always pictured Basil and their families loading up a trailer and trucks and moving their meager belongings to a tiny shiny new house with a yard, perhaps a patch of woods on the outskirts of town. Now, they were packing alone and setting out on a journey into the unknown with no safety net. They weren't seeking new and shiny. They'd be following wrath and destruction, immersing themselves in it, and profiting from it. Perhaps Basil was right. Man and man's greed had taken so much from them, namely taken their hope and dreams of that shiny new house. Maybe following God's wrath and destruction was the best option, even if it meant not knowing where they'd lay their heads, make their tea, or play 'restaurant'.

As the last day in the trailer unwound and each detail was handled, packed, signed, and sorted, the knot in Darcy's stomach grew. Dinner with her parents was emotional. Jackson's visit afterward and a string of apologies unleashed tears she didn't expect as she thought she had expelled them all. As Jackson, Harlan, and Gemma smothered the kids with kisses and Basil accepted a handshake and quick hug from Jackson, Darcy started to shake. She knew this was the last moment for a long time that they'd be together. Jackson leaned into her, pressed his forehead against hers, and let out a long exhale.

"I love you, sis. I love you more than anyone." He said with a shaky voice. Darcy pressed her head harder into his and held tight to his cheeks.

"I know you do, Bubba. I know." She squeezed her eyes and tried to prevent more tears from flowing down her cheeks.

"I've never lived here without you. Anywhere, actually." He started to shake.

"You'll be okay. You have mom and dad. You'll do fine. Just look up when you need me. You know where we are up there, holding hands just like Castor and Pollux. We're together forever in the night sky," Darcy said as the tears stopped, and a slight smile appeared. She felt him smile, too. All wasn't healed between them, but Darcy was certain their connection was still unbreakable.

He nodded and their foreheads rubbed more. Darcy remembered their secret language as kids and secret games. It seemed like yesterday that all they had was each other. They were each other's world, each other's protectors. Now grown, they were separating, and Jackson turned out to betray Darcy in a way no one else ever had. Instead of protecting her and her family, he had taken their box of dreams, their future. While Darcy kept reassuring him and her family that they would be leaving regardless of Jackson stealing from them, there was a small part of her that did blame him. She tried to press it down deep in her gut, but she knew he knew it, too. As their foreheads meshed into one, she remembered him as a boy hiding her toys, watching her scramble for them, watching her cry. She forgave instantly back then. She couldn't help but forgive him now. Even though they'd still hold hands in the heavens, they had to stretch their arms more to stay joined. It was no longer an effortless connection.

"I forgive you, Jackson." She whispered. He nodded again. "Look after them for me."

"You need anything, you call me. Promise. I'll move heaven and earth to get to you," He said. Jackson peeled himself from her and reached in his pocket. He pulled out a wad of cash and placed it in Basil's hand. "It isn't much and it sure as hell isn't all I owe you. But it's all I got now. Everything." Basil shook his head and held onto his hand a few moments.

"Are you sure, brother?" Basil asked. Jackson nodded. Darcy didn't need to know how much was in the wad, just that it was all he had. Her shoulders relaxed a little. She glanced around at the ceiling and floor, any place but Jackson's eyes or Basil. She thought *if this is what goodbyes are always like, I'm never doing this again.* Harlan cleared his throat.

"Well, it's time you guys get back home for your last night there. Everything's loaded, right Basil?" Harlan said. Basil nodded. Hugs were distributed and Basil and Darcy made their way to the truck. They didn't speak on the way back to the trailer. They were both exhausted. Darcy was letting morsels of doubt creep into her mind and heart again. She wondered if Basil was also. Darcy wondered if he was still as dedicated to the plan when he was sober. She glanced at him several times with words dangling on the tip of her tongue. She bit them and swallowed them. Part of her didn't want to ask Basil if he had any doubts, not because he might say no, but because he might say yes. They were in too deep to change the plan now. They had given up the lease of their tiny home. She quit Bakers. He quit job searches. They had dates to disconnect utilities and packed everything they held dear. Darcy knew if they were ever going to leave Winsockette, it would be in the morning or never at all.

Once Darcy got the kids settled into the sleeping bags on their bedroom floors, she joined Basil in the living room. He sat on the floor drinking the last of a six-pack he still had in the fridge. She gingerly lowered herself next to him. He put his arm around her and stared up at the ceiling fan.

"We had a lot of good times in this damn trailer." He said.

"Yeah, we did. It was our first home as a family." Darcy rubbed her belly. She wondered if they'd ever feel this at home again.

# CHAPTER 9

Sleep didn't come for Darcy. She twisted, stared at the ceiling, settled Orion after a bad dream, and rolled off the air mattress to pace around the nearly empty trailer for a while. With first morning light piercing through the remaining sheer curtain, she rose and pretended she wasn't up all night. They went through the motions of breakfast, dressing and doing Cassie's hair, and double-checking suitcases and totes that still needed to be loaded in the trailer. Once there was no more business to tend to, they looked at each other. Both seemed to read the other's minds. It was time to go. Darcy looked around again. Basil double-checked the trailer hitch. He made a few adjustments to the car seats and overnight bags that would lie at the children's feet. He did another walkthrough in the bedrooms, bathroom, and kitchen cabinets. Darcy knew it was empty and clean, ready for new renters, but she understood he needed to absorb his memories there just as she had. She picked up Orion and his sippy cup. He took Cassiopeia's hand and shrugged.

"Ready?" He said matter-of-factly.

"Yeah." She answered as she adjusted Orion on her hip, peeling his leg from her belly. They both looked up and down, scanned the walls, and then back at each other. Basil folded his bottom lip inward. Darcy shrugged and let out a deep breath.

"Let's go." He said.

"Alright." She responded. The little family who had never known anything or anyplace else walked toward the door. Darcy paused on the porch. She looked at the mill, silent and still. A flash of anger consumed her. All the time and energy her family had devoted to the mill, to making paper from the great pines that surrounded them. It was all for naught. It got them nothing in return except fewer trees and silence where the stability and security of the noisy valves and plumes of smoke had once filled the air.

The silence that rolled over the mill seeped into the truck until Basil turned the key. Darcy looked at Cecelia's trailer as they descended the hill. The best friends said their goodbyes earlier, but Darcy needed to see if she'd wave once more even though she made Cecelia swear not to. Cecelia honored her wish. No curtain moved. The door didn't fling open followed by a blonde teary waif yelling for her to stay. Cecelia had decided to move to Massachusetts in a few months, which comforted Darcy a little. No one stirred as they approached town. It was moments after dawn on a Saturday. Shops were still closed, including Bakers. The mill parking lot had a few scattered cars left from bar patrons who were wise enough to know they shouldn't drive home. The sidewalks, with spring weeds sprouting through the cracks, were also empty of Winsockette residents. It was as if the mill had sucked the life from town when it closed weeks ago. It was May, a time when people and the town would normally start to come to life a little earlier thanks to the warming high sun. It seemed like now there was no reason for anyone to stir early, or later for that matter.

Darcy tried to memorize each crack in the painted store signs, each pothole, each bright yellow forsythia lining the alleyways, just as she had memorized every crevice of their home. She compared the scene of that Saturday to the scenes of Saturdays when she was young, and she and Jackson would skateboard those streets. It was evident the silence was killing what was left of Winsockette. She glanced at Basil and wanted to thank him for getting her away before it took its last dying breath.

As the morning wore on and Basil fiddled with the radio going back and forth between three stations, Darcy kept glancing at the rearview mirror. She couldn't see Winsockette anymore, but she knew it was there faded into the background. Every town they passed along the way was interchangeable with hers. Those towns were also hanging on for dear life. Darcy found herself wondering how many young couples like them had packed up and left over the last year. Since the recession hit, it seemed everything the tiny Maine towns thrived on no longer existed. They were an endangered species and no one but their kind seemed to care. She wondered if any national news outlets bothered to notice or if schools in big cities or tiny farm towns in the plains of Nebraska discussed the fall of the paper mill industry. As teens salivated over their new smartphone, did their parents know anything about the industries dying as that one exploded? Darcy wondered if the men on Wall Street, the ones bemoaning losing millions and billions in the crash, ever thought about the small towns dealing with a recession that overtook them like a tsunami. Were any of them from towns like Winsockette? Did any of them call home and say, 'sorry mom, dad, uncle so-and-so about the tech bubble and market crash that ruined our hometown'? Did they go to bed at night and wonder what paper mill workers would do next? Did they consider the domino effect of closing the only real industry a town had ever known and the generational impact when people knew nothing else? She knew the answer. The silence was her answer. No one was coming to save the town, the mill, or them. No great sport or tourism company was moving in with adventurers to open bed and breakfasts, restaurants, guide services, and outdoor gear stores. The town was on life support as they got further away. Darcy thought, *if anyone is thinking of coming to the rescue, they better hurry the hell up.*

As she day-dreamed, the children napped. Except for pulling over and filling the gas tank, there was no noise, no conversation. The trees still surrounded them. Darcy noticed as they got a few hours south, there were more buds. It was as if Darcy was able to watch winter let go of its grip in real time. Spring was finally here. The landscape was transforming with every mile. Towns were closer together. It was greener, fresher. Darcy wondered if Winsockette was the last place on earth that saw spring flowers. Fresh, new light green leaves sprouted everywhere on both sides of the road. Houses were closer together. Darcy already felt a little claustrophobic by the increase in people they were seeing.

"What?" Basil said as he readjusted his hands on the wheel.

"Nothing. I'm just thinking how different everything looks already and we're still in Maine." She said towards the window. "Well, not everything. The pines are still the same." Her eyes scanned the tops as they swooshed by. Darcy noticed many were crooked on top, leaning to one side or sticking up awkwardly pointing at an angle. It was like those trees also lost their way after a certain point or forgot where they were headed and why. She used to look at those Maine trees and forests as sustenance, as most look at crops and water. It dawned on her that she was moving from them, too, not just Winsockette. She was leaving a land of a million trees for open plains. An entirely different landscape. An entirely different life, existence. She reached over for Basil's hand as he barreled down the highway and closer to their new life. Her eyes once again scanned the treetops then upward to the sky. That sky and the destruction it was capable of unleashing would soon become their new source of sustenance. She grew up always hearing God will provide. Now was the time God would have to prove it. Basil believed it with all his heart, and with all his drunken rants. Now, she just needed to.

The hours slid by as they sailed through a sliver of New Hampshire and onto the Massachusetts turnpike. Darcy struggled to remember when she had ever seen so many cars and trucks. The fresh pine air was replaced by truck exhaust. Orion and Cassiopeia grew restless. Car snacks and fast food stops only temporarily soothed their longing for freedom from car seats. Darcy fully understood and had the same need to stand, stretch, and stop the momentum of being trapped in the truck. Basil agreed to stop for the night and find a decent restaurant for them to enjoy a sit-down dinner. Having calculated and recalculated every dollar and dime, they decided they could spring for a real family meal at the end of each leg of the journey. Fast food and convenience store snacks would keep their bellies full for the other meals. Darcy even found hotels online with free breakfasts, which would help them reduce the need for fast food even more. Despite craving the occasional greasy burger and fries when pregnant with the others, Darcy found the smell of burger joints revolting while carrying Elara. She needed, craved, desired fresh fruit above all else. She had spent every hour at Baker's eating bananas, oranges, and picking grapes off the bunches every time she sprinted past the produce section on the way to the bathrooms early in her pregnancy. She was sure the collection of peels on the truck floor annoyed Basil, but she needed what she needed. To his credit, he was smart enough to never argue with or deny the cravings of his pregnant wife.

"Well, I think day one will be in the books soon. I'm gonna get a hotel once we get to Connecticut. These kids have been stuck in here long enough."

"Yeah, and me too. My legs hurt, honey." Periodic bathroom breaks at rest stops weren't enough to relieve her leg cramps.

Basil reached over and touched her belly. She laid her hands on his. "How's she doing in there today?"

"Good as any other day. She's beating the tar out of my bladder though. I've only gone, what? Three hours at the most without needing to stop?" Darcy laughed. Elara curled up under her rib cage. Darcy stretched her back. The elastic of her maternity jeans was cutting into her hip. Her stomach itched. "I can't believe she's due in less than six weeks. I can't wait to meet the new doctor in Franklin."

"They got your records, right? Last week?"

"Yeah, Dr. LeFleur faxed them. They said to let them know when I get there, and they'll squeeze me in for evaluation." Darcy looked out the window again. "I know it'll be okay, and the doctor and hospitals are just fine there, but it's weird, you know?"

"What? The doctor out there is just as capable as the ones at home. Plus, you said it yourself, women have been having babies since the beginning of time."

"I don't mean that. I mean, we're gonna have a baby born outside of Maine. I just never thought that would happen."

"Hell, Darcy. We never thought any of this would happen. Jesus, when we started dating, you were leaving Winsockette to chase stars and look through telescopes somewhere in the desert or wherever. I was just gonna work at the paper mill forever or whatever. Now, look at us. Nothing is as we planned." Basil said into the sun which was descending on the horizon to their right.

As Hartford came into view, Darcy turned around and nudged the kids' knees. "Hey, Cassie, wake up honey. Look out the window." She said. She let Orion continue to play with the car he had been slobbering over for the last hour. She watched Cassie's eyes widen as the truck twisted and turned past skyscrapers and towards the tunnel. As they entered the tunnel, Cassie tensed up and looked to Darcy for reassurance. "It's okay, baby. We're driving underground." Darcy smiled. She knew this journey was going to show her things she had never experienced before, but she didn't expect the glow, rumble of the concrete, and the silence of a tunnel to be so captivating. As they re-entered the outside world, Darcy gasped. The buildings on the other side were towering and enclosed them on either side of the highway. The increase in cars made her feel as if they were stuck together, traveling in one big block of movement. She thought of watching a colony of bees buzz and turn together as a group, individual bees humming and conforming to the hundreds around them. They acted as one body darting, twisting, and doing loops above her head as she watched from the lake in Winsockette. The cars, trucks, mini-vans, work vans, and others were the same, confined to four lanes, little space between them as they zoomed along going the same rate of speed. She glanced into the windows of other vehicles, squinted to read their license plates, and wondered if any of them were like her and Basil. She couldn't distinguish between who may have traveled this stretch of highway every day and night and who may have just packed up their entire world and entered rush hour traffic with no frame of reference like herself, except for different plates on the cars. She smiled thinking perhaps people weren't all that different outside of Maine, south of Boston, and now south of Hartford. Maybe from the outside, they'd blend into the crowd in Nebraska, too?

As Basil slowed on an exit ramp, a surge of anticipation rushed through Darcy's arms and legs. She needed fresh air and to stretch. Leg cramps had plagued her during all three pregnancies. They were only getting worse as her time carrying Elara dragged on. The thought of making this journey over four or five days was exhausting for her. She saw the hotel they found online come into view. It had an Italian restaurant attached with a sign slanted and in cursive. They each climbed from the vehicle sluggishly and with groans, even Orion.

"I'll go in first, get us checked in, then we'll carry stuff inside for the night," Basil said. Darcy nodded as she led Orion and Cassie to a patch of grass next to the curb. She got a whiff the garlic and marinara in the air. Her stomach growled as her mouth watered. Cassie followed her lead as she stretched her arms over her head and tried to lean downward. Cassie's fingers graced her toes with ease while Darcy's arms barely reached past her stout, chubby knees. Darcy's legs tingled. Orion wobbled on the grass. For a moment, Darcy watched her two kids and wondered how they went from a life in Winsockette to a small patch of grass in a parking lot in Connecticut in less than a day. It sure wasn't the yard she thought they'd be playing in with her kids when she pictured life away from the trailer. Flashes of reality like that made her wonder what the hell they were thinking.

"Well, let's get stuff unloaded and get washed up for dinner," Basil said as he skipped to them. Darcy smiled. The sun was at his back. He had a heavenly glow encasing his entire lanky body. He looked like the 16-year-old boy she fell in love with. His light frame floated back then. He didn't walk so much as bounced or grazed the floor or ground. He was airy then even with the weight of life with his father on his shoulders. He hid it so well when she watched him from afar. She admired that about him. Darcy couldn't help but smirk a little when she realized that seven years after they kissed, five after marrying, with a third kid on the way, he was still airy, idealistic, and determined as he flitted through a hotel parking lot at dusk in Danbury, Connecticut. She wished she could absorb a bit of that surety mixed with impulsiveness.

Darcy attached Cassie's backpack to her shoulders and handed her the doll that was her whole world. She reached into the car seat to gather a handful of Orion's matchbox cars. She dropped them into a diaper bag and tossed them with his collection of sippy cups. As Basil took Cassie's hand, she hoisted Orion on her hip and followed her husband into the lobby and down a dark hall.

Exhaustion settled into her bones. The pregnancy was draining. Darcy wanted nothing more than to crawl into a comfortable bed, pull the covers over her head, and wake up once the world was realigned. Basil inserted the card key into the slot. Faces were wiped, teeth brushed, and a clean shirt was pulled over Orion's fat wobbly head. Basil made a few trips to the car to bring in more overnight supplies for them all. As he slid a duffle bag from his shoulders to the bed, Darcy laid back and stared at the ceiling. The name 'Sullivan' was written in capital letters in black on the duffle bag.

"I'm glad you have your Uncle Quincy's Army duffle to use for our stuff. I can't wait to meet him," Darcy said as Basil sighed and laid beside her.

"Yeah. You'll like him. He's good, the best of our family. I think it's because he never moved back to Winsockette." He muttered into the air as Cassie climbed on top of his legs.

"You haven't even seen him in what? Forever?"

"Not since I was a kid. I only met him once, when I was little, and he came from Kansas for my grandma's funeral. Guess after he got out of the Army, he wanted to stay there. Loved it. Better than Maine. I'm just grateful his friend has a house we can rent when we get to Franklin, one that wasn't hit by the tornado."

"Are you sure he's gonna help us out? I mean, how do we know for sure we can move right in? Plus, you barely know him. What if he's a bullshitter like your—"

"He's not, Darcy. He's nothing like my dad. I have all his contact info, number, address, even his cell for work. He's put the word out that I'm a hard worker. He said last week the place is all set. It's gonna be fine."

"Well, I hope so."

"Darcy, we have enough to pay rent when we get there. I have the tools I need for roofing and everything else. Once we get settled, get you to that doctor, and all that, I'll set out to repair whatever the storms damaged last time and what they bring on next."

"What if there are no more storms? What if the destruction you want to follow doesn't happen? What if they've already repaired all of Franklin?"

"There will always be destruction. We'll be fine."

Darcy closed her eyes and let his reassurances cover her like a blanket. Then a rumbling of guilt bubbled up over the surprise of being reassured that there'd be more destruction. Sun poked through the crooked blind as it started to set. It was well past dinner for the kids.

She dragged her feet as they shuffled into Caputo's Ristorante. The smell that had made her mouth water in the parking lot was now making her slightly nauseous. Her cravings and feelings of overwhelming disdain for certain scents and tastes were changing day by day, sometimes hour by hour. Darcy repeated her silent vow that Elara would be her last pregnancy. Even though they were still young, Darcy believed three was enough.

As they were seated and water was poured, Darcy removed a small book and a handful of crayons from the diaper bag. Coloring kept Cassie entertained. They clipped Orion into a highchair and gave him a handful of his favorite cars. Darcy warned him to keep them on the tray and glanced around. A few tables of fellow guests were staring at her and Basil, then glancing away as soon as she'd meet their eyes. She looked down at her lap and noticed a mustard stain on her jeans. Basil also looked a mess from an entire day in the car even though he put on a clean shirt.

"Why didn't you tell me I had a stain right on the front of my pants?" She asked in a whisper as she dunked a corner of her napkin in the water. As she tried to blot the middle of the stain, she saw Basil shrug. Darcy noticed the white tablecloths and shiny silverware that was heavier than any she owned. She looked up at the chandelier. The wait staff was impeccable, and all looked alike. Darcy realized that even though she had been to a few nice places to eat in Portland throughout the years, she had never been to a place this nice. It might have been right next to a hotel, but it was on a different level than she had ever seen. She tried to not let the stares throw her off-kilter. She found herself wondering if these same people would look at them that way if Gemma was at the table. Her mother could walk into any room, any crowd, any situation, and completely absorb all the oxygen. She was a force, a presence, one that nobody gave a cross look to. Darcy knew without a doubt no one had ever made Gemma uncomfortable. She sat up a little taller, sipped her water, and tried to ignore them. She accepted they didn't necessarily look like they belonged, but they weren't trash either. They were clean, kind, hard-working and deserved to sit at a table draped in white cloth as much as anyone else in Danbury, Connecticut or anywhere else for that matter. Basil ordered a beer. She tossed him a glance.

"What? I'm done driving for the night." He said without making eye contact.

"I know." She said back as she glanced around at the others again. Even though they were far from Winsockette, Darcy was starting to realize some habits would follow them anywhere.

Once morning came and everyone got moving, Darcy was anxious to leave Connecticut. She let anxiety bubble up and knew it would only go away once they drove far from Danbury, further south or back up north didn't matter. She was teetering in absolute limbo. Darcy was suddenly aware that they were far from home, far from all they knew, and anyone who knew or understood them. They certainly weren't well off. However, she had never thought of herself as less than anyone else because they were technically poor, at least in a financial sense. She wondered if she'd be seen as poor trash in Pennsylvania, their next stop, or Chicago—the stop after that. And how about Nebraska? While she had a picture of cornfields and farmers in her head, what if Nebraska was just as uptight and judgmental as Connecticut seemed to be in the twelve hours they spent there?

While Darcy wasn't sure what to expect once they drove away that day and the next few days, she knew she'd always double-check her jeans for mustard stains before they walked into more restaurants, white table cloths or not, and she'd always sit up a little straighter. For the first time in her life, she realized no one around her besides Basil knew she was Gemma's daughter. It was up to her to show people who she was, or who she wanted to be once she figured that out for herself. The only thing she was sure of was that she never wanted to feel out of place or like an eyesore again, even if she was.

# CHAPTER 10

Before noon they were out of Connecticut and cutting through New York to get to Pennsylvania. Once they crossed the border of the Empire State, Darcy realized they had officially left New England, something she wouldn't have believed a year earlier. So much about her life would've seemed like fiction last year—being pregnant again, the mill closing, Jackson having a drug problem that led to him stealing, Basil and Jackson fighting, and heading to the plains to chase tornadoes. It was almost like someone pulled various events out of a hat and handed them to her. None of it seemed real or like it was under her control, her choice. Of course, she thought, getting pregnant with Elara didn't just happen to her, it was a slip-up. Despite events seemingly being out of her hands, she rubbed her belly and felt love. Elara wasn't a mistake. Darcy glanced in the backseat. Orion and Cassie weren't either. They were just unexpected, like everything else that had happened the last year. May might have been spring on the calendar, but to Darcy, it seemed like New Year's complete with resolutions and expectations that things were going to be better.

As they crossed a bridge, Basil beeped the horn of the red, tattered truck. "Goodbye New York, hello Pennsylvania!" he yelled. Darcy laughed. The children laughed too.

"Pennspilbania!" Cassiopeia echoed. She threw her arms in the air. Her doll fell to the floor. Orion tried to follow by yelling "Pabana" He giggled and kept thrusting his tiny arms above his head. Granola bar crumbs were stuck all over his face.

"Oh, Jeez. Baby Orion, you're a mess." Darcy said. She reached into the diaper bag at her side and pulled out a package of wipes. She stretched to hand one off to Cassie. "Honey, can you reach his face?" Cassiopeia tried to wipe her brother as he squirmed and curled his lips inside his mouth. Darcy shook her head realizing it was useless to clean him until they stopped. The entire inside of the truck looked like chaos. Crumbs, wrappers, random items of clothing, all strewn in a tiny truck cab. Darcy had to repeatedly tell herself it was temporary. They wouldn't be living in the truck forever.

Darcy glanced outside the window to take her mind off the condition of the truck. Something inside of her had always expected each state to look drastically different from its bordering states, like on the maps of the United States she played with at school. She laughed to herself thinking how a few states where bright green, bright blue, orange, with pictures of their crops or symbols on them. She tried to remember what Pennsylvania had. She knew Maine had a moose, lobsters, and blueberries. She thought Pennsylvania had cows, a farmer, maybe? The Liberty Bell? She felt silly expecting the actual transition from one state to another to look different.

"You know, we're probably gonna see Amish on the way," Basil said.

"Oh, that's right. They're here and where else? Ohio?"

"Yep. That's one of the many things I remember from social studies." He said as he puffed out his chest. She smiled.

"You cheated off me in social studies. Remember that?" She said as she threw her head back and laughed.

"Not the chapter about the Amish." He boasted. "Hey, Cassie, there're people who don't drive cars. They drive horses and buggies on the road like the carriages in your princess book. Did you know that?" Basil said to the rear-view mirror.

"Nope. Where are they?" She asked as she strained her neck toward the window.

"I don't know, but I'm sure we'll see some soon." He said. "Just keep an eye out, okay?" Cassie nodded. Darcy reached back and was able to get a piece of the doll's yarn hair in between her fingers. She gathered the doll and handed it to Cassie. She grabbed her, hugged her tight, and kissed its head. Darcy smiled thinking how nurturing Cassie was with her dolls, her brother, and her little friends. She hoped wherever they ended up there was another little one her age for Cassie to bond with.

Darcy turned back to the front and reached over for Basil's hand. "How far will we make it today?"

"I think we'll get through most of Pennsylvania, stay the night then hit Ohio early tomorrow. Possibly tonight if we don't have to stop all that much."

"Well, I have to stop a lot including right now," Darcy said as Basil rolled his eyes. "I can't help it. Your newest daughter is making it difficult for me right now. Maybe if we had moved during my first trimester instead of the last, I would be able to hold it longer." She quipped.

"Your first trimester wasn't during tornado season. Hold on. I'll find a place here." He said. His tornado reference hit Darcy like cold water. She had almost forgotten the journey wasn't just to start to a new life somewhere away from Maine, it was to chase storms, rebuild devastation, and follow more storms. She pictured the wrath and chaos they had seen on the news just a few short weeks ago. It seemed more real once they had left the comfort of a television in a living room and loaded their family into the truck to drive in that direction. While her rational mind understood they wouldn't drive right into a tornado as they crossed the Nebraska border any more than they drove right into a cow or apple when they crossed into Pennsylvania and New York, something was foreboding just thinking of that border. *Ohio? I have no idea what the picture or symbol was for Ohio*, she thought. Darcy felt heavy as if weights bore down on her shoulders and pulled her face downward. She wanted out of the truck. She needed Basil to stop barreling towards anything for a minute.

"I think we should stop more, eat in real places, let the kids stretch. I don't think we need to push it to get to Ohio tonight at all. Okay?" Darcy said.

"Okay," Basil said with no show or concern for why.

The initial excitement of crossing into Pennsylvania dissipated after lunch in a diner off Interstate 80 West. It looked the same the hour before and the hour after. There were solid green plots of farmland broken up by freshly plowed brown plots with sprigs of green protruding from mound after mound after mound. There weren't shades of green like in Maine or brighter patches that crept to the border of darker green patches of grasses, mosses, or wildflowers. It was a continuous flow of one shade like a child had dedicated a great deal of time to ensure an even job of coloring that plot. With the clean, strict, and straight lines that defined the browns and yellow plots, Darcy started to wonder if it was a life-sized version of those maps she used to put together. The green was broken up slightly by a rolling hill here and there. Then a barn, a very large faded barn, followed by a larger barn with a silo attached. The only real deviation that erased the sight of farms were the mountains and huge billboards, which didn't exist in Maine. The mountains were grand protrusions of rock jetting up from the side of the road and curving along with it in sections. The rocks also had streaks of color not found anywhere else in the landscape.

"Wonder what they did to all the rocks, the trees, and stuff." She muttered a few hours after lunch.

"What do you mean?"

"When they made the road. When they cut these mountains. What did they do with it all? All the earth?"

"No idea."

The concept boggled Darcy as she pictured blasts sending shards of multi-colored rock soaring into the air only to land at the feet of workers who feverishly gathered it to be removed. Now, it was streaks of color leading straight from a road. No extra to be found anywhere. Man had done that. It made her think of the paper mills and the trees they swallowed up, spitting out reams of paper. Man had done so much to Maine, Pennsylvania, everywhere all in the name of progress. *Look where it got us.* Darcy thought. It got them on a highway in the middle of nowhere heading towards flat straight roads to the middle of even more nowhere. She knew they'd have to make a somewhere out of nowhere. Winsockette was now no different. The trees that were sacrificed over the decades for over a century meant nothing. Same with the mountains that were sacrificed to make this road. Destroyed by man just to give man a way through, a way to get out. At least where they were going and what they were chasing was God's wrath, as Basil said. They weren't watching man destroy anything. They were cleaning up after God. Somehow, that made the idea of a profit a little more palatable for now.

The hours folded in on each other. The children after only two days on the road seemed to have adjusted. The whining was minimal if toys and snacks were within reach. Following the sun and aware dinner time was approaching, Darcy knew she was the most uncomfortable member of the journey. Her legs were cramped. Her bladder suffered as she begrudgingly asked for Basil to find a restroom more frequently than the day before. She was parched and blamed a scratchy throat on the car air. Darcy was hard-pressed to find anything she loved more than fresh air. She hated dry heat, blasts of air conditioning, car air, store air, any enclosed space where the air was still, stale, and used. She cracked her windows a few times to let the rush of a breeze fill her nose and lungs. Even though it mostly left a lingering taste of car and truck exhaust, she still preferred that to the dry car air. The more she thought of her discomfort, the more uncomfortable she became. Darcy exhaled loudly, then inhaled deeply trying to keep her inner-toddler from escaping. If the children are content, she knew she must pretend to be also.

"Cresson Creek 15 miles," Basil said. "Sounds like a good place to stop for dinner. Whattaya think?"

"Sounds good to me," Darcy said. She glanced back at the kids. "Orion is asleep. I'll rouse him when we get a little closer. I think he's full of cheese snacks though." Basil let out a laugh.

"Cresson Creek it is."

As they pulled off the exit, Basil turned toward the sign for food and lodging. Once they slowed down and stopped at a light, Darcy saw the sprigs of wildflowers, shades of different trees surrounding them. The off-highway view of Pennsylvania was shaping up to be much more pleasant than the highway view. She thought it silly to believe it was all farms and mountains sliced open for roadways. A diner that looked as homey as anything they'd had seen in days came into view. A motel with flashing lights and bright pink doors along a line of single-story rooms flanked the other side of the road. The sunlight that bounced off the silver walls of the diner blinded Darcy. Once Basil put the truck in park and she unstrapped herself, Darcy prayed it would be a while before she strapped herself and the kids back into their seatbelts. She had been feeling bigger during the last few weeks. Once she was free of a seatbelt, Darcy felt like a balloon that someone held tight to their chest then unleashed to float freely at full size, bouncing on the ground and skimming the curb. She stretched, ached, and cracked. Darcy wobbled to the curb and sidewalk as Basil gathered the kids.

She pushed on the glass door to the diner. A bell rang above her head. Darcy saw a few patrons and waitresses turn to look at her then look away. She glanced at her pants and shoes. A large woman in all white scuttled past her and turned to her head to flash a giant smile. She had cherry-colored hair.

"Be right with yunz." She said with a wink. Darcy smiled back and relaxed her shoulders. The sweet smell of fresh-baked pies filled her bloated body. Basil and the kids came up behind her right as the beefy red head walked back toward her with that giant smile. She led Darcy, Basil, and the kids to a booth near the window. "One highchair?" she asked. Basil nodded. As she returned with a highchair, she pulled a box of crayons from her apron and placed them in front of Cassiopeia. She had two kids' menus in front of the kids before Darcy had time to pull her shirt further over her belly. Basil thanked her.

"Where's the—"

"Right over there, Momma." The woman answered as she pointed to the right by the entrance. Darcy smiled and scooted back out of the booth. "My name's Merna. I'll be your waitress. My other half, Tiny, is the cook. Welcome to Yoder's." Darcy heard her say as she made her way to the restroom. Any looks she noticed were smiles and nods, nods of acceptance—something she hadn't noticed in days or even longer. Darcy walked a little taller as she stretched her back and made her way back to the table. The kids smiled as Merna swarmed them with sippy cups of chocolate milk and crackers to keep them content. "Well, there's your Momma. What'll you have to drink, ma'am?" she asked Darcy.

"I'll take an iced tea." As everyone ordered and Merna disappeared, Darcy leaned her head on Basil. He patted her thigh and kissed the top of her head. They were off the highway, away from the exhaust and noise, and together for a real meal. Darcy almost forgot they were on a cross-country journey as she watched Cassie color and Orion zoom his cars across the highchair tray. For a moment, it was as if they were at their old dining room table enjoying dinner alone as a family with the sun setting right behind the smokestacks of the mill.

As they finished dinner, Merna asked them about their travels. She stood, towering above them, wide-eyed and with her hands on her giant hips. Darcy wasn't sure if it was the whiteness of her uniform or her sheer size that made her look like a cloud floating above them, a cloud filled with kindness and care. She was inches from embracing them as Basil dove into more detail than necessary. He went beyond the where they came from and where they were headed storyline they had grown accustomed to sharing when someone at a rest stop commented on their Maine license plate. Darcy stared at him in amazement as he told Merna of his quest to chase storms and clean up God's wrath. He explained the fall of the paper industry and the impending demise of Winsockette.

"Well, it sounds like a well-thought-out and noble plan there, Basil. Good luck to you and your little family. Due in June, huh?" She asked Darcy. She broke her trance from Basil.

"Yep. June. Another girl."

"You make a beautiful young mother. I mean look at these two angels." Merna said as she picked up Darcy's dinner plate. Darcy struggled to remember the last time a stranger called her beautiful, if ever. Darcy smiled at her kids and reached for a napkin to begin cleaning their tiny faces. A bell on the metal counter rang out. Darcy looked to see sprigs of red hair sticking out of a small, pale head behind the warming counter. He was almost elf-like in his presence. "Well, that's Tiny callin' me. Good luck to you guys. May the stars and moons bless and guide you." Merna meandered from their table and turned sideways to barely slide behind the counter where plates of food awaited her.

"Did you tell her the kids' names?" Darcy asked as Basil pulled out his wallet and studied the bill.

"No, why?" he said without looking at her.

"Because she said about the stars and moons blessing us."

"Maybe that's just a common thing here. Hey, she didn't charge us for the kids' meals." Basil said. He turned the paper over. In large, loopy writing befitting a colossal woman such as Merna, the words 'Stars and moons guide the way for good folks like yourself! Stop back in Yoder's someday' were written. Darcy watched her float around the diner and smiled. Darcy couldn't shake the idea she was meant to be wrapped in the comfort Merna Yoder oozed with ease.

"I think we can get in another two hours or so then find a hotel. You good with that, Babe?" Basil asked as they strapped the kids in their car seats. Darcy nodded and resigned herself to the fact that she would have to strap herself back in and breathe the stale air coming through the dirty vents. She drew in a last breath of fresh air from the outside and rolled up the window. Basil turned the key. Nothing happened. He turned it back, then forward again. Nothing. He twisted his face in confusion. Darcy raised her eyebrows.

"We aren't out of gas, right?"

Basil shook his head no. He removed the key, glanced up at the ceiling of the old truck, and reinserted it. He turned it with force. The tips of his finger turned white from the pressure as he tried a few more times as if he was letting the truck know he meant it this time. Basil threw his head back and let out a deep sigh. He reached down and pulled the lever for the hood.

"I know it's not gas. Let me take a peek." He said as unbuckled his seatbelt. Darcy bit her bottom lip. She heard Basil tinker for a few minutes. Then, he popped up by her window, which she had rolled back down to imbibe as much fresh air as possible. "I'm going inside and see if anyone can jump us. It's gotta be the battery."

"But we just got a new battery after Christmas. Dawson checked out the whole truck last week. Said we were good to go." Darcy said.

"Yeah, well apparently we aren't good to go nowhere at the moment. Wait here." Basil leaped up the steps of the diner. Within minutes, he reemerged with a man who had been sitting at the counter. The man brought over his truck and aligned it diagonal to their truck. Darcy smiled at him and he nodded back. He wore overalls and boots. He hooked up the cables. He and Basil stepped back and chatted for a few minutes. They shook hands as Basil slipped back into the driver's seat to turn the key. Nothing once again. He shrugged his shoulders as the old farmer shrugged his. "Dammit. I thought for sure that was it." He said to both

Darcy and the farmer. Darcy heard him tell Basil to go back in and ask Tiny where Mitch was. Mitch was their son, a mechanic in Cresson Creek. Once again, the men disappeared into the diner as Darcy grew anxious. The sun no longer bounced off the diner's shiny metal exterior. It was behind it and casting an orange glow over everything. Luckily, Darcy thought, they weren't alone at night on the highway when whatever went wrong occurred. Basil remerged alone. Darcy knew it was a bad sign that he dashed to her side and opened the door rather than getting back in.

"Well, here's the deal. Mitch, their son, owns the only garage in town. He's closed for the night cause it's Sunday, but he'll come tow the truck to his shop. It'll be morning before he can fix it or figure out what the hell happened. Looks like we're staying the night in Cresson Creek." Basil drummed his fingers on the windowsill of the passenger side with his eyes cast towards the dirt parking lot.

"Okay. Can we get a room over there?" Darcy pointed across the street to the motel with the pink doors. "I mean there are worse places we could get stranded for the night, I guess," She said.

"Yep, Merna was calling them already after she hung up with Mitch. Her brother owns it. Go figure. Small town, I guess."

Darcy looked up at the main window of the diner to see Merna standing by the cash register, phone in hand. She smiled and gave a slight wave as she talked. Darcy smiled back at her. As she stood up outside the truck, Merna opened the door to the diner.

"Dutch says you've got a room. Mitch is on his way so yunz will want to get out your bags and get them over across the way."

"Thank you, Merna. You're a lifesaver. You didn't have to go out of your way," Darcy said.

"Trust me. It's no trouble. My brother has been doing what I tell him for 52 years!" she shouted with a boisterous laugh. Cassie and Orion laughed because Merna's laugh was contagious.

Darcy and Basil gathered their overnight bags, the backpack of kids' toys, and the giant duffle from Basil's uncle. Basil picked up Orion, grabbed Cassie's hand, and told her to grab Darcy's. They formed a chain and shuffled across the road to the hotel. From the parking lot, Darcy saw a sign in the window that said, "There's Always Room at Dutch's Place." As they crossed the threshold into the little lobby that jutted out from the rest of the building, a small bell rang over her head. It was the same as the diner. Dutch hobbled up from an old recliner that sat to the left of the counter and where an old cash register sat. He threw his arms in the air. "Well, you must be the Sullivan family?" He was a male version of Merna. His hair was the same cherry color and his voice could fill a concert hall. He was bigger than she was, which Darcy didn't think was possible, but the same build. He wore beefy well. His shoulders were as broad as the counter.

Darcy and Basil nodded as Darcy tried to keep the kids at her feet. She noticed Cassie's eyes widen as Dutch leaned over and smiled at her. She prayed Cassie wouldn't comment on his size.

"I got a room ready for you folks. I also got one of them portable cribs for the little one. Looks like I might have to dig out another if yunz stay here too long," Dutch said while he shot a wink to Darcy. She smiled at him and rubbed her belly.

"Well, I got a few more weeks, sir, so no need to worry," Basil laughed.

"This one will be a Nebraska baby if everything goes according to plan, Mister," Basil said.

"It's my experience that nothing goes according to plan," Dutch said. "If yunz need any snacks or supplies, we've got a few vending machines out back and a small store about half a mile down the road. I know you got no car, so I can give you a lift if need be. Tiny opens the diner at 6 a.m. so yunz can surely get a good breakfast there." Dutch reached behind him and pulled a key from a pegboard. Darcy noticed it was mostly full. She figured not too many others were guests at Dutch's middle of nowhere western Pennsylvania motel.

As Basil unlocked the door and they stepped into their room, the musty smell took her back to the trailer. She was slightly pleased even though she spent years trying to cover it with sprays, candles, and countless attempts at shampooing the old carpet. When Basil flipped on the light, she was even more pleased to see the carpet was the same dark brown color. She heard Basil smirk as he lowered Uncle Quincy's duffle onto one of the beds. She suspected it was because the sight and smell took him back home also. The bed made a sinking creak. The bedspread, thin and faded from years of washing, had tiny yellow flowers throughout. There were random green leaves and vines if you looked closely enough. Darcy lowered herself next to the duffle as she let go of Orion's hand. The mattress absorbed her. The creak indicated she was one of many who had been swallowed by that bed. The enveloping of the old motel bed was strangely soothing, just like everything else about Cresson Creek.

Basil's cell rang. "Hello?" he said as he paced and placed more of their bags on the bed next to Darcy. "I see. Yep, I'll be there in a second." Basil slid the phone into his back pocket. "Mitch is there to tow the truck and trailer. I'm gonna make sure we got everything, see if he has any ideas." Darcy laid back. She could still lay flat on her back for a few minutes before the pressure of Elara grew too great. "I hope it's something minor," She muttered to the ceiling.

"Me too," Basil said. "Guys, be good for Momma." He dashed out the door. Darcy sat up and turned on the television. She reached for the pamphlets on the nightstand next to her. Shade Mountain Valley Railroad Museum. Amish Crafts and Markets. Hiking Trails of Western Pennsylvania. Caverns of Shade Mountain. A varied landscape flanked each page. Mountains, lakes, caves, families huddled in horse and buggies, quilts, candles, trails overlooking magical sunsets. It wasn't only farms and cows like the Pennsylvania map of her childhood. She brought Orion onto the bed as he reached for her. Cassie flipped through the channels, stopping on cartoons. The momentum of traveling in the truck subsided. She relaxed for the first time in what seemed like weeks. The key in the door drew her attention from the pictures of dreamy adventures and mountain scenery.

"Well. Mitch loaded her up. He thinks it's the starter. No surprise. But thinks it might be more than that. He'll call me tomorrow with an estimate."

"Okay. I mean, it is what is. We can't do anything but wait, I guess." Darcy was learning to resign herself to things she couldn't control anymore. She stood and walked into his arms. He exhaled as she wrapped her arms around him. He slid his around her shoulders and kissed the top of her forehead like he always did when she needed comfort. Regardless of their surroundings or circumstances, that kiss on her head made the world better, smaller, gentler. It made the outside world stop for a moment, which she needed more than ever.

# CHAPTER 11

The morning sun poked through the dusty blinds much sooner than Darcy wanted. The slightest bit of light roused Orion regardless of where they were. He whined and needed to be changed. Darcy moaned and rolled to face him. He was already standing in the portable crib, which smelled as musty as the carpet. Probably from years of storage, Darcy figured. Her back ached, not from pregnancy, but that ache of sleeping somewhere new for two nights in a row. She pushed herself up on her side and slowly stretched her arms above her head. Two nights. It's only been two nights, she thought. It seemed they left Maine a lifetime ago. After she retrieved Orion from the crib, she called Gemma to check in. Darcy told her about the truck, the diner, the motel, and people. She assured Gemma they were safe, content in Cresson Creek until they could once again pile into the truck and head further into the unknown towards Nebraska. Her mother said, "Come home if you need to."

The tiny family, freshly showered and bathed, opened the motel door to a blinding sun. The air was still, warm. Birds chirped. There were flowers in the window boxes that Darcy didn't notice the night before when they settled into the temporary shelter. Basil once again scooped up Orion, grabbed Cassie's hand and led them across the street to the diner. The "Yoder's" sign was bright and welcoming. They stepped inside and the smell of bacon, pancakes, and warm syrup engulfed them. Coffee cups clanked, voices rippled from one end of the fake marble counter to the other. Tall red stools squeaked. Laughs echoed. Darcy stopped in her tracks on the way to a table. She filled her lungs with the comforting smells and felt warmer inside than she had in months. They slid into a booth by the window with a view of the motel. Before she had time to look at a menu, Merna cast a shadow over the four of them. Her smile swallowed them whole and her laugh covered them like a cozy quilt. Darcy had the urge to nestle herself into Merna's bosom. Just as she laughed at Merna asking about the old beds at her brother's motel, Darcy saw something out of the corner of her eye that made her whip her head around, nearly hitting the window. It was a black horse-drawn buggy with jet black and auburn brown horses pulling it gently down the street they had just crossed. Darcy gasped as Cassie squealed and pointed. Darcy wasn't sure if pointing was considered rude or if it made them look uneducated or touristy, but at that moment she didn't care. She was just as fascinated. Her heart started to race, and Darcy fought the urge to slip out from the booth and run outside to gawk at the sight of an Amish family closer. She saw a gentleman with a long beard and black-rimmed hat perched at the front of the buggy and a blue bonnet sticking out from the inside. The clomping of the horse was steady and hypnotic. Darcy had never seen anything like it. The buggy was regal-looking, sleek, and clean. The man sat straight and held the horses under his command. The world seemed to part as they made their way through the main street. Darcy held her breath afraid to disturb the scene or miss a moment of it unfolding before her. It wasn't until the buggy passed out of sight that she realized the whole family was in the same lingering sense of awe at the timelessness of the buggy passing.

"Pretty cool to see, huh? First time seeing Amish, I take it?" Merna said, which snapped Darcy from her trance.

"Yeah. I mean, we were hoping to see some, but didn't expect them to just come up the road out of the blue," Darcy said. She strained her neck to see if the buggy was still within view. She could barely make out the orange triangle on the back.

"Don't worry, Darcy. You'll see plenty more in this area. They're all over. You know, if you guys get a chance, you can always visit Bellamead over Shade Mountain and check out a whole town of Amish. There's a bunch of Amish shops right down the road here, too."

"A whole town?" Basil asked.

"Yep. The whole town is Amish. Pretty land. No telephone poles or electrical wires stringing each house and road together. And they've got awesome pies, jellies, cheeses, meats, quilts, gifts, all kinds of stuff for sale in their little shops. They welcome the English, mostly welcome English money." Merna said. She poured coffee for Basil and Darcy.

"English?" Darcy said.

"Yeah. That's what they call us. Us modern folk. The non-Amish," Merna said. "chocolate milk for the kids? Or OJ?"

"Oh, milk is fine. Thanks. Maybe we'll check it out. Well, if Mitch can fix the truck today, that is," Basil said.

As they indulged in home-cooking, Darcy watched the easy interactions of the locals. She kept trying to get a closer look at Tiny in the kitchen. She found it hard to imagine that behind that bobbing sprig of red hair peeking from behind the metal kitchen divider was a man who measured up to Merna in any way. She was a presence, a force. It wasn't just her size that made it impossible to not notice or become enraptured by her, it was just her. She was big in every way—body, personality, and heart. Despite her overwhelming physicality, she glided from one end of the diner to the other. She floated in and out of conversations and clusters of old men pouring coffee, removing plates, and giving out winks. She seemed to get every inside joke she interrupted. Without even asking, Darcy could tell Merna was a lifer in Cresson Creek. She had probably never considered ever leaving. She had most likely been a steady shoulder to cry on, rock to lean on, and a lifter of melancholy for everyone in that diner, in that town. Every bit of Cresson Creek was part of her DNA. Darcy was drawn to her, to everything in this little corner of western Pennsylvania.

A plate with a greyish-brown square was slid over in front of Basil. The Sullivans, including Orion, stared at it with bug-eyed confusion.

"Scrapple. It's the official breakfast food of Yoder's Diner. Go on, Basil. Give it a taste," Merna said. She placed her giant hands on her wide-spread hips. Basil looked at her, then at the plate, then her again. She nodded. "Go on. It won't hurt you. Yunz can't leave PA without tasting scrapple." Darcy noticed a few gritty farmers watching. One nudged another as they grunted. Basil picked up his fork as Cassie scrunched up her entire face in pure disgust. He gathered a good size lump of the mystery brick on the plate and slid it into his mouth. Darcy held her breath waiting for a recoil, a gag, anything. His eyebrows rose as he chewed.

"Not bad, Merna. Not bad at all." Basil scooped more and ate it while the rusty crowd at the counter gave Basil an approving nod. "What's in it?"

"Well, you know how they process the meat from a pig, get all the good stuff, grind it up, and boom, you got a good hunk of pork?"

"Yeah," Basil said. He shoveled another heaping forkful.

"Well, scrapple is everything else from the damn thing."

Darcy furled her bottom lip in complete rejection of the idea of tasting it too. Basil sat straight up and swallowed.

Once breakfast was cleared and the last of the coffee poured, Mitch pulled into the parking lot with his tow truck. He stopped in the parking lot to wave and chat with each person who filtered out of the diner. Mitch was red-haired like Merna and tiny. He was tall like Merna but built small and wiry like Tiny must be. He had the same infectious and all-encompassing smile as his mother. He nodded upward when his eyes caught Darcy and Basil at the end of the row of vinyl-covered booths. Mitch stood at their table with his hat in his hands. It was a ball cap with grease stains. 'Yoder's Towing and Repair' was embroidered in cursive.

"Well guys, I've got good news and bad news," He said as his eyes darted between Darcy and Basil. He flashed a quick smile to Cassie and patted the top of Orion's head. Darcy's heart nearly stopped mid-beat. Basil set down his coffee cup.

"Spill it. What are we looking at?"

"Definitely need a new starter. But your oil pan gasket has shit the bed, too." Mitch cleared his throat and glanced at Merna who was standing a few feet away. "Sorry about my language," he said to Darcy, but she sensed he was saying it because Merna heard him. Even though he was a man in his early thirties, Darcy understood he was the type of man who didn't swear in front of his parents. "So, I have to replace that, or you won't be making it too far highway driving without a major issue."

Basil drew in a long breath and tapped the rim of the coffee cup.

"How much we talking? And can you get it done today?"

"Today? Hell no. I gotta get my hands on a starter for that truck. That'll mean a trip to Pittsburgh possibly if I can't wrestle one up closer. I'll put in a few calls and see. And the gasket, well, I gotta get my hands on a suitable one too. I can order the starter through a parts dealer I work with though, put a rush on it," Mitch said. "Best case scenario, two days. Worst case, a week."

"A week?" Basil said. "Jesus. How much? I'm almost afraid to ask."

"If I get it through my guy and get on it tomorrow, I can cut the price a lot. I'm thinking ballpark $500 but that's low-balling so I can get you guys back on the road for as little as possible. I know yunz are on the move, got time constraints, obviously." He said as he nodded at Darcy's belly. She bit her bottom lip.

"$500? Jesus," Basil said.

"I'm surprised you guys made it this far without an issue, to be honest with you," Mitch added.

"It was looked over before we hit the road, but I guess not as thoroughly as I expected."

"That's the best I can do and that's if I don't find any other problems.

"Well, do me a favor and don't go looking for other problems," Basil said with a laugh. "I guess we'll stick around here and wait while you do what you gotta do. I mean, really, we don't have much choice," Basil said to both Mitch and Darcy.

Numbers started to swirl in Darcy's mind. $500 to repair the truck. Motel for $59 a night. Breakfast, lunch, dinner at the diner for another day, another day on top of that and possibly more. This stay would put them behind on the timeframe for getting to Franklin. They'd need more diapers. More car snacks. More everything than what the original plan called for. This diversion in Cresson Creek would easily cost them more than $1000 in unplanned expenses. Darcy looked across the street at the motel. In room 17 tucked behind her bras in a zip pocket of her overnight bag was the envelope, her insurance from Gemma. $3000 sat safely concealed from everyone. Darcy let out a sigh and looked down. It was impossible to see further down from her belly. That insurance from Gemma would cover the cost of the truck repair, the food, motel, supplies, anything they needed before getting back on the highway and more. Darcy bit her lip harder and strummed her fingers on her belly.

"What? What is it, Darcy?" Basil asked. All eyes were on her. She could save the day by telling Basil what she had. Then she imagined his first obvious question—where did you get $3000? How would Darcy tell him Gemma gave her the money so she and the kids had a way to flee if she discovered he was truly crazy, a drunk like his dad, or she couldn't take another minute of following his half-baked plan to chase storms? The disappointment in Jackson and what he did rushed through her veins. She remembered the look of devastation on Basil's face the first time they saw Jackson after the fight. He had lost his best friend just as she had lost her brother and other half that night. Darcy's heart broke for Basil as much as it did for herself. Even though she understood her mom's intention, Darcy knew Basil wouldn't. It would crush him to learn Gemma didn't have the same faith in him that she did. He had promised Harlan and Gemma he'd protect and watch over Darcy and the kids. If he learned Gemma doubted that, he'd be devastated. Darcy believed that doubt would sink Basil to a place so low he may never recover. Darcy couldn't bail them out of this, she reasoned. Basil needed to do it himself. She didn't for one second want Basil to think she took the money because she might need to flee him and take his children with her. Then again, Darcy deep in her heart thought she may need to use it for its intended purpose another day.

"Nothing. I just...I just can't believe this," Darcy said. She glanced back at the motel.

"So, you want me to call you when I get an answer from my guy about the parts? You could always ditch her and get a new ride next town over, finance something newer, or rent a car to get on the road sooner. You got options, you know."

"Yeah. Just see what you can do, and I guess, get on fixing it. We'll stay at the motel and just wait. I can't get something else. We've got limited funds for this trip and to get a place once we get to Nebraska. We'll just fix her up best we can," Basil said. Mitch nodded and jetted out of the diner as quickly as he appeared. Basil and Darcy both expelled the air left in their lungs. Darcy picked up a remaining piece of toast from the highchair tray and gave it to Orion.

"This is really gonna put a dent in things." Basil put his head in his hands as he rested his elbows on the table. "Seriously, what the hell else could go wrong this year?"

"Don't do that. We'll be fine. We've got enough to get there still, pay for that place. You've got tools to get to work right away, storms or no storms. Plus, we can always just go to your uncle's in Kansas if we have to."

"The last thing I want right off the bat after leaving Maine is to call my uncle I haven't seen in forever and ask him for more help than I already have," Basil said.

"We'll be fine," Darcy said again. She was reassuring herself as much as Basil. Merna walked over and slid the check on the edge of the table.

"You guys need anything else this morning?"

"Nah, we're good, thanks," Darcy said.

"Hey, I heard what Mitch said. I think Tiny and I can help out some, or you could help us out in a way," Merna said.

Basil and Darcy looked at each other. "We don't need charity, Merna, really. We've got enough money for everything we need. No one pays our way. We can take care of ourselves and our kids," Basil said.

"I know. I get it. Trust me. You just look like good people. I just think you need a break. If yunz are gonna be in Cresson a few days, it's gonna add up. All I'm saying is if yunz scratch our back, we'll scratch yours." Darcy and Basil again looked at each other confused. "Listen, I need help here, especially with dinner time. Help back there." She nodded her head back towards the kitchen. "If one of yunz can handle the dishes for the four-hour dinner shift, you can eat for free while you're at the hotel."

"Nah, we couldn't do that, Merna. If it's all the same, we'll pay just like everyone else."

"Suit yourself, but at least think about it." Merna left to follow the ding of the bell on the metal counter. Tiny beckoned with plates sliding across waiting for homes.

Darcy hung her head and patted the top of Orion's head. Basil slurped the last of his coffee.

"Maybe she's got a point, Basil? I can help back there today and tomorrow. The repairs are gonna put a real dent in our money."

Basil put down the cup. "You're almost eight months pregnant. You need to relax. I'll do it. You and the kids wait over at the hotel, hang out, watch tv, and I'll pitch in." Basil took a napkin and slid it across Cassie's syrup-dipped lips. Parts of the napkin stuck to her face. "Dammit," Basil said as Cassie giggled. He smiled at her and dipped the remaining napkin in his water and tried again to clean up the four-year-old. She laughed harder as she put up more resistance. "Come on, Cassie. Let me wipe your face." Darcy loved it when he tried to act serious with Cassie even though he couldn't wipe the smile off his face. She loved seeing him lighten up a little with the kids. The last few months had been too heavy on them both.

"Alright. I'll hang with them. You can help out, maybe get a full glimpse of Tiny back there at dinner time," Darcy said. Basil motioned for Merna as she balanced plates on a tray perched on her wide hips.

"I'll do it, Merna. I'll do dishes so these guys can get dinner. That is if the offer still stands?"

"Damn straight it does. Tiny, we got a dishwasher!" She yelled over her shoulder. The greasy spatula banged on the top of the bell wildly. Darcy, Cassie, and Basil laughed. Orion squirmed in the highchair, more than ready to go. Darcy saw strands of red wispy hair sway from the back. "Be here at 4, okay?" She said. "And don't stress too much about your truck. Enjoy a bit of Cresson Creek. Trust me, Mitch will take the best care of that truck and Dutch will make sure you have everything you need."

Darcy exhaled. Despite the obstacles in their way and the uncertainty that lay ahead of them, she knew they'd be okay for now. There was safety and comfort in Cresson Creek. It felt like home or like it could be, unlike Danbury. Darcy looked around at the others in the diner, the older men at the counter in green khakis and dirty boots, the older women gossiping over tea that cooled a while ago. She watched another young couple juggle two kids who had syrup lips like Cassie. She saw the other waitress, a younger woman, slim and quick, dash from one end of the diner to the other with a smile that never retracted even when no one was watching her. Everyone was content. There was no strife, no grumblings of mill closings, no suspicions of drugs infiltrating town, no signs of struggle. Even though Darcy understood Cresson Creek, like Winsockette or any small town in America, had to have its share of problems and the recession had surely infiltrated its border, something seemed different here. She couldn't put her finger on it, but she wanted more of it. Darcy realized at that moment that despite the cost and worry over the truck, part of her was happy they'd be stranded in Cresson Creek for a few days. She needed to be still for a bit.

Once they joined hands to cross the road back to the motel, Darcy looked up at the cloudless sky. The sun warmed her face. "Let's take a walk, to the main part of town down that way," She said before she realized she was thinking out loud. Basil shrugged his shoulders as he led them to the other side.

"Alright. We gotta get the stroller." She was thankful for a man who remembered to take the kids' things out of the truck before it was towed. "It's what, half-mile that way?" Darcy nodded as Basil fished for the motel key.

"I think. I'll take Orion and ask Dutch to be sure."

Dutch was laying back in his recliner watching the news in a plaid robe. Darcy felt bad for disturbing him. He confirmed it was a straight shot to the main part of town. There were a few shops, Amish craft stores, a coffee shop, book store, market, feed store, and of course Mitch's garage. He offered to give them his car for sightseeing, but Darcy assured him they wanted the fresh air. Plus, she also didn't want to accept more charity than she needed. Part of her felt odd about accepting meals for Basil doing a few hours of dishes. Even though Basil would be working, Darcy recognized the offer was because of their situation, not a need for a dishwasher.

They strolled down the two-lane road into town. Darcy's back ached, but she was still thankful for the distraction and way to pass the time other than corralling two kids in a motel room. As they approached a wooden carved sign saying 'welcome visitors', the sound of clomps came up behind them. Darcy's heart raced as she turned around to see an Amish buggy coming right towards them. She and Basil pushed the stroller off the road and moved Cassie over to the side as it got closer. With her mouth agape, she made eye contact with the driver. He was younger than she expected, younger than her and Basil. Maybe 15, she thought. He nodded and tipped his hat. Next to him was a little girl, roughly Cassie's age, in a dark blue dress and black bonnet. She had stark white hair poking out from under the rim. Her eyes were ice blue, just like the boys. Siblings, Darcy thought. The little one bounced in the seat as the young man directed the brown horse. The little girl smiled and waved. Cassie slid her hand from Darcy's to wave wildly at the girl. It was like stepping through time. They were silent as they passed except for the clomping. Darcy couldn't get over how such a new sight seemed so natural and ordinary in this little part of the giant map she was getting to witness. The idea that her eyes were absorbing a sight she had never seen reminded Darcy of why she wanted to be an astronomer.

Once they rounded a long twist in the main road and as Darcy's legs tired, the town opened before them. There were awnings with brightly painted signs lining the clean sidewalk exactly like she saw in the pamphlets in the motel. There was a yellow caution sign with the outline of a buggy and horse on it, something Darcy didn't know existed before their journey. There was a barber pole spinning, a cobbler sign swaying, and a mortar and pestle in red against white for the pharmacy. It looked like a scene from a movie or time warp, just as the horse and buggy did. Darcy's eyes followed the sounds of more clomping. There seemed to be as many buggies as cars making their way in and out of parking spots on either side of the road. Basil smiled and glanced at Darcy.

"This is pretty cool, huh?" He said. "Different than Winsockette." Darcy nodded as she helped Cassie step onto the curb.

"Everything, since we left, has been different from Winsockette," Darcy said.

They stopped and simultaneously filled their lungs. Darcy smelled the lingering scent of manure, but it was mixed with an earthy scent that cut the sting to her nose. It was clean air, fresh, not heavy with the weight of paper mill waste and crushed dreams of an entire community.

They wandered into an Amish craft store. The store smelled like cinnamon and berries. Before Darcy glanced behind the counter, she noticed the three women in the back were making jam. It reminded her of her childhood when Gemma tried canning blueberry pie filling. An older woman, short, stout, and with thick red cheeks and hips waddled out and smiled at them. She had a stained apron over her long dark blue dress. Her white bonnet was simple, not as elaborate as the little girl's had been. She reached under the counter and pulled out a tray of whoopie pies.

"For the children?" She said in a dusty voice with an accent Darcy didn't recognize. Basil nodded and said "thank you" as he took one and tore it in half for Cassie and Orion. Cassie squealed with delight and devoured the dessert in seconds. Orion squished his between his tiny fingers and slurped chunks from his palms as he settled back in the stroller. Darcy glanced at the shelves of canned beets, pickled eggs floating in purple beet juice, vegetables, jams, and pickles. Then she saw the quilts. Along the back wall hung ladders lined with the most beautiful quilts she had ever seen. The patterns and colors set each one apart. Interlocking circles with fabric containing the tiniest flowers, blue blocks, reds, yellows, and a mix of sizes made each one look like a masterpiece. Darcy ran her hand over one. It was much thicker than she realized. Her eyes scanned upward. They covered every inch of the wall. Along another wall in the back of the store were shelves filled with wooden toys and dolls. The dolls were simple fabric, stuffed, and dressed like the Amish children Darcy saw in town. They were both delicate and heartily made. The toys were simple blocks with letters painted on the side, horses with leather straps and wheels for gliding along the floor, farm animals all with the same painted eyes. Darcy smiled as she ran one lightly across the shelf. It was a cow with a pink nose. As she debated which one to buy for Orion, she heard the woman call out. She was motioning them to come back to the counter. In her hands were two plates with pieces of pie on each. One was blueberry and one was rhubarb.

"Oh, thank you. How much?" Basil asked as he reached for one of the plates. The woman shook her head no and unloaded the other plate onto Darcy's hands. "No, no. we couldn't." Basil insisted as he tried to hand her back the plate. She held up her hand.

"Yes. Take it. I have too much in the back. Take it. You look too thin and the wife is with child. Eat." She said as she pushed the plate back towards Basil and motioned for Darcy to taste it. Darcy obliged. She and Basil exchanged wide-eyed glances. It had a flaky texture and purity of sweetness that neither Darcy nor Basil could put into words. She knew by the look on his face that he shared her thoughts. It was the best pie they had ever tasted.

"Basil, can we get a quilt? For our new place?" She said as she swallowed the last piece of her slice. "They're kinda pricey, but they're gorgeous."

"Yeah. I think we should. Hell, she's fed us. The least we could do is buy something." Basil wiped his face with a napkin then proceeded to wipe Orion in the stroller. Darcy made her way with Cassie back to the quilts. As she pushed one aside and ran her hands over another, a younger Amish woman came up behind her. She was sleek, tall, and had dirty blonde hair held back in a tight bun. She wore wire glasses and looked to be Darcy's age.

"Those are wedding quilts. The circles are knots. Wedding knots." Darcy nodded at her as she explained the family colors, flowers, and lap quilts with squares. "They are calming, for women and kids."

"I think I'd like that one," Darcy said. She picked out one with blue stars for her and Basil. It was over $100. Basil saw her hesitation.

"It's alright. We'll have it forever as a reminder of this place. It's not like we'll have another chance to get an Amish quilt."

"I know. It's just with the price of the motel and the tru—"

"Stop. We never splurge. Today, we can splurge," Basil said. He picked up a doll and asked Cassie if she wanted it. Her eyes lit up with suprise. She knew he was right. They had always been responsible with money. They held off on unnecessary purchases, then eventually didn't purchase much of anything. Darcy couldn't remember the last time they bought anything they didn't need. They had always done the right thing, the grown-up thing, buying what the kids needed, food, paying the bills, keeping the fuel level above half for the oil tank and truck, socking away the rest, except for beer money recently. Darcy furled her lips when she realized what socking away that money had led to, where it had gotten them.

The little family of transplants made their way onto the sun-kissed street and gazed at the windows along the rest of town. As they crossed to the other side and started up again, more clomping gave way to the neighing of horses and giggles from Cassie. Darcy splurged on a few bars of lavender and goat milk soap and a few homemade candles. What started as a morning of helplessness and news of being stranded in an unfamiliar town for a few days was shaping up to be the most relaxing and carefree day they had had since the announcement of the mill closure. Time stood still in Cresson Creek. Her anxiety and fears faded more with every minute they spent in the tiny western Pennsylvania town. Basil looked more relaxed to her, not unsettled or anxious, and without a beer in his hand. He wasn't pacing as if that would alleviate the weight of the world on his shoulders. They were strolling down a quiet, warm, welcoming, and bright street.

As they finished their second dinner at Yoder's, Basil stood and kissed Darcy's forehead.

"I'm going to grab a smoke out front then I'm off to wash dishes," He said.

"Are you sure you don't want me to do it? I can do them, and you can relax with the kids."

"No, no, you go relax, watch tv and get off your feet. You don't need to be standing back there for a few hours. I love you." He winked at their daughter, "Cassie, baby girl, you be good for mom, okay?" Cassiopeia nodded as she slurped the last of her chocolate milk. Basil disappeared before Darcy uttered another word. She did her best to clean up the table before standing to unbuckle Orion from the highchair. As she lifted him out and down, Merna cast her massive shadow over Darcy.

"Oh hey, Miss Merna. Thanks again for letting Basil pay like this," Darcy said. She straightened her ever-aching back. "He'll be back in in a sec."

"No worries. He's helping us out more than we're helping yunz." Merna lifted Orion to her giant hip. "Let me help you get these youngens across the street."

"Nah, I've got it," Darcy said.

"Nonsense. I'm not gonna stand here and watch you walk across that road with two little ones." Merna used her free hand to adjust her giant hair net. Strands of cherry red and grey poked through in pure defiance.

"Okay. Thank you," Darcy said. Merna was large enough to stop traffic without even trying. After a quick kiss from Basil as he dashed back inside Yoder's, Darcy, Merna, and the kids made their way across the street. Merna let Orion slide down and gently tapped his butt as he scrambled into the room to chase Cassie. "Thanks again, Merna. For everything. I feel like we're some kind of charity case here. I wish I had a real way to repay you and Tiny other than Basil just doing dishes."

"Charity case? Girl, you're just a young family in need of a little help along the way. Ain't no shame in that." Merna motioned for Darcy to sit in the plastic chair next to the door. There was another one on the other side. Merna used a brick to prop open the motel door then lowered her body down carefully as if she realized she needed to introduce her weight to the plastic chair a little at a time. Her hips barely fit. The overflow squeezed through the sides. "So, I was talking to Tiny," Merna said. She stared off at the diner across the street. Darcy glanced in at the kids as they flipped through the channels. "I think you guys should think about staying in Cresson Creek, at least until you give birth."

Darcy sat up straighter. "Oh, you don't need to worry about us. Basil's got a plan. We're fine." Darcy looked at the ground.

"I just think a rest stop along the way to Nebraska is no place to give birth. Plus, Cresson Creek is a good place, a good place for families. This idea of you kids riding off into a tornado alley is just plain, well, it sounds like one hell of a crazy plan. I can only imagine the worries your families back in Maine must be dealing with."

"They worry no matter what. But, seriously, it's fine. I know it sounds crazy. In fact, I seriously struggled with whether or not it *was* crazy. But, like Basil said, there's nothing back there for us." She rubbed her belly. "As for this girl, I'm not even due for another few weeks. And well, I know Basil. I know we'll be fine even if I don't know when or where we'll end up. He's got family in Kansas if we need something, once we get down that way. Plus, well, we're a team. We've been a team since we were in tenth grade."

"There might not be anything for you back there in Maine and maybe not in Nebraska for all you know, but there might be here. This is a great place to slow down, relish in the quiet, and be part of a hometown that'll help you when you need it." Merna nodded over to the diner, "Plus, if you're a team, shouldn't this storm chasing idea be a team decision?" Darcy looked over at her. The freshness of the day evaporated. She felt heavy again. She wanted to crawl into Merna's lap and stay there. There was safety in Merna's presence, her essence. She covered everything in her embrace, her orbit. It wasn't like being overshadowed in Gemma's presence, competing for air. Being sucked into Merna's world was entirely different, easy, and warm.

"Yeah, it is a team decision. I decided to follow him, do this, make it work out there. We aren't exactly going to chase tornadoes, you know. I'll be at home with the little ones while Basil works to rebuild what storms destroy."

"But it's still storm chasing all the same, right? He's gotta chase 'em to rebuild after them. Plus, those storms won't magically skip your house while he's rebuilding others. Why not just stop the chase here? You can stay here and not go another mile, you know?" Merna said with a steadfastness in her voice. It wasn't a quiver, a warning, or even pleading. It was a fact, more than an option to consider.

"I'm not saying I wouldn't mind staying here. I think I would love it here. But we have a plan," Darcy said. Her dedication to the plan was fading with each second of her conversation with Merna. Darcy was caught up in her, her world in western Pennsylvania. To her surprise, she didn't want to pry herself from Merna's world. Perhaps they didn't need to go one more mile like Merna said.

"Think about it. Maybe God's plan isn't for Basil to chase storms. Maybe breaking down here, getting stuck right here in Cresson Creek is God's plan." Merna pushed herself up from the chair. It clung to her hips as she tried to rise. Merna peeled it loose. "I gotta get back before Tiny thinks I've run off with the barber, Mr. Macks. Tiny is a jealous one, you know."

Darcy laughed. "Merna, I don't know how to thank you enough for all of this. Staying here would be nice, I have to admit." She let her eyes wander over the top of the diner to the trees in the ridge. They reminded her of the hills beyond Winsockette, the hills that lay at the feet of Mount Katahdin. "We had the best day walking around town. Everyone here is so, so nice. Welcoming. It's calm here."

"It's home. It's always been my home," Merna said. As Darcy sat staring across the street, Merna turned back and stood in front of Darcy. Merna looked up at the sky and told Darcy of her childhood in Cresson Creek. Merna described life on a farm, wrangling goats and cows with Dutch, bailing hay with her brother and cousins. Merna described a symbiotic relationship with the earth, but not one that could fade away, or be ripped away as with the paper mill. There'd always be a need for food, milk, even the Amish pies and quilts.

"People will always want a good rhubarb pie to cuddle up with," Merna said. Darcy smiled. She had always thought the same of paper, at least for most of her life.

"This does seem like a little piece of heaven, Merna," Darcy said. She glanced through the doorway to see Cassie and Orion intertwined on the bed watching tv, their bellies full and worries nonexistent.

"It is. Not that I've seen much else of the world, but it is heaven to me," Merna said.

"Now I'm gonna get back to work. First, I'm gonna peek in and yell at my brother." Merna walked towards the motel office door. Darcy exhaled and looked at the sky. Merna turned to her once more after she shuffled a few feet from the office door. "Hey, think about it, Darcy. Think about staying here. Think about that being a new plan. We'd take yunz in like family, everyone in Cresson Creek would." Darcy fought a tear as she watched Merna disappear into the lobby door.

The sun was starting to set behind the ridge that rose behind the diner. After Darcy bathed the kids and turned on cartoons, she propped the door open again to sit outside and look at the sky while she waited for Basil. The stars were starting to pierce through one by one. As soon as she'd get her bearings straight and identify one star, another would emerge. The sky was clear, sheer dark blue with a hint of pink peeking from the ridge. The day was fighting to hang on. Darcy smiled thinking she wouldn't mind if that day held on longer. It was a good day, one of the best, she realized. Darcy leaned her head back to get a full view of the sky and stars. She spotted her children's namesakes. Darcy could pinpoint their place in the universe even when she had doubts about their place on Earth, where they belonged.

She inhaled cool, clean air. There were no smokestacks. There was no hiss of the valves or hum of the machines. There was no sound to get used to only to have gone silent. There was no icy wind, billowing smoke streaking towards the stars. There was quiet. It was still, all of it. There was a streetlight and the Yoder's sign. No cars buzzed past. There was no

Gemma, No Harlan and Jackson, no drafty trailer door, no Cecelia a few doors away. Nothing was the same, yet when she looked straight up, everything was. Darcy thought of Merna and her stories. Maybe she was right. Perhaps they could make Cresson Creek their home as easily as Franklin, Nebraska. Maybe that was God's plan all along.

# CHAPTER 12

As she nestled next to Basil in the full-size motel bed that was oddly more comfortable than the bed they had at the trailer, his warm breath was on the back of her head. She reached for his arm and placed it on her belly. Elara was still as if she could already tell day from night, unlike Orion and Cassiopeia. She took a deep breath and tried to drift off to sleep, picturing Merna's childhood. Her mind drifted to the last day and a half, the bliss of being stranded where they were. Darcy held her belly and turned over. The weight of Elara made it more of an effort than earlier. Basil opened his eyes.

"What's wrong? You okay?" he murmured with his eyes still closed.

"Yeah. I'm okay. Bay?"

"Hmm?"

"What do you think about staying here?"

Basil opened his eyes halfway. "What do you mean?"

"Making Cresson Creek our home. Staying put after the truck is fixed?" Darcy reached up for his face. His blonde stubble was prickly. He hadn't shaved since they left Maine.

"The truck'll be ready tomorrow hopefully, the next day at least. Why would you want to stay here?"

"It's nice here, don't ya think?" Darcy said as Basil pulled his arm from her hip and sat up in the bed.

"Yeah, it's nice here. What's this about?"

"I was just talking about it with Merna today. She mentioned they'd help us out if we stayed here. It's just an idea."

"Well, staying in western Pennsylvania wasn't part of any plan. We broke down here. We're headed to Nebraska. My Uncle Quincy is ready to help when we get there." He looked over at her. "Listen, I know you're scared, but we're gonna be fine. As you said, we've got enough to pay for the truck, the motel, and get going and start new in Franklin just like we planned."

"But what if we just stayed here and I don't know, you became a farmer of something?" Darcy searched for his eyes.

"Farmer? Seriously? I'm no farmer, Darcy. Are you crazy?" He glanced at the kids once he realized he had risen his voice. He rubbed his eyes.

"Well, Jesus, Basil. You're no builder either, but here we are heading to Nebraska to rebuild houses." Cassie squirmed and whined. Darcy was startled by how loud she was.

Basil threw the blankets back and stood. He reached for his sweatpants and paced while he rubbed his eyes. She realized by the contortion of his face that words were on the tip of his tongue and he was trying to swallow them.

"I'm serious, Basil. Can we think about staying?" Darcy said as she rose from the bed.

"No. We're heading to Nebraska. That's where we're gonna call home. I saw it, Darcy. I told you that night when I saw the news that we're supposed to go there. I just know it. Remember?"

"Yeah, I remember. You were also wasted that night, and every other night you talked about this plan," Darcy reached for his arm. She turned him towards her and touched his prickly cheeks. He looked away from her. She knew he was still in a half-asleep fog. "But listen. What if we broke down here for a reason? What if making it here was what's supposed to be? What if we aren't meant to go further? Maybe this is far enough." Basil averted his eyes again as she stood on her tiptoes searching for them. "Think about it."

"Drinking had nothing to do with it, dammit. You know that." He pulled away from her. "We'll talk in the morning. I'm beat. I'm not having this conversation right now." Basil crawled back into bed under the thin pale-yellow comforter. Darcy stood alone in the dark for a minute before joining him. She crawled in and pulled the blanket over her increasingly swollen body.

Darcy's eyes glanced around the small room. She looked at her bag on the floor next to the small table with a black rotary telephone on top just like her grandparents had. Her insurance was in that bag. For the first time since Gemma pushed it her way, Darcy thought of using it. She could catch a bus in the morning or pay for a ride to Pittsburgh and get plane tickets. Basil and his truck would head to Franklin and chase all the storms he wanted. He'd be able to buy as many six-packs as he wanted each night. Then Darcy pictured herself and the children getting picked up by her dad. She pictured herself in Bakers working again, being in a hospital having Elara without Basil right there. She pictured her three children tucked into beds at her parents' or Cecelia's place while she falls asleep alone thinking of Basil.

As she fought tears and increasing fears, her concerns of 'why am I following him' shifted to 'what if I'm not with him?' Darcy couldn't picture her world without him, whether it was in Winsockette, Cresson Creek, or Franklin. There was no her without him. The man she loved was in there, underneath his scars and fears. The in-between Basil might be leading the way and there might not a clear-cut day when the man she knew him to be would emerge, but he was in there. Darcy believed with all her heart that Basil wanted to be that man too. He wanted to defeat the demons his father tried to infuse into him. She knew he wanted to be the father his father never was. She also recognized if she took that insurance money and ran, he'd fall into being the man she feared most, exactly like his dad. She tried to calm her breathing so he wouldn't realize she was trying not to cry. She closed her eyes and wished sleep would wash away her fears.

After the sun rose and the children were dressed, they sat in the diner shifting breakfast around on warm plates. Darcy kept looking out the window and watching buggy after buggy pass by. Merna filled coffee cups, tussled Cassie's hair, and asked if they slept okay. They nodded, sipped, and sat in silence. Darcy's mind was heavy, foggy, and she shifted in the booth trying to get comfortable. She was out of sorts in every way.

She wanted a home, safety, and she wasn't sure they'd find it if they left Cresson Creek. Basil winked at her. She smiled.

"I'm sorry I yelled last night," Darcy said when his eyes caught hers again.

"I wish you'd trust me. Trust in this plan," He said without looking at her.

"I'm trying to. But seriously, maybe this was part of it for a reason. We could make it here. I know it. We'd be happy here." Darcy pleaded.

"I'm not saying we wouldn't be. But you only want to stop now because you're afraid of going further," He said as he sipped the last of his coffee.

"Damn right I'm afraid." Darcy snapped back as she put down her mug. "I'm afraid you'll get hurt there, or me, or the kids. I'm afraid we're inviting bad karma or whatever into our lives by making money off people's trauma and loss. Honestly, don't you think about that?"

"Of course, I have. But you're looking at it all wrong. Someone has to rebuild for these people. Someone has to pick up what God destroys. The paper industry ain't coming back. Society ain't gonna care tomorrow or ever. They've taken away every opportunity we had back home." He leaned in closer and lowered his voice. "We gotta chase our own now, and I believe this is it, going to Franklin. I believe God is showing us this is the way, the way for us to make it in this world. We aren't stopping halfway there and giving up. We ain't staying in the middle of nowhere Pennsylvania and farming. Jesus, Darcy."

Basil's face grew red. Darcy noticed the redness spread under his stubble. Darcy looked around and saw others staring at them. She fought tears and fought the urge to apologize to everyone in the diner. She also fought the urge to throw her coffee cup right at his forehead. Darcy saw Merna stop mid-pour of coffee and listen. She was embarrassed and felt like an eyesore just as she did in Connecticut. Darcy paused and looked to the motel. She pictured herself running across the road with her kids clinging to her pregnant belly. She saw herself throwing open the door and grabbing the envelope of money. She could be on a flight to Maine before dinner. Or she could tell Basil 'no', she had enough money to stay in Cresson Creek alone with the kids. She looked up at him as a hundred different scenarios ran through her head. His eyes met hers. She saw him swallow a lump in his throat as one bubbled up in hers. So many words swam through her head. She was drowning in them, unable to breathe or speak.

"Listen, I want this to work for us. You've always been the dreamer, the one who was destined to leave Maine, the smart one. I'm the reason you never got out of there. I need to be the reason you get to leave now. I need you to trust me on this, trust that I got us. I got this." He said in a whisper as he glanced around.

"I do trust you. I know you want the best for us. But I'm scared of going further. What if this breakdown was a sign?"

"It wasn't. It was a shitty job of looking the truck over before we left. Our sign was that tornado happening on a day when I was staring blankly at the tv hoping to God something or someone would help me see the way for us. And yeah, I was drinking. I know I've been drinking a lot lately, for a while. But I've got that under control, too."

Darcy drew in a long, deep breath. She wondered how many times Basil's dad might've said the same thing. Then she thought of Jackson and his vow to stay clean. She didn't doubt either of them meant it. Darcy knew both men wanted to get everything under control, but whether they could was a different matter. Basil's outbursts and pacing at night, all with a beer in hand, made her wonder how far down he was sliding before he or they'd land on solid footing.

"Listen, I'm not saying you're gonna turn into your dad. I know you're a good father and husband, a good man. I know that."

"Then listen to me. I'm not crazy. I'm not having a breakdown, which I know everyone was saying back home. Trust me." He rolled his eyes. "We're supposed to go to Franklin." Basil bit his bottom lip. Darcy nodded and twisted her fingers in her lap. She didn't know what else to say. She knew it was pointless to tell Basil that people who are crazy or are having a breakdown always say they aren't. She glanced back at the motel door, the door that held her only way out. Then Basil slid his hand across the table. She slid hers into his. He squeezed. She met his eyes. She wasn't sure if it was her deep need to see it or if she was seeing a change in his eyes. He was clear. Determined. Driven. Steady. A man who needed to provide security for his family, security he never had. The man she needed him to grow into seemed to be looking back at her. Even if it was just her imagination or a manifestation of who she needed him to be in that moment, there was no denying it. He squeezed her hand again and she squeezed back. She wasn't going to run back to the motel and scoop up the babies and fly back to Maine. Sink or swim, storms be damned, she was going wherever Basil needed to go.

Just as Darcy mouthed 'okay', Mitch pulled in and walked straight to their table. Darcy wiped her mouth and wiped away a tear that had bubbled up out of nowhere.

"The part came in this morning. I can have you up and running by this afternoon, or night at the latest." Basil's eyes widened with suprise. Darcy looked through Mitch, past the men at the counter, past Tiny's sprigs of red hair, past Merna's apron. She looked at the window and to the motel. This little spot of earth that held them safe would soon be a memory. They'd soon be on the road and into the great wide open, into the unknown, together.

"Hey, you hear that? We can be on the road today, or head out first thing in the morning."

Darcy stared into the eyes of the only man she ever loved. They were halfway to their planned destination. They were days behind and days closer to having their third baby. Even if she didn't have all the answers she needed, he was right about one thing. If they stayed, it would be out of fear of going forward. She told herself the same sky that brought her comfort and balance over the trailer in Winsockette and Cresson Creek would be the same sky she'd see in Franklin. This place was a stop in their journey, a relaxing and soothing stop along the way. A place to settle their minds. It wasn't the destination, or at least it didn't have to be just because she was afraid to keep going.

"Can we come back someday?" Darcy asked as she glanced out the window again.

"Of course," Basil said. Darcy was sure they wouldn't.

They packed in the motel as they waited for word about the truck. Darcy sat in the chair outside the door and held Orion on her lap. He had eaten too much and was 'bacon drunk', as Basil called it. Orion had a habit of eating until he was nearly asleep, worn out from expelling so much energy at a meal. She ran her hands through his soft curly hair the same jet-black shade as hers. Elara pushed out from the inside almost as if fighting for a spot before she even met her big brother. Darcy adjusted Orion to give Elara's feet room to press against her belly. She winced.

Mitch pulled in with his garage tow truck and their truck pulled in behind him, driven by one of his mechanics. Even though it had only been two days, their old truck looked foreign to her for a second. The tow truck and their truck doors slammed shut simultaneously. Basil stepped through the doorway of the motel room.

"She's as ready as she'll ever be to get you guys moving to the Midwest," Mitch said. Basil sprinted to the men. They talked numbers and Basil fished for his wallet.

After one last dinner at the diner, which Merna refused payment for, they loaded up the truck that would once again be their home away from home. They paid Dutch. Darcy was taken aback when he shuffled from behind the counter to hug her and leaned down to kiss the top of Cassiopeia's head. She wasn't sure why he meant so much to her, why anyone in Cresson Creek did. As they made their way outside to the truck, Merna and Tiny came across the road. It was the only time Darcy or Basil had seen Tiny out from behind the counter. He was shorter than Darcy pictured. Seeing Merna and Tiny side by side holding hands reminded Darcy of black and white pictures of circus acts from the 1800s. He had to be under five feet. His few strands of hair stood straight up, yet he had the biggest smile of any man twice his size. He reached over and shook Basil's hand, then Darcy's.

"It's been nice having yunz and your little ones around the last few days," Tiny said in a voice that was low and deep, not fitting of a man his stature.

"Thank you, Tiny. Who's watching the diner?" Darcy said. She realized there were cars in the parking lot and patrons visible through the large plate windows, despite the glare of the sun.

"Oh, we told everyone to just hang on a minute while we came and said bye. They're all fine," Merna said as she rested her large hands on her hips. At that moment, Cresson Creek reminded Darcy of Winsockette. Darcy had that feeling of leaving home all over again. She remembered leaving the only open Baker's checkout lane unattended once when she needed to call Gemma and find out how Harlan was doing after he got hurt at the mill the winter she was a senior. No one in the store batted an eye as she yelled out the checkout lane was closed for a few minutes. There was a deep trust and sense of family in a place like that, both Bakers and Yoder's. The thought of taking off without paying never crossed the minds of the customers or the workers. Family wouldn't cross family. Then she pictured Jackson and realized the irony.

"Listen, yunz pull over when you're tired. Get plenty of rest when ya can. And please call the diner when you get to Nebraska and check in a hotel there. Just let us know you kids made it, okay?" Merna said. She shifted her eyes upward to avoid looking Darcy in the eye. Darcy nodded. Cassie lunged forward and latched onto her legs. Merna looked down at her. Darcy saw tears were dangling on the edges of her plump, red cheeks.

"We will. I promise. Listen, we can't thank you guys enough for making us feel like family, taking care of us while we were here," Basil said. He slid his hands back in his pockets and looked at the ground like Tiny did.

"Merna, Tiny, please know we'll never forget your kindness," Darcy said. Merna reached over and pulled her in for a bear hug. Darcy let Merna's pillowy breasts suffocate her for a minute.

"Yunz come back anytime. If you need anything, ever. Okay?" Merna said as she released Darcy. Basil said they needed to get settled, buckled, and hit the road to get to Ohio by dark. A few wayward glances were tossed around meant to delay the inevitable. Basil took the first step away from the group and put Orion in his car seat. He made sure the straps were tight and snacks were shoved down enough below his feet for the boy to kick freely. He handed him his blanket, which Orion immediately pulled over his head.

"Come on, Cas. Say goodbye." He said. Cassie gave a little wave as wide smiles made their way across Merna and Tiny's faces. A few chuckles escaped as Cassie climbed into her seat with Basil's help. Basil then closed the back doors and placed his arm around Darcy's shoulder. She reached up and took his hand.

"Remember yunz are always welcome in Cresson Creek," Merna said in a low voice, fighting back tears. Darcy wrapped her arms around her again, then scooted around to the passenger side. She smiled and waved. Basil gave another handshake and slid into the truck right after her.

Merna patted the top of her wild cherry red hair down as the wind picked up. She waved as they backed away. Once they pulled out onto the road, Darcy saw Dutch come out in his robe and sweatpants. He placed his hand on Merna's shoulder. She reached up and patted it as her eyes watched Darcy's in the rearview mirror. Merna was physically the opposite of Gemma, yet Darcy couldn't help but see her as a mother figure. Her comfort, her smile, her wisdom, and protective nature gave Darcy a sense of safety she hadn't experienced in months, possibly longer. Gemma was everything Merna wasn't, but she was everything Darcy needed and always needed her mom to be. Darcy wanted to reach back and wrap herself in Merna's arms for a minute more, maybe longer. She wanted to experience her softness again. Darcy wanted to grab the bag of money and run back, stay, live in Cresson Creek with the kids forever. She knew she couldn't. There was no use pining for a place or life she'd never have. She watched Cresson Creek in the rearview mirror until they reached the ramp for the highway and Basil accelerated. Darcy accepted as the town and comfort of the last few days faded that she'd never see Cresson Creek again. Merna, Tiny, Dutch, the Amish would fade into the recesses of her tired mind. A home she'd never have.

"Boy, she sounds like a dream. I can feel the difference. Can you?" Basil said with is eyes forward as the highway opened to them.

"Yeah. I can." Darcy said. She swallowed a lump. Elara won't get to meet Merna, she thought. First, the lullaby of the mill was taken from her unborn daughter. Now, the warm giant hugs of Merna from Cresson Creek would be nonexistent in Elara's world, too. They were 85 miles from the Ohio border, another unknown spot on the map. Darcy squinted as they barreled forward, and she tried to remember what might've been pictured on the map for Ohio. Pink, she thought it was pink but couldn't imagine anything else.

Darcy jumped as the truck heaved over a bump in the highway. She shook her head and rubbed her eyes in a hurry as she realized she drifted off.

"How long have I been asleep?" She asked as she glanced back at the children and then Basil.

"A few hours." He said without taking his eyes off the wheel. "That bump was nothing. Just a change in the road pattern entering this highway."

"Where are we?"

"Illinois."

"Holy shit. I missed most of Ohio? What time is it?" Darcy tried to wrap her mind around where they were on the map with where they came from and where they were headed.

"It's 2 a.m. The kids have been out for just as long as you. I gotta stop to pee though and didn't want to wake you."

"We need to stop to sleep," Darcy said. She instantly realized the absurdity of saying that seconds after waking. "Well, you need sleep, at least." She glanced around. "what part of Illinois? I didn't miss the Chicago area, did I?"

"No, you didn't miss it. I'll find a gas station to pull over. We've lost enough time, and I think we need to just keep driving."

"You want me to drive awhile? You can't just drive straight through the night like that," Darcy said. She readjusted herself and tried to stretch her legs. Basil slowed the truck and exited the highway. Once he stopped in a convenience store parking lot, they both opened their doors trying to remain silent. Basil stretched his long lanky arms above his head. Darcy remembered how he touched the ceiling of their Maine trailer. She wondered if their next ceiling would be just as low. She tried to bend back and forward as she stretched her stiff, swollen legs.

"I gotta walk a bit. My legs are aching like crazy. This baby needs to come soon, or I won't be able to walk anywhere." She stretched her calf muscles as she slowly stepped in circles. She hadn't been this achy any other time. Then again, she realized, she had never ridden so long in a car without stopping before, much less during the last few weeks of pregnancy. She hated driving to town and standing at Bakers for a few hours when she was pregnant with the others.

Basil strolled inside as Darcy made careful strides around the truck. She heard the trucks whizzing by on the highway through the thin line of trees. The lights were glaring and pulsating like a strobe light through the branches. Darcy could forget it was 2 a.m. between the noise, headlights, and streetlights. Darcy tried to look down at her feet. She had to lean to the side to see past her belly. Her swollen ankles were bursting from her shoes. Darcy looked up to the sky. Buildings, treetops, and lights enclosed her. She couldn't see stars. It was a haze. Basil came out with two coffees in his hands and a bag of chips under his arm.

"Hey, look up, Babe." She said. He stopped and looked at the sky. "How on earth do the people here star-gaze?"

"They don't." He answered. Basil placed the coffees on the hood and stretched again. That idea was a punch to the gut.

"Alright, you drive a few hours. I'll nap. Then we can stop for breakfast, maybe take turns sleeping and driving and we can get to Omaha by lunch?" He leaned toward her and rubbed her shoulders for a minute.

"We'll see how far I can go." Darcy reached for the coffee and sipped. "Let's get going before the kids wake up." She said as she opened the driver's side door and pulled her bloated body up to the seat.

Darcy gently eased the truck and trailer back onto the highway. She hadn't driven it much since they left Maine. Her pulse quickened as she increased speed. Darcy kept glancing back in the mirror to be sure the trailer was still attached. Their whole lives were in that trailer, at least what little they had left.

"It ain't going nowhere, Darcy. Relax and just drive." Basil said. He tapped her thigh. Darcy saw him lean his head back and to the side. She knew within minutes he'd be asleep. The streetlights of the highway seemed one long line of suns guiding her way. Nighttime and darkness seemed like a far-off myth they were chasing. It only grew lighter and lighter the further she drove. There were eight lanes. She tried to remember if she had ever driven on such a wide road.

Darcy was torn between drinking adequate coffee to stay awake and having to stop and pee again so soon or deprive herself of coffee to get further through Illinois. She couldn't remember a damn thing about Illinois on the map she played with as a child, other than Chicago and that it bordered the great lakes. A picture of a steak? A cow for the cattle industry? Pizza for Chicago? The Sears Tower? Nothing popped out at her. She wished she had paid attention in social studies. She was always looking upwards at the sky, not downward at a map unless it was a map of constellations. Giant signs for Chicago came into view. Multiple lanes veered into the dark abyss and toll booths appeared. There was an immeasurable number of cars on the road for the middle of the week. Darcy marveled at this unknown part of the world while she strained her eyes to stay focused on everything around her, including the trailer. Where was everyone going, and was she the only one who had never been there before?

Darcy turned up the radio slightly to fill the air with noise other than Basil's snores and the children's breaths. She wished it was a reasonable hour to call someone, anyone. She missed mindless conversations with Cecelia. While she still touched base with her each day, this was the longest they had gone without catching sight of each other coming or going from the trailer park. She called her mom each day since they left Maine, but not to just chat. Darcy couldn't wait to tell Gemma about Merna. Then at the same time, she knew telling Gemma about Merna would only result in hurt feelings. Darcy realized there was no way to describe her impressions of Merna without making her sound motherly. Even though Gemma was physically the most gorgeous resident of Winsockette and surrounding towns, all of northern Maine in fact, any adoration towards another older woman made Gemma jealous. She was jealous of teachers Darcy would openly admire and emulate. She was jealous of Cecelia's mother and the desserts she would whip up to please Darcy. Gemma was snarky with Darcy when the college admissions counselor gushed over Darcy's scores and ambition to be an astronomer. She always wondered if Gemma was slightly pleased Darcy ended up pregnant and losing her scholarship because it meant Darcy wasn't going anywhere. There would be no other accomplished woman to swoop in and mystify Darcy with her charm, intelligence, and essence. Darcy recognized Gemma was devastated they had left Maine and that she loved her more than anything. But she also understood Gemma quietly loved being the object of Darcy's awe and ire when it came to Gemma's mesmerizing beauty. Darcy decided she'd call Gemma in the morning and unabashedly gush about Merna's cherry-colored hair, boisterous laugh, and limitless wisdom.

Darcy glanced back at the first streaks of sunrise in the rearview mirror. She heard Cassie stir and knew it was only a matter of minutes before she'd need to stop and pee, too. Darcy sipped more coffee and decided to soak up the last few minutes of silence and contentment of her little family.

Just as Basil stirred and the children collectively whined to welcome a new day on the road, Darcy could see the city fade from view. The exits grew farther apart as did the signs. Green replaced brick and cement. The view of ground spread out before the truck and on the sides. Soon, as she chose an exit for breakfast, gas, and bathroom breaks, the sky opened more, and the air looked cleaner. Everything looked fresher. The cars that surrounded her on the outskirts of Chicago at night faded to a few. Darcy wondered where they'd eventually end up, their sleepy little family. She grasped this journey was about more than a new home, a new state, new job. It was a change in circumstances, destiny. It was the two of them and their children breaking away from all they knew in life, all that nurtured them, all that held them back. By leaving everything they knew, Darcy believed she and Basil would become who they were meant to be away from their families, away from Winsockette. Even though Basil fought to be the opposite of his father and had resisted that man's pull since he kicked out Basil, Darcy believed in her gut that moving a thousand miles from him would save Basil. It would ensure Basil would become his own man, and she'd become her own woman. Nothing terrified and excited her more. The prospects of who they might grow to be were as limitless as the sky above them along the way.

She glanced around before finding a place to stop. They were as far from Winsockette as they'd ever been. While a tiny part of her heart still had the urge to turn around and drive right back to their trailer park, a twinge in her gut wanted to see how far away they could get and how fast they might get there.

After a stop, food, and the feeling of being normal again came over them, Basil decided to drive the rest of the way. Darcy was anxious to sleep a little and give her eyes and mind a rest. Basil talked to his Uncle Quincy again after their stop. The house to rent was a done deal. It was owned by the sheriff's mother who lived in the small Kansas border town Quincy called home. The sheriff's mother had to move in with the sheriff and his wife because of failing health. They had tried selling the house, but the recession made that impossible in rural Nebraska. It seemed no one was looking to plant roots in Franklin except for Basil and Darcy.

Quincy talked the sheriff into giving him the keys and letting Darcy and Basil rent it for a one-month trial period. The sheriff would visit in June and if he liked the way they were taking care of the house and land, he'd let them sign a year lease. While Darcy had overhead this plan as it was hashed out over the last two days, part of her wondered what if she didn't like it? Everything seemed to depend on what the sheriff thought of them as renters, with no thought as to what she thought of him as a landlord, not to mention what if the house was a piece of shit and unfit for their family? She realized it was a waste of time and energy to let herself grow resentful or carry disdain for a man they hadn't met yet. Basil assured her that if Uncle Quincy thought the house was a good place for them, then it must be. He had a good gut. Darcy reasoned he must because Quincy left Winsockette for the Army instead of working at the mill and he never looked back. That alone, Darcy thought, made him smarter than everyone else she knew in Winsockette. Quincy had made a much better life for himself than Basil's father had.

The idea that they had an actual house to drive to made it a little easier for Darcy to close her eyes and relax once they were back on the road. At least, in theory, they had a place to set up as a home. She had a place to bring a new baby home to. Darcy faded into sleep as she stretched out her naked feet. She let the sight of rolling green hills, red barns, cornfields, and wind turbines hypnotize her to sleep knowing Nebraska would be the next site she'd see whether she was ready or not. She hoped the night sky looked better than the one over Chicago. As much as Darcy was trying to be prepared for all the changes they were barreling towards, she needed to believe something would be the same, familiar. Something would feel like home, even if it was only the view above her and the stars she couldn't touch.

# PART III

# CHAPTER 13

Darcy drifted out of a dream as Freebird played on the radio. Before she could focus her mind or her eyes, she knew they were almost out of Iowa, perhaps just miles from Omaha. The rolling hills and giant silos were everything she had imagined Iowa to be. It was green, wide, and wild-looking. The silos seemed as tall as the giant pines. Those pines provided paper and sustenance for an entire region, just as those silos held the same for these communities. Darcy had never realized it before, but so many places they saw and absorbed along the way were no different than Winsockette. Basil squeezed her knee. She shot him a gentle, sleepy smile. Darcy glanced at the kids, who were more content in the back seat of this journey than she expected them to be. She wished to be as worry-free as they were.

"Almost to Omaha, Babe," Basil said with his eyes glued to the road. There wasn't much traffic considering it was possible to see for miles ahead and to either side of them. Even with the hills and changing shades of green, their line of sight was seemingly endless. Darcy grabbed a water from the back in between the kids and drank it down in a few gulps. Then, she cringed with the realization that she'd surely have to pee in a matter of minutes. She rubbed her belly as Elara readjusted herself under Darcy's ribs. *About a month to go,* Darcy thought.

A bridge spanning over a wide, brown river was laid out before them as they barreled along I-80. As the truck and trailer rattled over the bridge, Darcy noticed train cars situated on inclines on either side of the highway. Large stone structures flanked the sides of the road. Letters sprawled across the trains read "Welcome" and "Omaha" on the other side. The rolling green hills and silos were replaced by more lanes of highway, buildings jutting into the sky on both sides and evidence of industry—warehouses, train tracks and cars, high-rise buildings clustered together broken up by side streets, and people. Darcy noticed the clusters of people and parks, and city life taking place on both sides of the highway. There were suddenly multiple exits, tractor-trailers veering on and off, clusters of cars slowing and speeding up. It was an entirely different world than they had been surrounded by only minutes earlier in Iowa. Darcy had a hard time focusing on where they were supposed to be. *This is Nebraska?* She thought.

Basil glanced around, darting in and out of cars as he tried to keep an eye on the trailer. Darcy was aware Cassie and Orion were trying to absorb the sights also. The four of them seemed as hypnotized by the busyness of Nebraska as they were by the rolling hills, silos, and calmness of Iowa.

The bulging city of Omaha just over the bridge started to flatten again. As quickly as it appeared, it started to fade away. The buildings grew sparse. The exits were fewer. The lanes narrowed. The tightness and chaos of the tiny city started to give way to land again. Cement ceased and grasses and fields reappeared. There were clusters of housing developments complete with winding cul de sacs and manicured lawns. It was almost like an oasis in Darcy's mind. The kids settled back and became disinterested again. Orion squirmed and whined for another snack.

"Once we get to Lincoln around dinner, we'll stop for the night. Then, Quincy will meet us at the house in the morning. Okay?" Basil said. "Tomorrow, we'll be home." Darcy smiled and squeezed his hand. She looked out at the fields on either side of the road. It was stark, wide-open, and soon, it would be home.

Lincoln was much smaller than she expected. It looked old. The buildings were connected and had facades that varied in height and stature. They had ornate tops with scrolls and dates etched in stone and brick. Others had giant bronze plaques with stately names and purposes spelled out: opera house, post office, hotel, library. There were signs for the University of Nebraska—Lincoln. The brick buildings had colorful awnings and clean sidewalks. It looked quieter than the outskirts of Chicago or Omaha.

The motel they reserved from the road was on the other side of town. Slowly progressing through the incessant line of stoplights made Darcy's stomach queasy. She had grown too used to the constant high speed of the highway. She watched the GPS attached to the visor and willed the truck and trailer through each light and on to the next block. When they pulled into the motel, Darcy scanned the long single-story building with bright blue doors with numbers nailed to the top. The first door had a neon sign that said 'office' dangling from the top gutter. It swayed slightly in the wind. There were a handful of cars and two trucks scattered throughout the parking lot. The lot seemed to take up more square footage than the motel.

"Hurry, Babe. I've really got to go. Elara is kicking the shit out of my bladder." Basil hopped out and sprinted for the door. Within seconds, he reemerged from the doorway with a key and a wide smile. Darcy grinned at him as he slid back in the truck. He was her hero in every situation, she thought as they lurched the truck to the other end of the building. Darcy noticed the faded paint was peeling from the top. Basil jumped out and opened the door for her as she struggled to slide her pregnant body from the truck. She waddled towards the door as he passed her to get the kids from the truck. He tossed her the key. Darcy flipped on the light and made her way straight to the bathroom. It was bright, clean, and was surprisingly big. The tube-like building was deceptive. As she sat to go and noticed how swollen her ankles were, Darcy wondered if the bathroom in their new 'home' would be as big. It had to be bigger than the trailer in Winsockette. She rolled her eyes and thought she'd be grateful for any structure to call home at this point. Darcy knew it would be a long time before she'd be ready for another long road trip, even if that meant not seeing her family for many months, or longer.

As she flushed, washed hands, and glanced around, she heard the kids file into the motel room and the television click on. She looked at her reflection, her pale round face, her choppy black hair. She hadn't done her eyeliner, mascara, or anything in days. She missed getting dolled up, or more honestly, having a reason to make herself look girly. Then she smirked. *What's more girly than being eight months pregnant?* She thought. Perhaps once they were settled, Elara was born, and they felt comfortable, Basil could take her out for a nice dinner and afterward they'd slow dance like they used in the living room of the trailer.

The idea that tomorrow she'd learn the layout of their home, the size of the bedrooms, kitchen, and color of the shutters helped her relax. She'd know more than she'd known since the day they got word of the mill closing. Darcy would find a grocery store she loved. She'd find a pre-school for Cassie. Maybe she'd even make new friends. The world was suddenly filled possibilities she hadn't given much thought to before she was in Nebraska. However, every time she realized the small nuances of her soon-to-be new life, twinges of guilt would creep in. The worst thing that could happen to them is no wind, no storms, no destruction other than what had already occurred in Franklin. That was the storm that led them to Nebraska. Darcy feared both—the possibility of no more tornadoes to cause damage worthy of repair and more storms sweeping through causing her new sense of home to get windswept and tossed around before her eyes. She wanted normalcy, a sense of home, security. Darcy was sick with the realization that security, financial security, would only be possible if more destruction rolled through. It was a plurality she couldn't make peace with. It gnawed at her conscience more and more as they barreled closer to their new home.

Despite her inner turmoil, Darcy slept like a rock, as did the kids. Laying on a mattress as opposed to crinkled and twisted in a car seat and passenger seat was like heaven. She and Basil felt like kings stretched out on soft white sheets and claiming every inch of the queen-sized bed. Even with Orion in between them, space seemed like a luxury. Having immediate access to a bathroom as opposed to asking Basil to find a gas station was also a luxury. Before Basil turned off the tv for the night, Darcy watched Cassie drift into a dream, a dream that made her lips turn up almost into a full-fledged smile. She, too, was sprawled out, stretching her tiny body to take advantage of her own bed. Darcy let her eyes slide closed as she stretched one last time. Her muscles twitched, not used to the chance to expand. She found herself half-smiling as she listened to Basil and Orion breathe in unison. She took a relaxing deep breath and settled on the realization that her first day in Nebraska was a good day indeed.

When the sun rose the next morning and Darcy began to stir, she realized they weren't moving. They were still in a soft bed that held them through the night. Basil reached over Orion and ran his hand over her back and onto her belly.

"How you feeling, beautiful?" He muttered. Darcy reached down for his hand.

"Good. I'm sore, but it sure felt nice to sleep in a bed," Darcy said.

"Well, once we get moving and meet Uncle Quincy, we can get our stuff unloaded, and hopefully have our own bed set up. At least our mattresses."

"Yeah. I'm not sure our old mattress will feel as good as this bed though," She said as she slid out from underneath his arm. She didn't want to wake Orion in between them. Darcy waddled to the bathroom and closed the door. She noticed her belly looked even bigger, heavier, and Elara was killing her back. Pregnancy had never been hard on her short frame before, but the third one was testing her limits. She saw new stretch marks appear each day even though she was diligent about using lotion.

After she showered and the kids were cleaned and dressed, they made their way to the office and paid. The clerk offered them coffees, juices, and donuts. Darcy was queasy from the sugar but grateful to not have to stop and pay for breakfast.

Basil hoisted a powdered covered Cassie into the truck as Darcy lifted Orion into his seat. He squirmed and whined as she strapped him. As she reached across and pressed her belly into him, she said, "Don't worry, Baby Orion. After today, we don't have to ride anywhere for a long time." After she buckled him, she slid herself into the passenger seat. She groaned as she reached back for the seatbelt. She knew her promise to Orion was a lie. They'd need to go back to town for groceries, cleaning supplies, her new doctor, and God knows what else. Even though the trailer was packed with the sunken couch, beds, a crib, a high chair, toys, a dinette set, clothes, sheets, towels, cookware, pictures, curtains, and a rocking chair for their new porch, they would still need a shower curtain, trash cans, and cleaning supplies. They'd need more furniture once they saw the house and assessed what they had room for.

Darcy didn't know if there was even a place for the rocking chair, but she couldn't leave it behind. Gemma had given it to her when she and Basil moved to the trailer park. It was the chair Gemma used to rock Darcy and Jackson as babies. The dark stained wood was streaked with scratches. The back was wicker. It looked old, tired, a piece that no one would currently choose to have in their home or on the porch, but Darcy couldn't let it go. Gemma could barely let it go. Darcy hoped they'd have a porch for it or at least a corner in whatever room they'd use as a nursery.

Basil drove through the endless grid of lights to find Route 27. Once the lights ceased, the natural landscape swallowed the cement sidewalks and mismatched buildings. The world once again opened. Darcy could see forever, on all three sides of the truck. There was tall grass, corn, fences lining the cracked road, and the occasional collapsed barn and home. Everything seemed abandoned, left to fall where it was all alone. A few sparse houses would look lived in, modernized with flowers out front, cars in the driveway, a swing set in the field adjacent to the homes. There'd be a silo, a large barn, and a few pieces of equipment every few miles. The freshly planted corn waved as they passed crops that went on further than the ocean. The small, sturdy stalks rippled together like a symphony was playing. She marveled at the desolate views. Even though other parts of their journey had looked similar, Darcy was refreshed and awake enough to take in the scope of it all. She saw a crossroad ahead. There were no trees on either side, no curves, no blind spots. Just a straight shot to wherever. That wherever would be her family's new home.

Darcy squinted her eyes as the sun reflected off the giant silos ahead. More buildings sprouted through the fields off in the distance. They were approaching Franklin. She noticed two cars heading toward them, the most she had seen since they left the gridwork streets of Lincoln. She let out a small gasp as a farmhouse came into view on her side of the truck. It was mangled. Half the roof was sheared off like the top of the sardine cans her father used to eat in the kitchen late at night. However, this debris wasn't old, decades of neglect that left a property looking lonely and desperate for love. This was new. It was bright yellow siding strewn across a well-maintained yard. It was flower boxes broken to bits and nestled next to the road. There were the remnants of a swing set across the field. There were pieces of cabinets, a mattress, chunks of what must've been the linoleum floor. Darcy scanned the debris and tried to picture how it must've looked before the storm. Her mind tumbled back to the night Basil watched the breaking news and called her to see what he saw, feel what he felt. Here she was less than two months later driving by the very site of the devastation. It was only one property out of hundreds, one house out of hundreds, one family out of hundreds. She wondered where the family was now and how they got there. Had they moved into a hotel, with family, or fled Nebraska for good? Darcy squeezed her eyes shut and reached for Basil's arm.

"It's okay, Darcy. I'm sure they're all fine."

"But you don't know, do you Basil? None of this is fine."

"Well, honey. That's why we're here. To help make it fine," Basil said with an inflection of hope and purpose.

For the first time since he spewed out his plan, his vision for their future, she saw it as real. She saw it through his eyes, as a calling, as something they needed to do. She fought tears as she tried to picture the sheer terror and panic that family in the farmhouse must've felt in those moments. If they had children to protect, family heirlooms, or a way of life, how horrible it had to be to watch it get destroyed in moments. Did they have time to mourn, to cry, to comfort their babies? Did they have spare moments to warn family or neighbors nearby? Did they pray? Darcy couldn't remember the last time she prayed. What if they were atheists who didn't believe in God at all? What if they were believers but now hold God responsible for this wrath and have become unbelievers? Darcy couldn't figure which might make more sense. She thought of the many times Basil said this was God's plan, for them to move to Nebraska and help these people rebuild. She saw it as a job opportunity, one that required the suffering of innocent people to unfold first. Darcy saw it as profiting off the misery, pain, and ruin of others. She saw it as using God's wrath as their personal windfall. That was until she saw the farmhouse. Suddenly, Darcy got it. She wanted to jump from the truck and help gather a random family's belongings. She wanted to do anything humanly possible to piece back the lives of strangers. Maybe they could make a difference in Nebraska. Perhaps God needed them to step outside of themselves, far from Winsockette, and do this. Darcy thought of her babies, her own little family coexisting on this earth with a family who lost everything. What if that family lost one of their babies? She looked at Basil. His eyes widen. Darcy realized his mind was racing with ideas and anticipation of helping these people. But, she thought, at what cost? Not only were they following God's wrath with a somewhat noble plan of helping those who needed it, but they were also placing themselves and their babies in the middle of it. Would God want them to do that?

As the farmhouse and what was left of its littered life faded in the rearview mirror, other scattered evidence of the storm sprang up on either side of the road. Clothes seemed to make up the most of it. Bits of wood, broken and splintered, lay exactly where they landed weeks ago. Darcy stopped trying to figure out what comprised the various piles peeking out from the fields. She focused on Franklin growing before her eyes. It wasn't a cityscape like the outskirts of Chicago or the instant liveliness of Omaha. It was subtle. It was muted, quiet, still. She heard Cassie shift in her booster seat.

"Mama, we there yet?" Cassie asked for the millionth time. Darcy reached back and tapped her knee.

"Soon, baby, real soon. You see those buildings up there? That's our new town." Darcy was trying to convince herself as much as Cassie. She saw Basil rub his forehead as he drove.

"You tired, honey?" She asked.

"Yeah. I just wanna get there and get settled. Hand me my phone," Basil said. Darcy reached in the console. Basil pressed in Quincy's number.

"Hey, man. Just making sure you're there. I think we're just a few miles away." Darcy heard Quincy through the phone. He rattled off a few road names, numbers, and mile markers. Basil nodded. He always nodded when on the phone, which always made Darcy smile. She knew if he was nodding 'yes', everything was fine.

Darcy leaned forward slightly as the buildings came to life. Three more cars came toward them and one appeared behind. A Nebraska traffic jam, Darcy thought. A sign next to the road made it official. "Welcome to Franklin, The BEST of the GOOD LIFE!". She smiled. It was prettier than she pictured. The main street was lined with grand brick buildings attached to each other. There were faded awnings over shops and town services. There was a giant red building with a massive engraved sign at the very top. It was an Opera House, or it had been at one time. There was a tan and brown brick building with intricate masonry work running along the top. The Hotel Franklin. The streets, the light posts, and the shops reminded Darcy of a movie set from the 1950s. There were pickup trucks parked in spaces that jutted out to the road at an angle. Despite the picturesque details, there were a few piles on corners, piles of wood, plaster, and shingles that had peeled from the historic roofs and facades. Basil leaned up to get a closer look at the road signs and seemed to tune out the evidence of the storm in town. He muttered numbers to himself.

"How far are we?" Darcy asked.

"Not far at all. I think I turn left off the main street in a sec. Then we go straight out of town for 12 miles."

"12 miles? We'll be 12 miles out?"

"Come on, Darcy, that ain't far. That'll be nice." Basil said. He glanced at her and turned the wheel. "We were in the middle of nowhere Maine our whole lives. 12 miles out of this town is fine."

"Yeah, but our middle of nowhere was still somewhere. We could see Winsockette, see the mill, hell, see other houses."

"Trailers, Darcy. We could see trailers. This will be a real house, brick, and foundation. It'll be better. And there's no use living within sight of that mill now. It'll just rot before our eyes. It would only remind us every second of every day of what Winsockette lost, what Winsockette was. At least here, we don't have to be reminded of it, you know?"

"Yeah, I guess. But it was home. Our home." She said as she looked out the window, searching for a familiar feeling.

"This will be, too. You'll see," Basil said. He reached for her thigh again. She smiled and swallowed a lump in her throat. She believed he was right, or so she needed him to be. Just as she got used to seeing more than six cars at once, traffic lights, and actual people walking down a sidewalk, the truck turned left, and the buildings once again became sparse. The road turned to dirt. Darcy rolled up her window. Even though it was dirt that was packed down over decades, a layer of dust still rolled along the sides of the truck. It coated her throat. Orion coughed as Basil rolled up the driver's side window. Darcy thought about the back roads of Winsockette, the ones she and Basil used to race down in his old beat-up car. The hills would make her stomach flip. The pine needles along the side of the road would tumble and swoosh to the sides. Trees lined both sides of every road she ever loved, grand old white pines with the occasional baby spruce peeking up from time to time. The smell was invigorating. Now, there were no trees, no needles, no fresh smell. Just dirt and grasses and crops waving as they barreled down a straight, flat stretch of road. Darcy struggled to give this road any redeeming characteristics. Quiet, she decided. Quiet was all it had going for it. Quiet was good.

# CHAPTER 14

A few houses and farms appeared. Darcy wondered what it would be like for kids growing up in those houses and at those farms. How did they play hide and seek? There was nowhere to hide, much less a gang of kids to play with. Her heart ached for her kids. She rubbed her belly. She was getting leg cramps from the ride, and Elara was getting restless because of Darcy's stillness. She looked down and whispered, "Don't worry baby girl. We'll be there soon." She saw Basil smile out the corner of her eye.

"Right there. See it? Up ahead? I think that's it." Basil said. He pointed his finger from the top of the steering wheel. Darcy scooted forward a bit and tried to straighten her ever-stiff back. A farmhouse was on the left. It looked ancient, almost abandoned by the last few decades. Just beyond on the right side was a two-story brick house. Darcy saw the posts from a front porch jutting out. She saw a small barn next to it. The red bricks looked faded, more of a light brown. There were lots of windows. Darcy squinted and noticed window boxes on the first floor. A wavy sidewalk led to a paved driveway. The sight of a paved driveway leading to a dirt road made her chuckle. There was a pickup truck in the driveway and a man waving next to it.

"Uncle Quincy?"

"Yep, that's him. Hasn't changed a bit." Basil said. He beeped the horn. Orion and Cassie jolted to attention.

"Look, guys! It's our new house," Darcy said. The words warmed her insides and temporarily alleviated her leg cramps. Basil pulled in as Quincy walked to meet them. Basil threw the pickup in park and jumped out to embrace his uncle. He was lanky like Basil. But he had jet-black hair and lots of it. It was short but bushy, like an accidental afro. He tossed a cigarette to the side and wrapped his arms around Basil. The men slapped backs. Darcy slid out from the passenger side and opened the door for the kids. She reached in to unstrap Orion and slid him onto her hip as she took Cassie's hand. Cassie jumped out of the truck and raced to be by her father's side. Darcy brushed off her balloon-like shirt and tried to freshen up as she approached the men. Before she could speak, Quincy wrapped his arms around her and held her close.

"It's so good to see you kids. Darcy, you look radiant." He said with a gruff, raspy voice. He sounded identical to Basil's father. His eyes were the same, too but there was a kindness in them, not pain or anger. Darcy wondered how two brothers could turn out so differently. Her mind instantly drifted to Jackson. She missed his voice, his forehead against hers.

"I don't feel too radiant. I feel huge. I'm ready to get this girl out." She said as she let Orion slither down her pale and puffy legs. Darcy noticed her ankles were instantly swollen twice the size they were in the truck—another sign Elara would be coming very soon. She exhaled.

"Well, let's get you in there, show you guys around and get this lady off her feet. You got a doctor in Franklin, right? New fella, pretty young, but everyone seems to be happy with him. Got a good practice and well, I hear good things about the hospital."

"Yeah, Dr. Patrick. I have an appointment with him in two days. My old doctor already faxed over my records to him. He sounds nice on the phone, his nurses too. I just hope I make it the next two days. She's definitely ready."

"You due in about a month, right?"

"Yep, but I went early with baby Orion here, so I'm sure Elara will be here soon, especially after this long road trip. We would'a been here a few days ago if we didn't break down in Pennsylvania."

"Well, you kids are here now." Quincy scooped up Orion. He let him, which made Darcy feel even more at ease.

Quincy opened the door. The screen door squeaked. Darcy exhaled realizing she had room on the porch for Gemma's rocker. She couldn't wait to call her mom and tell her. She ran her hand along the brick as she entered the doorway. It was soft, worn, but sturdy feeling. The smell told Darcy the house had been closed for a while, possibly since winter. A loveseat and small table sat in the middle of the living room. The floor was wood, not stale old carpet. However, there were streaks from the constant sunlight in the middle. It was a faded square. Scratches crisscrossed each plank. Quincy opened the windows.

"Come on to the kitchen." His voice echoed. Darcy smiled and ran her hands along a small island in the middle. The cabinets were dark wood with God-awful white nobs, but there was plenty for everything they needed. The sink was deep and white. The countertops were a beige, neutral and unexciting. But Darcy noted they were in perfect shape, no nicks, chips, or scratches. Either someone never used the kitchen much or they were overly cautious. She had nicked and scratched the countertops at the trailer on a near-daily basis with her clumsy knife skills. The floor was a multi-colored linoleum that was made to replicate stained glass. It was ugly, old fashioned, but clean. *Beggars can't be choosers*, she thought. They were getting this place for dirt cheap rent for at least a year. She appreciated a solid roof and clean floor even if the details didn't look like her taste whatsoever. For a minute, she missed the musty carpet.

They wandered down a narrow hall to a bathroom painted green with a pink flower border along the top. There were watermarks on the ceiling. The tub was pink. Darcy's eyes widened. Basil smirked.

"The owner's mom didn't change too much from the 80s, but hey, it all works," Quincy said as he closed the faded floral shower curtain. He squeezed past them to continue down the wood panel-lined hall and up a flight of stairs. The stairs squeaked. She wasn't sure if that normal wear and tear or if she had gotten that large since her last appointment. There were three bedrooms, small but also clean. There was a dark wood ceiling fan setting the master bedroom apart from the others. There were end tables on either side of a darkened rectangle on the floor. The master bed had never been anywhere else. The floor was faded around it. Quincy opened more windows as he darted in and out of the room, rattling off dimensions.

"Oh, trust me, it's bigger than the truck and much bigger than our trailer in Winsockette. This more than works for us," Darcy said.

"Good, glad to hear it. Now you sit in the living room while Basil and I unload everything." He motioned for her to get comfortable on the loveseat he tapped as he walked back towards the front door. Darcy sank into the brown couch. Orion curled up next to her. Cassie followed the men in and out as they made countless trips. Darcy was amazed how fast her furniture, clothes, her entire life seemed to appear in the once empty space. She got up to put away items from the kitchen boxes. Each stretch radiated throughout her body. *Please give me a few weeks to set up house, Elara."* She thought to herself.

As she put away sippy cups and forks in an empty drawer, she gazed out the kitchen window. It led to a blank canvas. The grasses swayed and a single tree jutted out in the very back of her line of sight. The sky was endless, light blue, and completely clear. She wondered how such a blank and quiet sky might unleash the fury she saw scattered on the ground before and in Franklin. It was an openness she had only seen in movies and recently from the truck window. But standing still in a kitchen made it feel different. Darcy put down a fistful of spatulas and walked to the back door. She heard Basil and Quincy struggle to move their mattress up the stairs and around a corner. Darcy opened the back door and stepped outside. There was a small cement patio. Then, grass. Grass forever. It was long and restless. A breeze blew through her hair. It swayed in the same direction as the grass. She squinted to see beyond the line where the grass met the sky. It seemed to go on forever as if they were on a planet alone. No noise other than the wind, no people, no structures other than the house behind her. She walked to the side of the brick house and saw the remnants of a garden. Her eyes rose to the house on the other side just down the road. It was farther than she expected, but she could make out details, colors, porch furniture. Neighbors, she thought. Darcy instantly missed Cecelia. She missed the other trailers and even the mill. She saw a car pull into the neighbor's house and watched as a woman walked inside. Darcy was relieved at the sight of a person who wasn't family.

When she walked back inside, the space which was echoing with foreign creaks mere hours ago was suddenly a home. Her family pictures were laid across their small dinette set, ready to be hung. Basil was taking towels to the bathroom as Quincy placed stools around the island. While there was still so much to buy to make it cozy, it would work. Out of the blue, it seemed familiar, safe, settled. She sniffed and fought back a tear. She didn't want to cry but her body needed to express the relief and sanctity of what was before her. Her kids were both pushing cars from the box of toys, playing and darting around the corner as if they had never lived anywhere else. Basil positioned a baby gate in front of the steps. Quincy brought it realizing they probably weren't prepared for a two-story home. He smiled at her. Darcy knew Basil recognized that look on her face. He bit his bottom lip and came to her, drawing her in close. He ran his hand across her hairline and to her shoulders as he kissed the top of her head. She was ready to make Nebraska their home.

Quincy and Basil loaded Cassie into the truck and set off to Franklin for groceries and everything Darcy said they still needed. They left her alone to nap with Orion in her newly assembled bed in her new master bedroom. The breeze and the quiet made it difficult to fall asleep for a few minutes. Then, her body and mind surrendered. She needed the rest. She needed days-worth of rest and let her body force her into a deep slumber.

Darcy dreamt of the mill nestled in the valley below the trailer park. She heard the hum and saw plumes escape the smoke towers. She felt warm and protected by the pines and neighbors. She was surrounded by family and friends she had known her whole life. She squinted to see Bakers and the plate glass windows that held Sale signs, signs that changed each week. She saw snow blanketing the town, muffling the sounds of nature, spreading quiet except for the mill. Out of nowhere, the wind whistled and drowned out the sound of the mill. The wind increased to a scream. Darcy held onto the railing of her little front porch. Her knuckles were white, numb. There were swirls of pine needles mixed with flakes making tiny tornadoes in the road and her driveway. They grew bigger. Her hair whipped in front of her face. Her babies were lifted from the porch and caught up in swirls. They screamed and reached for her. She tried to grab their tiny hands, but they kept going in circles, slowly rising above her head and beyond her reach. She stood on her tiptoes and reached with all her might. They were gone. Everything around her started to break apart—the porch, the trailer, Cecelia's trailer, the stop sign at the end of the hill, then finally the mill. The mill cracked. Cement and brick disassembled in a fury. Reams of paper unfurled and snaked like ribbon alongside the smokestacks. They too broke off piece by piece, little by little until they were brick nubs sticking out from the floor of the mill. The roof was gone. Her family, friends, and all of Winsockette was gone. Her heart seized and she was nauseous.

Darcy jolted awake to find Orion tapping her shoulder. A trail of snot oozed dangerously close to his top lip. She gasped. She reached up and touched his tiny, plump face. He was thirsty. She reached for him and they slid to the side of the bed. It was the worst dream she had since the storm infiltrated their lives through a television set over 1700 miles away. Before she stood, she took Orion's hand and looked around the bleak, quiet room. This was home or at least home for now. The thought didn't rattle or scare her as much as she expected it to. Then, she replayed the dream in her head. Maybe it was false comfort, a calm before the storm so to speak? Or hopefully, it was only a bad dream.

The slamming of the truck doors prompted her to hurry as she made her way to the kitchen with Orion shuffling behind her. Basil and Quincy carried loads of groceries and home supplies. She reached in one bag and pulled out new dish towels. They had sunflowers on them. She smiled.

"Basil, we brought some kitchen stuff. You didn't need to buy more towels." She said as she handed Orion a sippy cup of milk from a gallon Quincy placed on the counter.

"I didn't. Uncle Quincy did." Basil nodded his head back at his uncle who flashed a smile. "He refused to let me buy any of this. I told him we saved just for this and we had our bases covered, but he wouldn't take no for an answer."

"Consider it my 'welcome to Nebraska' gift, a housewarming. Plus, this guy goes into town tomorrow to work on a guy's crew I know from Kansas. You'll need to be fully stocked being out here without a vehicle. He'll probably be working 12-hour days roofing and such until end of summer. And, well, I wasn't around much when this guy was a kid. This makes up for what, 23 missed birthday presents?" Quincy put another armload of bags on the already covered counter.

"Hell, you sent me plenty when I was a kid. I still remember those Army t-shirts and MRE's you mailed for me to show off in Winsockette," Basil said as he unpacked the bags.

"Quincy, seriously, this is too much. We saved, planned. We could've gotten this all ourselves," Darcy said. She pulled a banana from a bunch.

"Bullshit. You broke down in Pennsylvania and you got a new baby on the way," Quincy said as he picked up Orion. Darcy was surprised at how quickly both kids seemed to warm up to Quincy. She wondered if kids can just sense family without being told. She missed Jackson. He had been the only uncle the kids knew. He adored them. They adored him. She hadn't spoken to him since she left, however, Gemma insisted he was doing well. That didn't bring Darcy much comfort as she knew Gemma would say that no matter what.

After Quincy left, and the house was looking somewhat like a home, Darcy and Basil cleaned up from a quick dinner with the kids. She could breathe and move freer than she had in weeks. It felt strange to walk around a house and not prepare to climb back into the truck. She stood at the sink. Darcy stared out the kitchen window as the sky turned bright orange.

"Come on. Let's go out back and watch the sun set," Basil said. He took her hand and led her out the back door. Orion and Cassie followed. It was calm, not too windy. They stood in what seemed like a new world and watched the sun they'd always known set in a field they'd never seen before that day. Darcy slipped her hand into Basil's as they watched the sky transform from their first day in a new home to their first night. Basil went to the front porch and brought her rocker around. He motioned for her to take a seat.

"I'll get these little buggers inside and ready for bed," He said as he chased a giggling Cassie. "If I can catch her!" Darcy laughed. She loved Cassie's giggle, especially when she ran and was borderline breathless. Orion bumbled after them. Those three were her whole world, and this was their new world. Darcy looked up and spotted the first stars of the evening. Her eyes scanned the horizon. The skies of Nebraska looked limitless. No pines obstructing half the constellations or mountains keeping certain stars hidden.

Darcy leaned further back. She opened her eyes wider as if she needed to drink in the entire view. Darcy vowed to call Gemma in the morning and tell her about the sky, the house. She watched the outline of Cassie bobbing in and out of view from in front of Basil. His long and lean shadow was followed by the tiny son who would follow him anywhere, just as she vowed to do. The stars started to pop more. They crisscrossed in the patterns she had always studied. They were the same, unaware of the changes in her life or that she was watching from somewhere new. She glanced at Basil's outline as he chased the kids. He looked like the same man she fell in love with at 15. She knew he had heavy weights on his shoulders, ones he hid well back then. Maybe the Nebraska air or sky would lift that weight, she thought. Despite her uncertainty and unease about this adventure, he was still her constant, faults and all. He was her home no matter what the coordinates under their roof said. New dish towels, old ones, old bed frames and mattresses, new shower curtains, rocking chairs handed down from her mother, new window boxes for daisies to grow facing a road barely anyone traveled, all of it could swirl above her head and get sucked up into space and time. All of it could crash around them. All she needed to feel safe, loved, and purposeful was to be within eyesight of that long, lanky shadow of a man and the babies they made together. She strained her eyes to see more stars poke through the now dark purple sky. They were infinite. There was so much left to discover up there and at her feet. Darcy rocked more and had a twinge of anticipation for tomorrow, for this new life in Nebraska.

# CHAPTER 15

Believing everything is okay is one thing. Having a doctor say the words is another. Once the doctor examined her, uploaded her patient info and squeezed her hand just as the doctor who delivered Cassiopeia and Orion had done, Darcy felt lighter. Despite the weight of her belly and the strain on her short, stubby legs, she filled her lungs with relief. Elara was the perfect size, perfect heartbeat, and she would come into the world within the next few weeks. Darcy made her way back into the waiting room to tell Basil and the kids everything was perfect.

Darcy drove Basil back to the chapel he was helping to re-roof. She barely fit behind the steering wheel anymore, another sign she was due soon. He leaned over and kissed her.

"You sure you want to drive yourself back home? I can drive and drop you off, then come back here."

"I'm okay. You can't afford to miss out on hours here. How's it going anyways?" Darcy asked as she peered past him. Two guys on the roof waved to her. She waved back. Basil had told them about her, them, their journey. The foreman of the building company knew Quincy from his Army days and already credited Basil as a hard worker because of his bloodline. Darcy briefly wondered if she and Basil would've made it this far at all if they hadn't had the help of both family and strangers. They seemed to stumble into the kindness of others. She wondered if that was the way it was for every family who moves cross country on a whim.

"It's almost done. But the height of storm season isn't over yet. They say there'll be plenty more work especially in the towns south of Franklin where the tornadoes have hit the hardest. Plus, there's still plenty of homes needing repairs. The boss up there waving says four homeowners are waiting on bids after the church is roofed," Basil said. Darcy looked up at him and marveled at how her impulsive and sometimes reckless husband could also be the hardest working man she knew. He leaned over and kissed her pale forehead before hopping out of the truck.

She smiled and brushed her black hair from her eyes. Her smile faded when she realized that for there to be more work after that, there needed to be more destruction, more storms to uproot what someone else had already built. More roofs needed to be ripped away in a violent flash. More homes or churches needed to be destroyed, decimated for Basil to rebuild, for any of these men to rebuild anything. She remembered Basil's words from that night in Winsockette. "God's wrath will provide…"

"God's wrath," she muttered as she drove away. How could she relax with the thought of a perfect pregnancy and new home knowing that all of it was dependent on God's wrath? Slivers of guilt cut through her. It was a church. Would a righteous God destroy the home of his flock just to put cash in Basil's pocket and the pockets of the other men? Then again, she rationalized, those men might be that flock. Its dismantling provided for that flock. God's wrath might not be wrath after all. She and Basil weren't profiting from the devastation of others, just the devastation of wood and brick that could be replaced. At least, that's what Darcy needed to believe.

Darcy pulled the truck into their driveway. She was still struck by the irony of driving a dusty road from town just to pull into a paved driveway in front of their new home. The flowers Quincy brought for the flower boxes were blooming. She wondered if her old perennials planted in the tiny flower bed in front of the trailer were blooming. She realized she never asked Gemma or Cecelia who was living there, despite talking to one or both at least once a day.

As Darcy put the truck in park, she saw someone cross the road and walk to the driveway, a young woman. Darcy slid her tired, bloated body from the front seat and stood there waiting for the stranger to get closer.

"Can I help you?" she said as she opened the back door for Cassie.

"Hey, didn't mean to sneak up on you. I live at the house across the way. The only other place in sight," She said with a laugh.

"Oh. I've wanted to walk over and meet you guys. I've just been, well, busy getting this place set up."

"Yeah, I can see you have your hands full. When I got home from school the other day, I could tell you're ready to pop." The young woman said as she approached Darcy.

"Ready to pop?" Darcy said. She slid Cassie out from her booster seat. "I gotta go on the other side to get my boy out."

"yeah pop, you're preggers. My Gram guesses you're about close to having that one. Plus, you got these other two. Hands full."

"Yeah, I've got two weeks before my due date. June 14 to be exact. I'm Darcy."

"Yep. I know. We all know. Only about 5 new people come to Franklin a year. The whole town knows you guys are Darcy and Basil, right? You guys from way up north, like Canada or something?"

Darcy laughed. "Maine, but that's pretty close."

"I'm Talia. My grandparents, Ron and Barbara Pinkerton live at the house. They're raising me. I graduate in a week, so I guess I should say they raised me, not raising," Talia said as she waved at Orion.

"So, you're like 18?" Darcy said.

"Yep." Talia brushed her fiery red hair out of her eyes. A breeze seemed to blow through her. She was taller than Darcy, but not by enough to make Darcy feel small. Of course, at this stage in her pregnancy, Darcy never felt small. Darcy noticed her scattered freckles. Her cheeks and shoulders were like ancient maps detailing clusters of kingdoms.

"Do you want to come in?" Darcy asked. "I'm not much fun to hang with at this point, but I've got tea and stuff, snacks."

"Sure. I'd love to. We don't get many actual neighbors out this way. Last person who lived here was super old, like 80s. Guess her son in Kansas took her in," Talia said as she held the door open.

"Yeah, that's how we got this place. Her son is friends with Basil's uncle, and he helped secure it for us before we got here."

"Basil is a builder, right? Works with the crews to get the town built back up?"

"Well, yeah. He wasn't a builder till we got here though," Darcy said with a laugh.

Darcy pulled out a stool for Talia. "How old are you guys?" Talia asked.

"We're both 23. We were high school sweethearts, then bam, parents of two almost three."

"Wow. That sounds like a whirlwind."

"Yeah, everything with us is a whirlwind, you could say."

The two sat on stools at the kitchen island and chatted throughout afternoon as the kids played on the floor until Orion eventually laid on the couch and napped. For the first time since leaving Winsockette, Darcy seemed like her old self. Talking to Talia was as easy as talking to Cecelia. She felt like a teenager listening to another teenager talk about school, dreams, growing up in the wild plains. Darcy noticed Talia eyeing up her stack of old cookbooks Gemma insisted she take.

"You like to cook?" Darcy asked.

"Yeah, why? You caught me staring at those?" Talia asked as she nodded her head in the direction of the stack. She got up and started to thumb through the old books. "I collect them. Cookbooks that is. I like to stay up late and make odd things. I make a list for my Gram each week. She doesn't always get all of it cause some of the ingredients are too expensive. Mostly though, she can't find half the stuff cause we live in the middle of nowhere," Talia said with a laugh. Darcy smiled. She thought of Bakers. Talia told Darcy she loved to be all alone in a kitchen with a stack of random things to mix, chop, saute, or simmer down and make it look new. She told her of the rush she got after combining everything individually and making it into something completely different, unrecognizable. It wasn't so much about the food itself as it was a creative outlet, a way to offer up something to others, something they couldn't make for themselves.

"Food, you see," Talia said. "It's not just about filling your belly or staying alive. It's about feeding someone's soul, I think at least. It's about filling up the empty spaces everyone has inside." Darcy's eyes widened. She thought back to Gemma always mixing up something in her kitchen to make whatever was wrong alright again. She thought about Basil making his chicken potpie and always making Darcy sit while he brought her out a plate. There was a thoughtfulness to Talia that Darcy rarely noticed in other people her age, especially girls younger than her. "Everyone has empty spaces inside that someone or something needs to fill, ya know?" Talia said she put down one book and picked up the next in the stack.

After comparing stories of high school classes, mascots, traditions, and stories about the mean girls every school seemed to have, Darcy asked Talia why she lived with her grandparents. Talia's face fell and she stared ahead past Darcy. To Darcy, it seemed as if the air was let out of Talia's skinny, freckled body. She told Darcy she lost her mother three years earlier. Her mother, Sandy, died of a drug overdose. Talia always understood her mother was an addict. She had done a little of everything since before Talia was born. Talia spent most nights and weekends at her grandparents. Her mother partied every night. When Talia was in her care at night, she remembered seeing her mom stumble out the door with various friends, mostly men. She watched her mother light up crack in the living room once. Sandy and her friends yelled at Talia to get to bed and stay in her room. Talia ran, jumped in bed, pulled the covers over her head, and sang herself to sleep. She figures she was around eight at the time. Meth is what got its hooks into her. It was starting to be cooked and sold in the early 2000s. By 2005, when Talia was 15, it was everywhere. Talia had friends in high school whose parents made it at home, made it in RV's they drove on highway 80 cooking and selling from Nebraska to Iowa and up to Chicago. It was spreading like a brushfire burning everything and everyone in its path, including Talia's mom.

Darcy told Talia about Jackson. They both sat in silence for a few minutes. She told Talia how she always thought if her twin was in trouble, she'd sense it by instinct, she'd feel it in her gut. But she never realized it was that bad, at least not at the time he stole from them. Both girls nodded at the other as they shared how it hurt to be helpless when someone you love is going through what Sandy and Jackson did. Darcy let out a deep sigh. As much as they had in common and as cleansing as it was to bond with another young woman who loved an addict, a twinge of guilt raced through Darcy as Talia told her more about Sandy. Darcy realized she was so much luckier than Talia. She could pick up a phone and call Jackson. She knew she'd see Jackson again. Talia carried around an emptiness that couldn't be replaced or filled even with the most elaborate or decadent meal. Her mother was gone forever.

"You know what's bad, Darcy?" Talia said. "I knew from a young age, I mean young like 5 or 6, that she'd die from that stuff. I used to lay in bed and think 'what am I gonna do if she's dead in the morning when I wake up for school?' I'd plan out to call my Gram first then get dressed, call the school, tell them I'd be absent, and still have time to get breakfast before the house was crawling with cops, EMT's or whoever," Talia said. "When she did die, I was at Gram's and Pap's. She didn't die at home like I had always pictured. She was in a dirty hotel in Lincoln with two guys. It was heroin. A needle in her arm. I just always pictured it would happen at home and I'd be there." She sighed. "You want to know the worst part?"

Darcy swallowed. She wasn't sure a worse part was possible. She pictured finding Jackson that way. Instead, she found an empty cedar box. She'd take being robbed a thousand times if meant Jackson was still alive.

"I would always picture it, knowing how it would happen and I never cried. I just knew it was the way my mom would go. And I never told her, screamed at her to stop, or anything. It was a given just like some kids' moms go to work each morning. And well, I always pictured a peace in it. She'd be dead in our house and I'd get a few minutes in silence with her. No other druggies groaning or yelling at me. We'd be alone in peace and I could hold her hand without her pulling away. I was kinda looking forward to the morning we'd get to be in the quiet together. I pictured her clean and happy once she'd be dead. She was always angry, sad, even mean. Her face twisted as she yelled at me or threw food at me." Talia wiped away a tear. "How messed up is that? I hated that she died far away, and I couldn't have that alone time without her being high?"

"My God, Talia. That's awful. You were just a kid who needed a mom. I'm so sorry you went through that," Darcy said. She wiped away tears from both eyes. "Sorry. Pregnancy makes me cry easily."

"It's okay. And it wasn't all terrible you know? We had fun, some, I guess. Plus, I was lucky. I had my Gram and Pap. They gave me normalcy, well more normal I should say. They gave me love even if Pap is mean at times. He has a bad temper, which is why my mom ran away so young anyways. But at least he was always there and always clean. They were raising me all along before she even passed. In a strange way, it's been nice waking up and not worrying about her. Don't get me wrong. I miss my mom, mostly miss who she could've been. But, well, me, Gram, Pap, we sleep a little easier at night."

Darcy had the urge to call Jackson. She couldn't imagine ever sleeping easier if he was dead. She said a silent 'thank you' to God or whoever saved her brother, and she hoped she never got the kind of phone call Talia did. Darcy couldn't imagine a mom like Sandy either. She battled Gemma with all her might at times. She hated her beauty, her charm, and her overpowering energy. But Darcy loved Gemma with every ounce of her being. She needed her. She wouldn't be the mother she was without Gemma's guiding hand and advice. Darcy couldn't imagine a world without Gemma, without a mom at all. She wanted Gemma to walk in that door and hug her tight, hug Talia, too. Darcy wanted Talia to feel the love of a mom like Gemma. Everyone deserved that kind of love, even if Darcy had to admit she didn't always appreciate it. The family Darcy always wanted to escape was something she realized others dreamt about.

Darcy slid from the stool and walked to Talia. She hugged her tight hoping Talia might absorb some of the love she needed. Darcy never wanted Gemma more. She vowed to call her mom as soon as Talia left and possibly Jackson, too.

As the days melted in a routine and a countdown to Elara's arrival, Darcy spent more time with Talia either after school and most days after her graduation. Talia had a job in town but stopped by every day regardless. While Talia was a sweet kid, she didn't have many friends. She told Darcy she usually kept to herself because she didn't like asking her grandparents about having friends over. They were older, set in their ways. After years of chaos at home, noise all night from her mother's parties, strangers on the couch or surrounded by smoke in the kitchen, Talia liked being alone. She was independent out of necessity, a loner by choice. Talia told Darcy she wasn't sure what made her tell Darcy about Sandy the day she met her, but something in Talia told her it was time to share it with someone. While kids in school knew about Talia's mom and plenty of the kids had similar stories about family members, it wasn't shared out loud. Kids growing up with drug addicted parents or family members was a silent given. Just as tornado season came each year, so did the list of people who lost the battle of addiction in Nebraska, all over the Midwest.

Unlike most of the other kids her age though, Talia had no plans to just live and grow old in Franklin and watch the list of victims grow. Talia dreamt of starting culinary classes at the community college in Lincoln in the fall. The one obstacle was that her grandparents resisted any pleas to help her. While they loved and encouraged her kitchen experiments, they saw no reason to leave Franklin, to leave them like Talia's mom did. Despite their objections and longing for no waves to be made or plans of leaving to be discussed further, Talia did the work of getting the ball rolling on her way out. She intended to apply and go to school without much thought into the actual logistics. She had hidden the application for months. On a sunny day after she worked all morning at the only restaurant in town, Talia brought the application to Darcy. As she entered, a hot breeze blew in behind her waif frame. She laid the papers on the kitchen island that faced the window overlooking acres of grass, which eventually meshed into corn.

"I don't know how I'm gonna even afford this. Look at the fees and stuff? I can't save a penny here with my car payment and the cost of living on or near campus. Dammit."

"Don't be so discouraged. You can work in Lincoln, probably make more than any job right here. Plus, there's always financial aid. I had a full-ride scholarship before I found out I was having Cassie."

"Yeah. I called the financial aid office. They can help. But Gram and Pap won't. They don't think I should go off anywhere, ever. Say I'll end up like Mom if I do. Honestly, I'm more afraid I'd end up like my mom if I don't. I just want something away from Franklin. Don't' get me wrong. It's a great little town and I know the drug problems are here and everywhere else in between," Talia said. "But, staying here would drive me mad. I always pictured me and mom, after she'd get clean of course, riding a car out of town, never looking back till we got to the Grand Canyon or something. Even without her now, I still need to take that ride." Darcy understood perfectly wanting to flee small town life.

"Here's a pen. Fill out what you're missing. Want some iced tea?" Darcy reached for the fridge. She held her belly as she stood on tiptoes to reach it on the top shelf. She poured a glass and slid it over to Talia. Talia brushed her hair behind her ear. Then, hurriedly pulled it back to hang over the side of her face.

Darcy saw what looked like a bruise on Talia's cheek. Darcy reached for Talia's hair. Talia pulled back.

"What's that? A bruise?" Darcy asked.

"It's nothing. I hit my cheek on the cabinet door. Not the first time. I'm just a clutz at heart," Talia said with a laugh. Darcy went to the other stool and kept trying to catch glances at the bruise. It wasn't the first one she noticed on Talia. As they dug up dirt alongside the patio to make room for a few tomato plants the other day, Darcy thought she saw the greenish remnants of bruises on Talia's upper arm. She didn't ask but had made a point of looking whenever Talia was around.

"So, your grandfather is gonna be pissed when he finds out you've been accepted, huh?" Darcy said. She chopped up celery for the kids to slather with peanut butter and kept glancing up at Talia for a reaction. "You tell him you plan to go yet?"

Talia fiddled with the pen. "They know I want to. I brough it up again the other night. But gramps has a temper, you know. He doesn't want to hear it," Talia said without meeting Darcy's eyes.

"But he's going to find out when you get accepted. He's going to realize you're leaving when you pack, when you make a payment or accept the grants and stuff. They'll be okay with it then, right?" Darcy didn't want to believe Talia's grandfather was physical with Talia, but it was getting harder for her to come to any other conclusion as greenish bruises turned yellow then new ones appeared. They were hard to ignore as the days got hotter and Talia wore t-shirts and shorts.

"I guess. I mean, he does have a temper. But hopefully he simmers down once he realizes this is my dream and I'm going one way or another," Talia said. "But for now, if you don't mind, I mean, it's easier if I just fill this out over here, somewhere he isn't." Darcy tilted her head. "He'll be over it by the time I get a semester break and he sees I didn't run off to turn into an addict like my mom," Talia said with a confidence that Darcy sensed was just for show.

"Well, okay then. Let's get this ready to mail." Darcy said. She peered over Talia's long freckled arm. "So, I know you love to cook, but when did it start? Were you always the kid who loved to cook?"

"Well, not really," Talia shrugged her shoulders and let out a long exhale. "One morning, when I was, I don't know, like 10 or so, I woke to the sweetest smell. I followed it to the kitchen. Our kitchen never smelled sweet at that time. Plus, there was always like three or four other people crashed at our place eating anything I wanted for myself." Talia said. "So, I walked in and saw my mom in jeans and a t-shirt, no PJs like a normal day, or not a trashy dress from the night before. She was standing at the stove. She saw me and yelled, 'get over here, Tally. We're having French toast and cinnamon buns.'" Talia twirled the pen between her skinny fingers. "She was making breakfast. And, Darcy, it was the best breakfast I ever had. It was the only time I remember her making me breakfast. She was happy, smiling, singing. She let me pour a ton of powdered sugar on mine. She made rivers of syrup on our plates. It was too sweet, sticky, and the most delicious thing I ever had. I remembered looking around at the kitchen. It was a mess, spices everywhere, dishes, powered sugar, flour, all of it just a mess. And I remember thinking she made this huge mess to make me happy, happier than I've ever been. I want to do that."

Darcy inhaled deeply and her heart ached. "So, that's why."

"Yep. I want to give other people the chance to feel that." Talia put down the pen. "Is that dumb? Pap says it's dumb and she was probably high. He said I could learn all I need to know about cooking by helping Gram, reading my cookbooks and can just stay home and make whatever I want." Her smile faded. She looked down again.

"I say do it. Go to this school. Get in a kitchen there and smell that breakfast. Be that happy again," Darcy said. "Make others that happy." Talia smiled up at her. Darcy noticed she was on the verge of tears.

Talia picked up the pen and started to write. As she checked box after box, Darcy slid down and checked on Orion napping. He stirred on the couch and moaned his warning that he was waking. A spit bubble appeared in the corner of his lip as a slight, accidental smile slid across his baby face. Darcy's heart swelled. She thought it might burst. Darcy wanted to wrap that baby up in her arms and smell his head again like she did when he was newborn. She rubbed her belly and exhaled thinking how she'd have another newborn in a matter of days, or sooner.

Darcy was startled from her baby-worship trance when Talia dropped her pen.

"Shit, I didn't wake him, did I?" Talia said as Darcy turned around. Before she could answer, a stabbing pain radiated from her groin up through her giant belly and then across her back. She doubled over, holding her belly as if it would fall off. "Oh my God, Darcy!" Talia yelled as she hopped off the stool. Orion let out a yell. "Are you in labor?"

Darcy nodded. She straightened her back and glanced around. "Um. I might be. That was definitely a contraction. I need to sit a minute, time the next one." Darcy's eyes hunted for the clock on the stove. She slid her feet closer to the stove. Orion scrambled to be at her feet. Talia took her arm.

"Want me to get the kids in the truck? Where's Basil? Want me to call him to meet us at the hospital? Maybe get my Pap? Gram? Tell me what to do, Darcy," Talia said in one breath. Darcy held her arm tight.

"Just let me get to a seat. I'll be okay. I've kinda done this before," She said with a smile. "I think I'll call Basil though. Can you hand me my phone?" Talia released her arm and rooted for the phone underneath the pile of papers for her school and junk mail still in the name of the grandmother who owned the house. Darcy lowered herself into a seat at the tiny dining set. Orion slid his sticky fingers along her bare leg. Darcy patted the top of his head. He was sweaty. The breeze drifting in from the plains was hot, dry, and didn't yield any relief from scorching early June temperatures. Darcy had never experienced heat like that before July in Winsockette. Even then, it only lasted a few days. Cassie went to Talia and asked for more tea. Talia shot Darcy a look asking permission to get the tea first. Darcy nodded.

"It's gonna be okay, Talia. I swear. It could still be a day or two, or more. It might not be labor yet. I've just gotta wait and see if another comes." As the words left her mouth, the fire of another contraction started along her sides and spread to her belly button. She instinctively held her breath, even though she knew not to. She swallowed as Talia handed her the phone. Darcy looked at the ceiling then at the phone. She dialed Basil's cell. Darcy tried to calm her breathing as the phone rang.

She immediately told Basil it was fine. She had plenty of time to get to the hospital. He needed one of the guys to drive him there to meet her. She and Talia would get the kids. He told her he'd call Uncle Quincy to come get the kids just as they planned. She smiled as his steady words soothed her nerves. All she needed to do was get into the passenger side of the truck and trust her fresh out of high school new neighbor/best friend to get the kids strapped and get her to the hospital in Franklin. The dated paperwork for insurance through the state was already in the hands of the social worker in Franklin, so she could relax about the bills and medical care. Her new doctor was a calming presence even though she had only met him twice. Basil would be there. Everything was textbook, just a different textbook than before.

# CHAPTER 16

Talia ran into the bedroom to get the hospital bag. She also grabbed the diaper bag and gave Orion a fresh diaper in a flash.

"Talia. It's okay. You don't have to panic," Darcy said. She stood and scooted to the closet to find her slide-on clogs. Cassie danced around her, babbling that she was ready to meet her sister. She was singing a song she created for Elara. Talia shot her a smile as she pulled up Orion's shorts and pulled down his stained and sweaty shirt.

"I know. I guess I'm a little panicked anyways. I'm gonna call Gram and Pap and tell them I'm driving you." Talia stood from the floor and whipped out her flip phone from a back pocket. Darcy saw the shiny red phone and realized the world was changing. If a teen in the middle of Franklin, Nebraska had a cell phone, everyone must have one by now.

Talia loaded the kids and drove them cautiously. Her only visible moment of excitement behind the wheel was when they passed her grandparents' house. Talia beeped and waved wildly. Darcy wondered if Talia had ever seen anyone give birth. She was quickly saddened thinking that Talia had experienced death in a way Darcy couldn't imagine. She instantly thought of Gemma. Darcy fumbled for her cell phone and called her mom. As she rattled off the details about her contractions, which were exactly like the last time she was in labor, she paused to let Gemma's hushed calmness fill her ears. Gemma stayed on the phone as a virtual labor coach until Darcy was in wheeled into a room. Once a hospital band was attached and a gown unfurled on the bed, she let Gemma go. Darcy promised to call her again as soon as Basil got there, even though she knew Gemma was surely calling Basil next to be assured he was close.

As she hung up the phone, Darcy thought about the money from her mother, her parting assurance that Darcy would be fine no matter what unfolded during their journey from Winsockette. The money was still in a bag she unpacked and stored in the back of their bedroom closet. She had thought a million times about telling Basil where it was or of depositing in the bank and explaining later. But something always stopped her. Something made her check on it every few days and just stare at it. Darcy wondered if it was time to tell Basil for the simple reason that if something went wrong in labor, Basil should realize they have spare cash. If she didn't wake up from unexpected anesthesia or if a tragic blood clot or mishap took her life, Basil should know. As he rushed into the room covered in dirt from carrying packs of shingles from a truck to the ladder to be hoisted up a roof, she suppressed the urge. Nothing would happen. It was all textbook. A purpose, a clear reason to take the money out of the bag would appear before her any day now, she thought. Even though it might've been handy for setting up house, buying extra for the kids, or something nice for themselves, they had gotten by with what they saved on their own and what Basil was making each day working with the building company. Plus, Jackson had mailed them a few hundred. He was staying true to his word to pay them back. Basil leaned down to kiss her forehead and assured her she'd be fine. They'd be fine. The money would come up another day.

Talia kept the kids entertained in the waiting room. Quincy was on the way. Talia's grandmother was on the way with food and snacks for everyone. Gemma's voice was once again floating through the phone, along with the occasional well-wishes from Harlan. As the beeping of the fetal monitor picked up and the contractions came closer and fiercer, Darcy leaned back and watched the nurses flutter in and out. They were like hummingbirds buzzing and hovering close to her face, then darting back once they had their fill of information. She let them zoom and buzz, drinking the nectar of excitement she provided. They were all three happy women, beaming as if they were about to birth a child themselves. Darcy realized in a small town like Franklin, they didn't see births every single day. This was the type of shift they longed for, went to school to experience, and couldn't wait to go home to tell their husbands or boyfriends about. The chance to help her unleash this new life into the world is what they showed up to work hoping to experience each day.

Gemma was on speaker, never wavering for a minute. She managed to become a superstar to the nurses as she asked them endless questions about their lives. Unbeknownst to them, Gemma sprinkled these morsels of praise, amazement, and flattery of others just so she could interject with stories of herself and her life. As the contractions morphed into a painfully predictable wave of her body's efforts to expel the little girl she couldn't wait to see, Gemma stole the show. The nurses adoring gestures and smiles became glances of assurance as they strained to hear more about Gemma. Their wide eyes looked at the cellphone more than at Darcy. Basil shot her a knowing look, just as he had a million times before when attention was diverted from Darcy to Gemma. As much as Darcy loved her mother and wanted and needed her voice in that room a thousand miles away, just once she wanted it to be about Darcy and only Darcy. She was amazed at how she simultaneously missed her mother terribly and resented her very voice and constant need to be the center of attention. Then again, she thought, Gemma was fascinating whether it was in person in Winsockette, in any beauty contest in South Carolina and Maine, or as a disembodied voice filling a delivery room in Franklin, Nebraska.

Darcy noticed the daylight started to fade. Two of the nurses said their goodbyes as there was a shift change. They promised to stop in and gush over Elara in the morning when their next shift was scheduled to begin. They also made sure to take advice from Gemma, promised to look after her daughter, and visit her in Maine someday.

The night came right as the contractions became unbearable, each one indistinguishable from the next. The wavelength grew shorter and the peaks grew to be nauseating. Darcy started to sense this labor wasn't textbook. Basil kept reassuring her it was exactly like labor with Orion two years ago. He told her she had just forgotten. She had let the reality of the pain fade. She didn't have an epidural or anything extreme, just an IV drip of pain killers to "take the edge off", as they said in all three cases. No edge was taken off. There was no rounded sensation to any of the contractions. The burning and paralyzing force that gripped her uterus, back, and legs was becoming a state she never thought she'd escape. Panic bubbled up at the thought that something was wrong. It should be over by now. She should be able to push. She was fully dilated, effaced. Elara had a clear path out, nothing stopping her from entering the world and being seen for the first time, held, and loved.

Just as she believed Gemma's voice might be the last thing she'd hear and Basil's hand all she could feel as she faded from this world, broken and torn in two by a labor she wasn't built for, the doctor told her to push. The nurses rose the bed, chirped and echoed the doctor's orders. Gemma squealed through the phone as Basil squeezed her hand and kissed the side of her face with brute force. It was time to push and unleash the pain that had been ripping her body and mind apart. It was time to fall in line with what every voice around her shouted and encouraged. It was time to actively claim her swollen and exhausted body back. Darcy inhaled the most important breath she'd ever take. She scooted herself back a bit and bared down. She was willing to die and push out her own heart to make the pain stop. Darcy got light-headed and knew sweat was running from every pore. She was in the midst of what every mother before her had done naturally. She turned her head and saw the night sky over the plains out the window. Darcy was too exhausted to lament the view. It was exhausting peering through the reflection of the organized beautiful chaos that centered around Elara's birth. She had to be content believing in her heart all the night stars ever discovered were up there somewhere twinkling and exploding for her.

It was a few minutes after 10 p.m. when the last push yielded what they had been waiting for. A groan and muffled yell from Darcy was eclipsed by a piercing and familiar cry. The newborn cry that she had waited for months to hear. As Darcy fell back into the pillows that had propped her up for what seemed an eternity, she saw the doctor lift the fleshy and squirmy child they created. Basil gleefully reached to cut the cord as a crying nurse steadied it. The other nurse wiped Elara's eyes.

Her next cry echoed as her tiny arms and legs jerked. Before Darcy could catch her breath or center her tired mind, the doctor placed a freshly wrapped baby in her arms. Despite her exhaustion, her arms folded around Elara and drew her in close. Darcy shared her warmth. Basil leaned down and cooed at the baby like it was the first he'd ever seen. Darcy cried. She heard Gemma crying on speakerphone, then Gemma, Harlan, and Jackson burst into cheers and applause. Darcy was always amazed at the unique mix of emotions and bodily sensations that overcame her during and after giving birth. She figured it must be the same for every woman, or perhaps, she thought, each woman had her own way of handling the most naturally chaotic, frightening, and inexplicably beautiful trauma a body can undergo.

She looked into Elara's eyes and saw an entire universe. She saw her future, the past of a thousand generations of women, and the newness that is only found in those eyes for a moment. Darcy let her body go limp as she absorbed every inch of the baby, her scent, her essence. There were no words. There never was. She let Basil hold her while she held their baby just as she had done twice before. There was no safer place to be. While their lives never seemed perfect or settled or the time never seemed right, there was magic each time they had a baby. The world seemed to stop spinning. Their young age didn't matter. The size and state of their tiny trailer on the hill didn't matter. The doubt and worry of their families didn't matter. The journey more than a thousand miles away and the uncertainty of making a life away from Winsockette didn't matter. All that mattered was Basil with his arms wrapped around Darcy with her arms wrapped around their newest baby and knowing the others were safe. The paper mill closing, storms brewing, and conflicting feelings of purpose, guilt, and God's will as they profited from the wrath of those storms were outshined by Elara's eyes and suckling. As Elara wrapped her fingers around Darcy's and Darcy squeezed Basil's hand, a cocoon of love and hope surround her. Nothing could come between the little family they created.

The last few months of Darcy's life swirled around her head as the chaos of her body and the room settled. The uprooting of all they knew, the shock of Jackson stealing from her, the loss of the mill and the quiet that followed, Basil's obsession over the storm that led them to pack up and leave. In a blink they were in a hospital in Franklin, holding what Darcy was sure would be their last child. They were content, sheltered from any storm, if only temporarily. Everything seemed to align. The stars were fixed in the sky above them, and for now, that was enough.

# CHAPTER 17

Despite being away from everyone and everything they had ever known, Darcy found it easier than expected to adjust to the new baby. She started to feel settled, started to enjoy the quiet of the plains. She even found herself trying to remember what the mill sounded like her entire life. Now, it seemed silly to Darcy that she mourned the idea of Elara never hearing it for herself. It was just a noise. The absence of noise, except for the rustling the expansive acres of corn and grasses, was her new normal. Feeding Elara while reaching for a sippy cup for Orion and a snack for Cassie was also her new normal. Basil adjusted, too. He stayed home with them for about a week before Darcy insisted he go back to work. However, he did decline overtime and weekend work so he could give Darcy a much-needed break. Gemma's voice daily also gave Darcy a sense of connection to family when the plains felt too quiet. Even though Talia still had a job waitressing at a breakfast counter in Franklin, she also checked in with Darcy each day. Sometimes it was a few minutes on the phone to see if Darcy needed any supplies or groceries from town, other times it was an afternoon visit. Darcy grew to rely on her visits, Gemma's call, and Basil's incredible dad instincts.

During rare moments those first two weeks where all three kids were napping or occupied, Darcy would step onto the cement patio where they had placed two chairs and a small table. She'd look up to a bright blue sky with intermittent clouds drifting across. Darcy would watch as the wind whipped them faster into sight. Those clouds would fill up the empty spaces and enclose her view. She'd think back to the enclosure of the pines of Maine where she once felt protected, if not trapped. The exposure of the southern plains of Nebraska went from being too open, too bleak, to feeling powerful. It reminded her of trips to the ocean. The openness, vastness was unsettling, foreign at first. Then, she'd stand in the sand on the water's edge, letting it engulf her and lap against her calves, then thighs as she'd wade in further. Standing up tall and straight regardless of how the waves intensified was just as brave and courageous and standing in the gusty winds without wavering.

She was defiant and resilient compared to who she was years ago. Darcy remembered the feeling of meekness trying to stand out in Gemma's world. She would hunch her bulky shoulders and look down when she walked. She remembered the sense of reliance she had on Jackson to protect her when they were kids. He was her other half, her stronger half. Then she remembered the periods of self-doubt when she started to fall for Basil as she wondered how or why he was falling for her. She was no Gemma. Darcy smiled as the sun warmed her face and sweat started to trickle down her nose. She not only grew to love herself and believe in herself the last few years of marriage to Basil. She finally made it beyond those treetops lining the sky of Winsockette. She had left there and was happily making a home a world away from all the protections, barriers, and trees that held her back her whole life, making a home a world away from who she was back then and doing it as her own woman, and not just her mother's daughter.

Basil spent his days eating lunch on a partially finished roof or next to a stack of siding waiting to be attached to the chapel in Franklin and then the barn out of town that belonged to the largest cattle farm in the county. The storm that first captivated Basil on the news had wiped out the house, the barn, and every outbuilding on the farm except for the farmer's wife's potting shed, where they ended up hiding and surviving. Darcy could see how the reality of the storm damage was settling on his face each day when he came home. He'd shower to get the dirt and grime off, the smell of hot shingles. Then, he'd hold Elara while Darcy would get dinner ready. Darcy loved watching him play with Elara's wisps of black hair, black as hers and Orion's. The labor of rebuilding important parts of their new hometown aged him beyond 23. But it didn't age him in a distressing way to Darcy. She saw it as a maturing. He didn't just walk in the door exhausted or frustrated like he did from the mill, ready to crack open beer after beer. He came home with a sense of purpose in his eyes. A purpose he had never known before then. Even though he'd still have a beer, he'd have much fewer if any. Basil was doing exactly what his vision was the night the great Franklin tornado came on the news. He was taking God's wrath, picking through the devastation, and molding a new way with his hands, a far cry from his father's existence and the existence he'd be living if Basil had followed in his footsteps. He was rebuilding, rejuvenating a town that others may have given up on.

A few residents moved away when the wind stopped, and the damage was quiet and spread thin over an entire county. Some always do after a massive tornado. Others stay, rebuild, and keep a string of hope in their back pocket, hope that the previous storm is the worst ever. Basil didn't have the burden of hope. He hadn't lost anything in the storm like the others did. He gained from it. His family was eating, sleeping under a roof, and secure because of it. He walked in each night with deeper lines but also a sense of pride he never had when he rolled reams of paper or monitored vats of pulp.

Darcy found it easy to remove herself from the reality Basil saw each day. She didn't have to see any of the devastation if she didn't want to. She had picnic lunches of peanut butter and jelly in the green grass with her kids, not lunch on a half-built roof. She got to spend her days watching Cassie run like a wild colt through the tall grass as Orion struggled to keep up with her. She got to listen to the coos of Elara as Cassie colored and Orion dragged his favorite blanket to the patio. Darcy got days and nights of the best Franklin had to offer, while Basil got to see the worst it could unleash. Despite being in the thick of the devastation, he never seemed to think a storm would impact his family. Peak tornado season was over as June was ending. The heat was the only real danger, not the harmless yet powerful storms that rolled through every few nights.

That sense of purpose, security, and resolve that helped them both adjust and feel settled in Franklin would change in a blink when a band of storms starting in Oklahoma was on track to move northward and had already engulfed everything in its path. It was a Tuesday night. Elara was a day away from turning two weeks old. Basil came home late, tired, sunburned, and unfazed by the news reports. After his shower, he leaned down to kiss a sleeping Elara who had sweat beads on her tiny nose. Basil picked up Orion and tickled his belly. He had a mix of dirt and snot bubbling from his nose.

"It must be allergies. His nose hasn't stopped running since we moved here. When I take Elara for her shots Friday, I'll talk to the doctor about him. I think the dust in the air is what's making his voice scratchy, too." Darcy said while she chopped vegetables Basil bought at a small farmer's market on the way home from work. With only one vehicle still, Darcy was stuck at home all day unless she drove Basil to his work site early in the morning. He usually could bum a ride home with one of the other guys if he needed. But most days he took their truck and brought home whatever Darcy needed. Darcy didn't mind being stuck at home most weekdays anyways. It gave her a chance to snuggle with the kids and take care of the wildflowers that sprouted up around the house.

"Yeah, his voice makes him sound like a 60-year-old who's smoked for decades," Basil said with a laugh. Darcy laughed and Cassie joined in even though she had no idea what was so funny. Cassie slid up on the stool to pick at peppers Darcy had cut.

"So, that line of storms is supposed to come through this area tomorrow morning. Should we be worried?" Darcy said. Basil came into the kitchen.

"Nah, the guys at work were saying these things seem to break up, scatter, as they get closer. Chances are we'll just get hellish thunderstorms and wind. Just stay here at home and pay attention if you guys are outside." He leaned down and kissed Darcy's head. She loved the sensation of him being so close. It caught her off guard that she still noticed butterflies in her stomach from his touch.

"Well, what do I even do if something turns really bad? I know the basement is supposed to be a shelter, but, Jesus, it's small and dirty, and scary enough with spiders all over."

"That's still the best option. Toss the shit in there off to the side, get down under the steps, and cover the kids." Basil let Orion slither from his arms. "Cassie, baby, listen. If a storm comes when I'm at work and

Mommy says get in the basement, you get right down there. You hear me?" He raised his eyebrows, his signal for Cassie to take him seriously. She nodded as she grabbed another handful of peppers.

"Hey, little girl. Those are for the salad." Darcy said. It was too hot to cook. The air was heavy and made the world seem slow and thick.

After dinner and cleaning up, Darcy and Basil bathed the kids together, a virtual assembly line of tub dunks, shampoo bubble crowns, soapy bottoms, and rinsing with the sprayer. Then towels were lined up on the hall floor as each child was wrapped, dried, and released to run naked, except Elara. But Darcy knew after the first two kids that this time of immobility and easy control would fade quickly. In a blink Elara would be running behind the other two, leaving wet footprints from one end of the house to the other. As Darcy sat on the floor laughing and wiping up the trail, with Basil right behind her swaddling Elara, she realized she was picturing her tiny family in that house years from now. It was becoming home, not a reprieve from the downfall of Winsockette.

Basil rocked the baby in his arms down the stairs and through the hall to the living room and kitchen. Darcy watched him hold her close and whisper in her tiny face. She watched his gentleness shine through. He was madly in love with her. He turned and saw Darcy watching them.

"She reminds me so much of you. It's her eyes. Don't get me wrong, Orion is your little clone too. But this girl," He leaned down again and kissed Elara's head. "This girl has your eyes. She's gonna be something special." He smiled down at Elara. Darcy thought how she had never loved him more than when he was holding their kids. Saying 'yes' to dancing with him was the best decision she ever made.

"Yeah, she's special alright. I have a feeling she's gonna be spoiled just like the others." She said.

They shot a knowing smile at each other. Even though she knew they shouldn't make love for another few weeks, Darcy was filled with a desire to be close to him, to feel him all over her. After they put the older kids to bed and changed Elara, Basil placed her in the bassinette next to the couch, where she slept until they wandered to bed later. Basil stood up and reached his hand down to Darcy. She knew he wanted to dance. He drew her close and put his hand on her back and the other on the back of her head. He leaned down and kissed her forehead. Darcy's insides melted. She exhaled air she was sure had been pent up in her lungs since they left Maine. Basil swayed his hips and moved hers with him. He hummed as he pranced her around the tiny living room. It was dark, quiet, and it seemed as if her feet were no longer on the floor. Basil hadn't danced with her at night in months, not since they found out the mill was closing. She snuggled her face into his t-shirt. She loved his smell, his essence after a shower and after helping her bath the kids. It was home even when Darcy wasn't quite sure what home meant anymore. She glanced up at him. He was looking up at the ceiling. She remembered their first dance as teenagers and how he held her the same way even though there was much unsaid and unknown between them. That was the night he looked down and told her there was no place for dreamers and stargazers in Winsockette. He was jaded before sixteen. But as they danced in Nebraska, Darcy was beginning to realize Basil was just as much a dreamer as she was. And the stars at night in Franklin could make anyone a stargazer.

# CHAPTER 18

As dawn peeked through the blinds of their bedroom window, Darcy heard Elara shuffle her arms and legs. She heard Basil in the kitchen making his lunch. Darcy stretched and noticed she was already sweating and sticking to the sheets. Her pale body was still plumper and doughier than she'd like. *Time, Darcy, give it time and you'll get in decent shape,* she told herself. Darcy peeled herself from the bed and scooped up Elara to change and feed her before her stretches turned to yells that would wake up Orion and Cassie. Even though Cassie was a big help getting diapers and wipes, Darcy needed a few quiet minutes with the baby before the other kids joined her for the rest of the day. At times, she felt guilty letting the others sleep longer, but those quiet morning moments gave her time to plan her day without pulling Orion from stools and counters and keeping Cassie from escaping into the yard without her knowing. It gave her extra seconds to get to know Elara.

Darcy made her way down the stairs with her new daughter in her arms. Basil met her at the bottom and kissed her goodbye. He grabbed the keys and turned back to Darcy before he left.

"Hey, we gotta find a good tattoo place here. You need one for Elara now." He winked at her as he drew the door closed behind him. Darcy smiled at the closed door and already missed him.

As Darcy finished her new morning routine of dressing, feeding, and wrangling her fully awake little brood, while trying to get dressed and run a brush through her hair, she realized she hadn't listened to the weather. The lingering band of storms making their way from the southern plains was due to cross over Nebraska in the afternoon. She grabbed the remote, flipped through the channels and hoped for the best. Maybe the line of storms broke up, weakened, changed course altogether. No such luck. The weather woman sounded more concerned than Darcy heard the previous day. She had a lump in her throat as she struggled to make Orion stand so she could button his pants.

"If you hear those sirens, folks, get to cover and protect yourself. This is a big one. We'll be tracking it all day so stay tuned for alerts and instructions. Make sure your supplies are stocked." The petite woman with glasses and a loud print dress said. Cassie begged for cartoons as she fought the armholes of her sundress.

"Alright, honey. I'll put them on for a little bit while I get laundry going. But if a storm does come, I need to turn it back so we can do what the lady says, okay?" Darcy said. Cassie nodded and swooshed her hair out of her face. Darcy grabbed a brush and started to tackle the rat's nest in her daughter's hair. A knock broke her concentration and Cassie broke loose.

"Come in, Talia," Darcy called out. No one else had come to their door unannounced. Talia walked in. She strolled to the kitchen to get coffee and slid onto the stool. The two women chatted and laughed as Darcy cleaned up after the kids and fed Elara. Talia took the baby and rocked her in her arms afterward.

"You'll make a great mom someday," Darcy said.

"I don't know about that. There's a lot more to it than being able to rock them to sleep." Talia flashed a crooked smile. "I just want to get to school and figure out family stuff way in the future."

"You'll get there, Talia, to school, I mean," Darcy said.

"Not if my grandfather has anything to say about it," Talia said.

"He can't control you forever," Darcy said. "Come on, let's sit outside." They both put shoes on the kids. Darcy placed Elara in her pack and play next to the back door. The two women sat at the patio table and watched the kids roll, run, stumble, squeal, and play with trucks in the grass. The air felt electric to Darcy. "I'm kinda worried about these storms."

"Yeah, but you get used to it. They can be fierce, but we're past peak season. Plus, Franklin already got hit hard this year, so we should be good," Talia said looking up at the sky. She scratched a bite on her freckled ankle peeking out from her sneakers. Darcy noticed the clouds rolling in. They darkened before her eyes.

"Is that how it works," Darcy said as her eyes followed the procession of clouds building from the horizon. "You get hit once, then your town is all clear for the rest of tornado season?"

"Well, no not technically," Talia said. "I'm just trying to be optimistic. In all seriousness, there's nothing scarier than that roar when one is coming." Darcy tried to suppress fear bubbling in her gut. "Oh hey," Talia said. "I almost forgot. I put a few pots of herbs on the front porch before I came in. I wanted to give them to you. Wanna put them in the ground there where we dug up for the tomato plants or in the pots the old lady left in the garage? They'll really add to your dinners. Trust me." Darcy noticed Talia lit up when she was talking about food. While she still talked to Cecelia every day and no one else understood her better, there was a comfort and familiarity when she was with Talia listening and sharing stories. Darcy was beginning to realize that she didn't need to know someone for years to feel so close to them. She'd miss these talks and hours spent with Talia if she left for school at the end of the summer.

"Let's put them in the pots. That'll be easier." Darcy stood.

"I'll go grab the plants and you get the pots. We'll use the dirt from over there," Talia said as she pointed to what Darcy hoped would be flourishing garden.

As the women got the plants and pots spread out on the patio, they sat across from each other and got to work arranging sage, rosemary, parsley, and some mint in the terra cotta pots of all sizes. Elara slept with a light blanket draped over the pack and play as Orion and Cassie played in the grass that needed mowed. Darcy kept an eye on the sky. Talia brushed dirt from her hands and pulled a hair tie out from her pocket. Sweat beaded up on her freckled nose. She stood and flipped her hair over to tie in a pony tail. Darcy saw another bruise. This one was definitely new. It covered the part of her shoulder that peaked out from her tank top.

"Holy shit, Talia. How did that happen?" Darcy said. Talia looked around as if an answer would come running to the patio. Darcy could tell Talia couldn't catch her breath for a minute. "And don't lie to me again. I don't want to hear any bullshit about a cabinet or anything else. We're friends. Be straight with me," Darcy said. She put down the garden shovel she was holding and slapped her hands to shake off the excess dirt. Talia looked at the row of pots and slid a small one over. She started to make a mound over a few sprigs of mint that laid over the edge. "I mean it, Talia. I swear to God I'll walk over there myself and punch that rat bastard grandfather in the face myself." Darcy's temples throbbed. Her hands started to shake. She glanced over at Orion and Cassie to be sure they didn't hear.

"Honestly. It looks worse than it is," Talia said as she fiddled with the mint more. Darcy could tell she was fighting tears. Darcy reached over and put her hand on Talia's. Talia drew in a slow breath. "He found the acceptance letter. It came when I was at work. I told the school to email it, but they sent it both ways. He just…he just wants to protect me, stop me from ending up like my mom."

"No Talia, that's not protecting you. That's controlling you. He hits you and you end up feeling sorry for him. Feeling bad about his pain. I've seen that before. Basil's dad was the same way. Even after we married and he'd show up drunk fighting and yelling in our driveway. It was always Basil feeling bad for him in the end and believing he should do whatever he could to make his dad okay. It wasn't his job to make his dad okay any more than it's your job to make sure your grandfather is okay. He feels like shit that he lost his only daughter. He takes that out on you. He wasn't able to control her so he's trying to control you. You even told me once he broke your mom's arm," Darcy said.

"I know. But you know what, Darcy, he's right. I can learn everything I need on my own here. They do need me. They're older. And truth be told, even with the financial aid, what I've saved, and the grants they can give me, I'm still short a few grand. I can't pay for the room and board deposit they need in the next few weeks. So, I'm gonna just stick around here and try again next year, save more money," Talia said. She used the clean side of the top of her hand to wipe away a few tears. Darcy had a pit in her stomach thinking how Talia's grandfather would never let Talia go, never stop making her feel like it's her fault he gets angry. She closed her eyes and pictured the night Basil turned 17 and showed up at their doorstep. The blood from the knife wound didn't hold a candle to hurt in his eyes. Even after all of that, Basil still thought for years that his father would change, that he'd be a better man, and a better dad. He never did, and Darcy knew he never would. She was confident Ron Pinkerton wouldn't change either. He wouldn't help Talia leave next month, next year, or any year after that.

Darcy looked out at her kids playing in the grass, oblivious to their family legacy, their father's scars. They got away. Darcy knew Talia had to get away, too. She glanced up at the thickening clouds and realized the sky looked much worse than she had ever seen it before in her life. She had a sense of dread as she watched the kids and the clouds at the same time. Darcy's head pounded. Her mind was scattered. She wasn't sure if it was anger towards Ron or sympathy for Talia. She was off-kilter, dizzy.

"Don't you worry about me though. You've got enough on your plate. I'm gonna be okay," Talia said. She looked up at Darcy. "You alright? You don't look so good," Darcy nodded and moved the pots to the side of the patio. The dizziness increased. She lowered herself to the chair.

"Yeah, I think I'm just feeling anxious, dizzy. A headache maybe. Plus, I got a little anemic after each kid, so it might be that."

"I bet it's the barometric pressure," Talia said. "It gets bad before the storms. It'll be alright after it rolls through. The heat, now that's the real enemy out here this time of year."

Right as Darcy rubbed her temples and let Talia's words pierce through the panic that felt like electrical pulses in her brain, the yell of a siren rose from the depths of the fields. It started to build, slowly, then to a full scream. Darcy's body and heart froze. She wondered for a second if it was real or if it was a sound her mind conjured up out of fear. The kids jumped and scrambled to Darcy. Orion tried to crawl up into her lap. Talia stood straight and determined. She stiffened her back and faced the open sky of black, purple, and gray. To Darcy at that moment, she looked like a superhero ready to fend off the storm with her bare hands. Talia looked like the strongest warrior Darcy had ever seen. As the siren rose from unseen depths of the open field that led to town, so did the wind. It raced through the fields and straight to Darcy's face at the speed of light. The angry purple clouds propelled the winds faster. Darcy thought it would surely lift her and the children off their feet at any second.

"Come on. That means it's time to get inside," Talia said with a steady confidence that startled Darcy. She still couldn't stand. Her short, pudgy pasty legs were seemingly filled with cement. The fierceness of the wind only made standing seem more impossible.

"Darcy!" Talia yelled. Darcy shook her head and scooped up Elara from the pack and play as she tried to stand. The wind prevented her from taking a breath. It was as if the very wind in her lungs was being sucked out and swirling above her head. Her knees shook and knocked back and forth. Her head pounded harder as sweat began to pour from her body. The clouds rolled faster. The table slid on its own as Darcy stepped away toward the back door. Cassie clung to her as Orion hung on her other leg. The siren screeched louder. It seemed the faster the clouds rolled and rumbled in anger, the louder the siren became.

Talia grabbed the door and held it as she shoved Darcy and the kids inside. Once she slammed it shut, Talia dashed to the basement door. Darcy knew she and children needed to follow every move of her teenage neighbor.

"We gotta get down here," She said as she ran down the basement steps to shove boxes and old tools over to make room underneath the stairs. Darcy and kids followed. Talia turned around at the bottom of the stairs and grabbed Cassie's arm. "Cas, honey, go to the back under here. It's okay." Cassie huddled in the dark corner. Orion bobbled next to her. Talia turned around to Darcy as she made it to the last step with Elara tight against her chest. "Flashlight. Where's a flashlight? Blankets?" Talia said. Darcy shook her head. Words wouldn't leave her mouth. She had no idea where anything was. Talia darted past her and upstairs to the kitchen. Darcy heard Talia open and slam kitchen drawers, one after the next without closing them. Darcy squeezed in between her children under the steps and held Elara close. "Ha! I found one!" She yelled to Darcy. Talia ran to the basement. She clicked on the flashlight as she stood on the bottom step. Talia had the Amish quilt draped across her arm. "This is the only blanket I could grab. Here, you guys sit on this."

Darcy crouched on the quilt on the floor as the kids huddled next to her. She remembered the moment she saw it hanging in the shop in Pennsylvania. It was such an extravagant purchase for them. Now, it was on the dirt floor and possibly would cover their heads if things got worse.

Darcy tried to breath slowly as Talia stood directly in front of her. For a moment, the world was silent like the instant the mill stopped. Then the noise grew louder. It roared like a wave. Bangs sounding like rocks hit the ceiling and the sides of the house. The bangs drowned out the rising cries of the kids.

"It's hail," Talia yelled without looking back at her. Darcy nodded, but no words formed still. Cassie scooted closer to Darcy's side and burrowed her head. Darcy wrapped her arm around her as Orion forced himself up on her legs. She held Elara against her chest and Orion's back. Her three kids were essentially glued to her. Talia stood with her back to the steps. "It'll be over in a minute. Don't worry," Talia yelled. Darcy comforted herself with the thought that Talia had been through this her whole life. She knew these storms just as Darcy understood the intensity of a blizzard. Then she looked up at Talia. The flashlight showed her eyes, her face. Darcy realized she was lying. She wasn't sure if it was for her sake or the sake of the children.

"Sit Talia. Get down," Darcy muttered in a low, shaky voice. She was surprised at how weak she sounded and not sure Talia heard her. The noise beyond the basement increased. Cassie covered her ears. Orion started to cry louder. Elara squirmed, too. Orion's cries were drowned out in seconds. Darcy began to shake as she realized glass was breaking upstairs. The wind grew so loud that it muffled the sirens. It sounded as if a freight train was above them barreling through the house she was just starting to call home. "Basil" she whispered into the dark air. He was out there somewhere. It was as if she was choking. The hail, broken glass and God knows what else was swirling above them all. She wanted to go home. She wanted to grab her three kids, throw them into the truck, drive straight to Basil, throw him in and take off for the highway. She wanted to leave Nebraska, barrel right into Iowa, Illinois, Ohio, Pennsylvania, just keep going until they were safe and calm in the single-wide trailer overlooking the mill. They could lay on the musty carpet, sunken couch, and listen to the silence of Winsockette. She wanted Gemma in their old kitchen making tea. She wanted Jackson teasing her and leaning his forehead against hers to make up for it. Darcy wondered if their twin connection was making Jackson feel unsettled or worried a thousand miles away. She wanted to scream his name. Panic grew in her belly and she fought the urge to run from the basement. She understood it was the worst thing she could do, but her body started to shake. She struggled to breathe. She wanted Basil now, not in ten minutes or an hour. She wanted them gone from there. They'd find other jobs, other clothes, other everything if they could only hop in that truck and take off.

Tears dripped from Darcy's cheek onto Elara's face before she even realized she was crying. The mix of terror, helplessness, and regret burst like a damn and rushed from her eyes. She gasped for air as sobs overwhelmed her and Cassie. She realized she was making it worse for Cassie by crying too, but she sure as hell didn't know how to make it any better. Hiding her fear was impossible. The shaking of the flashlight told her that Talia was scared, too. Talia sat across from Darcy as she drew Elara close. She thought this was no world for a baby so tiny and innocent. It was no world for all of them. As the world around them crumbled, Darcy wondered what the sky looked like. Were the stars still fixated in their normal position even though the world around her was being windswept, engulfed in chaos? Would anything stay where it was, as it was and should be? Or would a storm like this uproot them and everything they knew? Darcy wondered if anything was permanent at all, including her tiny family.

The freight train whistling that pierced her ears and made them cry started to slow. It faded. The hail stopped. The sirens still roared. Oddly enough, Darcy was fine with sirens if the other noises subsided. She drew in a breath. Darcy wondered if it was the first breath she had taken since the sirens began. Her chest hurt. Her stomach was seizing with worry and terror. The air in the dark dirt basement was thick, hot, used. Cassie whimpered next to her. Orion was a stiff ball that Darcy knew would never be the same. Elara's big eyes danced around in the dark. Talia exhaled and placed the flashlight on the floor. She stretched her legs. Talia was shaking. The siren wound down. It was replaced by a deafening silence. Darcy's heart beat hard against her chest. She drew in quicker breaths as she realized they had survived. Her children huddled against her were all fine. Talia was fine. They stayed in the basement in utter silence for a few minutes. Cassie broke the silence.

"I have to pee, momma." She said in her tiny voice, a changed voice. Darcy nodded.

"Hang on, pumpkin." Darcy steadied her voice. "Is it safe to go up?" She asked.

Talia glanced at the ceiling. "Yeah, I think," She said. Darcy wanted her to sound surer. Darcy needed to be certain before she dared walked up those steps with her baby in her arms and the other two behind her. "Come on," Talia said. She motioned with the flashlight. "I'll go first and yell down if it's safe." Darcy nodded. She stood on the Amish quilt. Darcy realized the kitchen where she made a picnic lunch an hour earlier might not be safe, or it might not be there at all.

Talia walked up the rickety and creaking dusty steps. Darcy walked around to the steps and saw Talia's feet reach the top. The kids still clung to her legs. She heard the door creak open. Talia had stepped back into the world.

"It's fine. Come up, guys," Talia yelled to her. Darcy exhaled and tapped Cassiopeia on the head.

"Go on, baby. Let's go up," She reached down and helped Orion move forward as she clutched Elara with one arm. She watched Cassie step up one splintering step at a time, with Talia waiting at the top to take her hand. She helped Orion crawl up one step then another, waiting behind him to step and be sure he was balanced. Talia reached down and hoisted him up the last two then extended her arm to Darcy.

"You got it?" She said. Darcy nodded and stepped from the basement doorway back into her kitchen. It had only been minutes that they huddled together in the dirt under the steps of the basement Darcy had only gone into once. A lifetime seemed to have unfolded. Her heart raced as she glanced around. The glass of the back French doors was broken. There were huge, jagged chunks that were holding onto the doorframe for dear life. The rest on the floor was scattered, pulverized from the force.

"Honey, stay back, go through the other way to get to the bathroom," She directed Cassie. Darcy saw hail the size of golf balls laying on her welcome mat and kitchen floor. They were starting to melt already, leaving a little pool underneath each. Talia picked up Orion. Together, they stood side by side looking into the distance, amazed that was the only damage. The pots and herbs were gone. It was as if they weren't sitting there talking and planting mere minutes earlier, like the whole day had been a dream until the siren woke her. Darcy couldn't believe the noise that pierced her ears minutes ago was replaced by a slightly hot breeze, a few birds chirping, and utter silence. The silence seemed out of place, like an intruder that had the wrong house. Darcy could almost hear her heartbeat. Elara's slight cries broke them from the trance they were all in. It was feeding time.

Talia shook herself back to the moment.

"My Gram and Pap!" She said as if the world around them existed again beyond that kitchen. Darcy gasped. Talia ran toward the front door with Orion still in her arms. She flung the door open and stepped onto the sidewalk where the two women first met. Darcy stumbled behind trying to shush the baby at the same time. They stepped outside to see half the roof peeled off the only other house in view. Talia slid Orion down her leg and ran.

Darcy ran back inside to call 911 from her cell phone that was still on the counter. She saw missed calls from Basil. When she called him after giving emergency personnel Talia's address, he picked up immediately. He was out of breath. They hurriedly relayed that both were alright, the kids too, and Basil had darted into the post office across from the church he was rebuilding. He huddled inside with everyone else desperate to race back out and call family and friends. The half-repaired church, post office, grocery store, and school were as safe as they were yesterday. It didn't touch down in town like it had in April. He was racing home to be with his family just like everyone else in town prepared to do.

As emergency vehicles' sirens rose in the distance, Darcy walked the kids to Talia's. Barb Pinkerton had a broken wrist and nasty scrapes. She looked stunned. She assured her husband, Ron, and Talia that it looked worse than it was. Ron's back hurt, but that was a normal day for Ron. He refused medical attention. The house wasn't a total loss, but the roof would need to be fixed immediately. Other than that, the damage was mostly cosmetic. Basil pulled in as EMT's checked Barb over. He immediately assured Ron he and a few guys who were working at the church could start his roof repair the next day. Their insurance company would cover a hotel room after they were checked out and Barb was released from the hospital. Basil called Uncle Quincy to let him know they were fine and asked for his help with the neighbor's roof. He said he'd be there by morning. There were other houses slightly damaged, but no deaths reported according to radio and television reports. Darcy couldn't wrap her mind around the level of devastation that the houses, farms, and people could withstand in Franklin all with the knowledge that it could happen again, and again.

# CHAPTER 19

After Ron, Barb, and Talia came back from the hospital, they rummaged through the house for clothes to take to the hotel. Darcy and Basil walked over with the kids. The sun was starting to dip along the western horizon. The heat was breaking slightly. There was sweat on Darcy's nose, bubbling up as it had all day. Cassie seemed unafraid of what had happened, and Orion was his toddler self, rubbing his dripping nose across his face. Darcy suddenly remembered their upcoming appointments. She found it odd that life would just go on, appointments needed to be kept, and her newborn needed to be fed as if their world hadn't been upended. It was chaos before them, yet no one seemed fazed for long.

Darcy and Basil stood on the porch talking to Barb and Ron. Barb's wrist was cradled in a brace, and she had stitches across her eye and chin. Darcy cringed and Cassie hid her face.

"Oh my, this isn't as bad as 1984 when Sandy was in school. We got a twister that knocked down the whole house. We were alright and Sandy was safe at school, but my leg was broken, Ron's too. We made quite a pair trying to get around each other on crutches." Barb said as they both laughed. Darcy pictured them bumping into each other in the hall as they tried to pass one another. Cassie asked for Basil to hold her. He lifted her and pressed her head against his shoulder.

"I'll get to work on this roof asap. Tomorrow after work, I'll get the wood and tarps to get it safe enough to stay in while we get it shingled again. Don't worry about a thing." Basil said.

"Well, we appreciate not having to wait on it. The insurance adjuster will be out tomorrow, too. So, you'll get paid. Don't worry about that none." Ron said. Darcy's blood boiled when she looked at Ron.

"Nah, I'm not worried about that. I don't care if I get paid or not, I'm gonna fix your roof anyways. That's what neighbors do." Basil said. Darcy looked up at him. He spoke with a surety and determination she was getting used to since the mill closing upended their lives. Even though her contempt for Ron grew as she stood in front of him, she knew her husband would help him even if he knew about Ron's treatment of Talia. There wasn't a person in need that Basil wouldn't help. He seemed taller, stronger. Basil was simply a better man than anyone else Darcy ever met. Talia came outside with a small duffel bag.

"I've got enough for a few days, Gram," Talia slid her bag on the porch step by Darcy. "You got enough stuff?"

"Yeah, honey I do. We got a room already too. Not too many people needed to book one cause we're one of the few with roof damage," Barb answered.

Ron cleared his throat. He shoved his meaty hands in his pocket.

"Well Tally, I think this storm was God's way of showing you we need you here." He looked at Talia as Basil glanced at Darcy. "We need you more than that school in Lincoln does. Plus, you know damn well with this roof now and other things that need to be done, like the barn siding the insurance isn't gonna cover, we can't afford for you to leave. You work here for another year or two, save your own money and you can head out after that. Won't kill you to stay here in Franklin for a while longer. No need to go that far anyway," Ron said.

"I'm afraid he's right, honey. You can always take online classes, hell you already know how to cook. Maybe try and save to open a diner right here? You ever think of that? That would be something to be proud of. It's not like we've got a whole lot of choices out here," Barb said. She rubbed her wrist and let out a forced laugh. "I know you were looking forward to going, but we can't afford all that. It's not the right time and—"

"I think we should talk about this another time, Gram," Talia said. She reached for her bag. "I already said I'd stay anyways," Talia said. She looked down at her feet.

"God spoke to me, to us, with this storm. You'll be better off here anyway so no pouting about it," Ron said. Darcy noticed Talia's jaw tighten and her hands start to shake. Ron stepped forward and extended his hand to Basil. "Thanks again, Basil. We're gonna get to the hotel. I'll be back bright and early to start what I can." He shook Basil's hand. Basil nodded. "Tally, get in the truck." Ron's voice boomed. Darcy jumped. Talia gave a small wave and headed away with her grandmother to the other side of the truck.

"Um, Mr. Pinkerton, can Talia stay the night at our house? Just tonight?" Darcy said in a voice much shakier than she expected. "She was…she was a big help to me today with the kids and the storm. I was never so scared in my life. If it weren't for her, I don't think I would've been able to get the kids somewhere safe. I was paralyzed with fear. I just, I'd like if she could help me get them settled tonight and all? They love her and I could use the help. I'm kinda rattled myself still," Darcy said. Talia unclenched her jaw. Barb looked at Ron and shrugged. "Honestly, Mr. Pinkerton. I could really use a friend right now. Can she come back to our house?"

"I don't see why not, right Ron?" Barb said in a small voice. Darcy realized Barb and Talia both made their voices quiet and small to avoid giving Ron a reason to raise his.

Ron seemed taken aback and unsure of the gesture. He looked around at Darcy, Basil, and their kids.

"Just for tonight. If you want, Tally? I mean, you think she'll be a help to you?" Ron asked Darcy. "I guess since I can't pay you right away to start on my roof, maybe a free babysitter is what I can muster up as collateral at the moment." Basil smiled and nodded. Darcy strained to produce a fake laugh.

"Definitely. Elara is a handful. It would be a huge help if she'd stay the night." Darcy tried to mask the desperation in her voice. She sensed she needed to get Talia away from Ron. With each encounter, although always brief, the ominous energy about him only grew in Darcy's gut. It was the exact fear and anger she experienced every time she watched Basil in the driveway with his dad.

While everyone else just thought of Ron as an intense man, Darcy was unsettled by being too close to Ron especially since her gut instincts were confirmed right before the storm. Mentioning that God wanted Talia to stay infuriated Darcy. While Darcy and Basil weren't the most religious people, she knew enough to know God didn't want grandfathers to hit their granddaughters no matter how much anger and pain they carried around from losing their own daughters. Darcy knew it just as she believed God didn't want Basil's dad to hit him at will or cut him on his seventeenth birthday.

"Well alright then. I guess we'll see you tomorrow morning, Tally," Ron said. He leaned his head down and looked up at her overtop his glasses. Darcy saw Talia's hands stop fidgeting.

Darcy drew in a deep breath. She swaddled Elara a little closer. She, Talia, Basil, and the kids headed back across the road and into the house. Darcy glanced around as she adjusted Elara to feed her. She couldn't believe the storm blew out the glass but left the magazine on the kitchen table untouched. If not for the glass missing, there'd be no evidence of a storm. Talia thanked Darcy as Basil taped cardboard over the doorframe.

"It's no problem. I know you needed away from him tonight," Darcy said. Darcy suspected Talia needed more than a temporary break even if Talia didn't.

As Basil and Darcy finished dressing Orion and Cassiopeia for bed and giving them milk with exactly two cookies each, Talia showered. The kids slid under sheets with fans blowing and making the sheets look like mountains when the kids kicked up their feet. They giggled wildly from both rooms as they played 'see over the mountain', as they called it. Darcy and Basil laughed with them. Darcy stopped in the hall to listen a minute. She let their giggles wash over her and cast aside the fear she felt earlier. She could breathe again, move again, and knew the kids would be fine even though she might be traumatized by the storm, the noise. She wanted them to feel safe, free to giggle, unafraid of anything a storm could bring.

Darcy missed her own mother. She smiled as she recalled her mother's encouragement even in the form of being controlling all her life.

Her mind flashed to the money she gave her. Darcy wondered if that money was also Gemma's way of still having control from a thousand miles away. Gemma always needed to be in charge, set the tone, approve everything. As much as Darcy loved and missed her mother, she didn't want to be her. She wanted to mother differently, love differently. She also thought of how Gemma pushed her to be more beautiful, conventional looking and acting even though she wasn't. Gemma wished Darcy could be more, and Darcy knew that with every fiber of her being. Part of it was a mother's natural wish for her daughter. However, part of it was a way to mold Darcy into someone she wasn't, someone she could never be. Every day Darcy didn't see her mother making tea in the kitchen or chasing the children, Darcy began to see Gemma more clearly. She loved her with all she had, but Darcy realized she had to be away from her, out from under her crowns and sashes. As Darcy stood in the hall listening to her kids laugh, she realized she needed to be a different type of mom. Darcy needed to wear a different kind of crown, a different shade of lipstick if any, and she needed to raise her daughters without the glow of Gemma casting a shadow on them all. Gemma would swallow up Elara and Cassie as easily as she had Darcy and never even realize it. The world needed Gemmas but they also needed Darcys. As for her purpose besides being part of her tiny family in Nebraska, Darcy realized the possibilities might be endless. It wasn't too late to go to school someday, even if online. She might never recover that full ride to be an astronomer, but she could teach her kids about the stars, moons, planets, black holes, and galaxies none of them would ever touch. She could teach them all she knew and show them how to discover the rest. She could let go of the mill town and the noise that served as the backdrop of her life up until three months ago. Darcy would be her own woman and take her sweet time deciding who and what that would look like. She leaned her head back on the wall and let the fear of the day out of her lungs, along with the fear of the last few months.

Talia opened the bathroom door and startled Darcy. She saw endless possibilities for Talia, too. In that moment, a purpose for the insurance money hit her as hard as fear had when the storm came.

"Hey, come here a sec." Darcy motioned for her to follow her.

"What's up?" she said as she ran a comb through her wet, stringy red hair. Darcy motioned for her to come in to her bedroom.

"Close the door," She said. Talia quietly closed the door behind her and sat on the edge of the bed. Darcy pulled a small suitcase out of the closet. She unzipped it. It was filled with smaller totes and travel bags. Darcy pulled out a tote and reached in. She pulled out the envelope from Gemma. Talia sat up straight.

"Listen. When Basil and I were leaving Maine, my mom was worried I'd be stuck and worried about how I'd end up, or where, and worried about a thousand other things. She was convinced Basil was crazy and I was crazy for following him. She gave me what she called an insurance policy." Darcy opened the envelope and showed Talia. Talia jumped and put her hand to her chest.

"Holy shit, Darcy. How much money is that?" Talia said in a high pitch tone that told Darcy she was dumbfounded.

"It's quite a bit. Over $3000. More like $3500." Darcy slid the cash back in the envelope. "We saved after my brother stole from us. We managed to get here, pay for the hotels, gas, food, damn broken truck, and get a deposit on this place without touching it."

"Wow. So, what are you guys gonna do with it now?" Talia said.

"Well, the purpose of it was a way out, freedom I guess if things got bad or a way for Gemma to pull me back. I never told Basil about it. I should've but didn't. Plus, Basil would've been pissed at my mom for thinking I needed a way out. And well, Gemma would've had a dramatic breakdown if I didn't take it." Darcy sat back on her heels. She put the envelope on the bed. "I see what Ron is. I know you love your grandparents, but I see it. He'll never stop. I feel it in my bones—"

"No, Darcy, he's n—" Talia tried to spit out as tears welled in her eyes.

"He is. He's abusive. He'll get worse. He'll never let you be who you want to be."

"He's just in so much pain over losing my mom. He's afraid of losing me too. That's all," Talia said. One tear escaped and rolled down her freckled cheek. Darcy reached up and tapped her knee. She wanted to wrap her arms around this waif of a girl who had become her best friend in such a short amount of time. Darcy wanted to guide and protect Talia like an older sister. She had the urge to shield her from life like she and Jackson tried to do for each other.

"I know. But that's no reason to stop you from living a life you want. You deserve to be your own person. Not a replacement for your mom or a do-over for him as a father. You know that?" Tears start to bubble up in Darcy's eyes. Talia's knees started to shake. "It's okay. Everything will be okay," Darcy said.

"I don't understand," Talia said. Darcy glanced at the door and lowered her voice.

"This money, my insurance policy. It's yours. There's enough here for you to pay for the room and board, plus next semester's. Plus, any of the tuition your grants don't cover. Right?" Darcy said.

"Um, yeah. But I can't take this. You guys have three kids. You need all the money you can get. Seriously, Darcy. You barely know me. I can't take this."

"I know you enough to know you need to go. Go to Lincoln, start classes, live away from Franklin, cook and heal. cook and be happy. Give that happiness to others. If you stay, you'll end up like so many people I knew from school. You'll meet a guy, get married, have babies, stay in Franklin forever, never leaving to find or have anything of your own. Someone will always decide everything for you." Darcy fought tears. "I had a full-ride scholarship for astronomy. I had a way out. I was gonna discover something no one had seen before in the space. I wanted to name a star, find it out there, and pluck it for my very own. But I got pregnant."

"But you love your kids. You love Basil, right?" Talia said.

"God, yes. I love that man. But I lost my chance to leave Winsockette on my own terms, on my own at all. I think Basil would've followed me, who knows. But I'll never know what I could've been. Who I could've been." Darcy paused. "Listen, you have the whole world ahead of you," She said. "You aren't tethered to Franklin, to anyone. Let yourself get swept up by the wind and get the hell out of here. Go wherever. Do whatever."

"I can't take it. Use it for your kids or something," Talia said.

"We're fine. My kids will be fine. Jackson has been mailing money to pay us back slowly but surely. And hell, with this new storm, Basil will be roofing until next tornado season. God's wrath provides like Basil said it would." Darcy picked up the envelope again. "My destiny is already written. Take this and write yours. Go to Lincoln first thing tomorrow. Pay the bills, get what you need, and make your way out there, away from here. We'll take care of Barb and Ron. I promise."

She slid the envelope to Talia. She picked it up and held it to her chest. Darcy could see Talia searching for something to say. "I'll pay you back someday. I promise." Darcy nodded. She stood and embraced Talia.

"Go put it in your bag before Basil wonders what we're doing," Darcy said. As Talia left the room, Darcy looked around the room. Despite the intention of the money, the mixed feelings of needing and loving her mother and also wanting to reject everything she represented, Darcy smiled and thought Gemma would be proud of her. Gemma would want Darcy to help Talia, to give her the chance Darcy let slip away for herself.

# CHAPTER 20

Darcy slinked downstairs to find Basil as the children slipped into dreams and a hush fell over the house. He was sitting on the patio. He had found their table and chairs in the field before it got dark. He had a beer in front of him and was staring up at the sky. He also had a cigarette. He barely smoked since they got to Nebraska. Darcy slid out from behind the cardboard covered doors and sat next to him.

"I'm glad you found the chairs and table. I kinda like them, and I like sitting out here." Darcy looked up at the clearest sky she'd ever seen. Basil took a swig of his beer. While it still bothered Darcy, he had drunk a lot less since they settled in the plains.

"Darcy, I've been thinking. I know this isn't what you signed up for. That storm and all. Man, when those sirens went off, I was scared shitless for you and the kids. All I could think was that if anything happened to you guys, it would be my fault for dragging us here. Hell, Elara is only two weeks old and she was already in danger."

"Basil, we're fine," Darcy said.

"Thank God. But honestly Darcy. Say the word and we'll head back to Maine. Just say the word. I know this isn't what you wanted. It was reckless, dangerous to come out here and put us through this. I can find another job back home." Basil looked up at the sky after another sip. Darcy exhaled and strained her neck further toward the sky.

"You're right. It is dangerous. I didn't sign up for this. I didn't sign up for much that has happened to us. We didn't sign up for the mill to close, for me to get pregnant, then pregnant again and again. Now that was reckless according to most people back home. But I did sign up for being with you. No matter where, no matter what happens to us. I signed up for you." Darcy reached across the wrought iron patio table and took his hand. He swigged his beer again and tossed his cigarette.

"But these storms are no joke. We, you, the kids could've gotten hurt."

"We can get hurt anywhere, Basil." Darcy leaned back further. Her upper back cracked. She exhaled. "We could've ended up anywhere." She paused to look up again. "Years ago, before Cassiopeia, I wanted to run off to school, never look back. I was sure I'd lay eyes on something no one else had ever seen. I was going to discover the next great star, or a whole galaxy."

"I know, honey. I know things didn't go as we planned back then. When I get paid for the new jobs I'll have, we'll get a better telescope. I promised you that. I just wish I could go back and find a way to have us, our family, and still give you those dreams you gave up by being with me."

"Thank you. But I realized something when you placed Elara in that bassinette tonight and when I saw you help the Orion and Cassie play 'see over the mountain'. I realized my dream did come true. I did lay eyes on something no one else had ever seen. I had discovered something entirely new."

"What do you mean?"

"Our kids, Basil. When I first laid eyes on them as they were placed on my stomach. When I saw your eyes light up as each one came out. As I watched you cut all three cords, shaking and all. When I held each one and they grabbed my finger and looked up at me. That was it. That first look into their eyes. That was what I needed to discover. We created those little stars and showed them to the world. They were ours first, ours to see first. They came from us," Darcy said. Basil huffed and took another swig. "But I still want a good telescope." She said with a smirk. Basil laughed and nodded. "There's still a lot more out there I want to see."

Darcy pointed out Cassiopeia for Basil. She told him once she had a better telescope, she'd find Elara, too.

"Did you know they have storms on Jupiter?"

"Really?"

"Yep. Just like tornadoes or hurricanes. The giant red spot I showed you once. That's a spinning storm like a tornado that has been rotating for over a hundred years. Elara the moon was originally a chunk of an asteroid that got sucked into the gravitational pull of Jupiter. So, you see? There's really no escaping storms, or the wind in general when you think about it." Darcy looked over at Basil. "Everything looks fixed and still up there. Quiet. Safe. Like never-ending silence with sparks of light poking through. But it's just as chaotic. It's just as unsettled as anywhere else in the universe." She glanced around for more constellations. "Whether it's the sky above Winsockette, here or anywhere else, it's all just chaos. There's nothing stable or permanent about it." Darcy said.

She strained her eyes to see more piercings of faraway lights. Basil huffed. Darcy thought of Winsockette. She thought of always looking up for the answers when she didn't understand what was happening in the world around her.

"Those stars aren't forever either. They're just the light of what exploded, reactions of energy, released as a light that's so hot it glows. They're just as windswept and lost as this patio table was earlier today." Darcy said.

"So, none of it last, here or there, huh?"

"Nope. None of it. And going back to Maine isn't gonna make anything more secure for us, safer, or longer lasting." She turned towards him. "Listen, I'm not sure if it was God's plan for us to move out here and fix what broke or blew away. I know it's been hard for us to process why everything happened, why the mills closed and nothing else opened for us back home. You're right about man's greed taking what we thought we had, what we counted on, and you're right to be mad as hell about it." Darcy looked at the stars above them. "And maybe God did bring us here make up for it all." Darcy drew in another deep breath and exhaled as Basil swigged more of his beer. "Despite everything, I do know one thing, we're needed here. Even though we can't stop a storm or stop the wind, we can help others pick up the pieces while we start a life of our own."

She turned to look at him. "Listen, Babe. I know who we are and who we'd be back home. I think I wanna find out who we can be here, who we could be away from our family, away from Winsockette. On our own. If you want to stay, we stay. Got it?"

Basil let out a long sigh. He swigged again and swallowed loudly in a way that Darcy knew would drive her crazy when they were old and rocking on a back porch somewhere.

"Okay. We'll stay. For now. We can always go where the wind takes us if we decide to leave later. We aren't trees. We can move anywhere," Basil said. He pointed. "That one, that's the north star, right?"

"Yeah, it is. See, stick with me. You're learning," She said with a laugh. He laughed, too.

She watched him in the moonlight, his smile, the crinkle of skin on the sides of eyes when he laughed. He had the face of a man who has worked too hard for his age. He was more tanned than during Maine summers, she thought. Basil squinted. She could tell he was looking for another star to point out and quiz her about. For once, Darcy wasn't looking to the stars. She looked over at the only sight that mattered— Basil. Darcy realized she was making a dreamer and stargazer out of him yet regardless of where life would take them. They had become windswept, caught up in everyone else's storms, but for now they were home.

# ABOUT THE AUTHOR

Karri L. Moser currently resides in Maine. She has lived all over the U.S. as an Army wife and daughter, which has provided an overflowing well of inspiration for characters and settings in her novels. She is the author of three previous works of Maine-based fiction.

When she is not writing, Karri can be found running, gardening, snowshoeing, and exploring the beaches of coastal New England all with a hot hazelnut coffee in her hand.

# NOTE FROM THE AUTHOR

Word-of-mouth is crucial for any author to succeed. If you enjoyed *A Home for the Windswept*, please leave a review online—anywhere you are able. Even if it's just a sentence or two. It would make all the difference and would be very much appreciated.

Thanks!
Karri L. Moser

Thank you so much for reading one of our **Women's Fiction** novels.

If you enjoyed the experience, please check out our recommendation
for your next great read!

*The Apple of My Eye* by Mary Ellen Bramwell

"A mature love story with an intense plot.

This book has something important to say."

**-William O. Shakespeare, Professor of English,**

**Brigham Young University**

View other Black Rose Writing titles at
www.blackrosewriting.com/books and use promo code
**PRINT** to receive a **20% discount** when purchasing.